Love at the Wrong Time

L.J. Crowe

Original title: A DESTIEMPO First Edition: July 2013
This novel is a work of fiction. Names, characters, and situations are the product of the author's imagination and are fictional. Any resemblance to real events or people, living or dead, is mere coincidence.
The author previously published a series of online episodes of this story titled, Mrs. Margarita, on the website http://novelasemanal.com and titled Obsesión, on the blog http://luiscrowe.megustaescribir.com

Published by Ibukku
www.ibukku.com
Cover design: Diana Patricia González
Copyright © 2013 L.J. Crowe
All rights reserved.
ISBN Paperback: 978-1-68574-029-0
ISBN eBook: 978-1-68574-030-6
ISBN Hardcover: 978-1-68574-031-3

To you, who has known how to love
by devoting everything.

She is so beautiful, Lord,
and so soft, and so light,
that it would be a great sin
if I did not love her.

And therefore, forgive me, Lord,
for she is so beautiful, that You,
who made water,
and the flowers, and the stars,

You, who hears the mourning
of this nameless pain,
would love her too,
if you could be a man!

José Ángel Buesa
Poem of Guilt fragment.

PROLOGUE

"Eddy!" My business partner called out to me, poking his head out of the improvised tin office window, while I closed the door of the small freight elevator that would take me to the 19th floor to check the newly installed beams in the new building we were constructing in the city of Los Angeles.

"What's up?" I questioned. "Are you going to floor 19?"

"Yes," I said, as the elevator started to ascend.

"Okay, I'll talk to you later!" he shouted.

"Is it important?" I asked as I continued to go up.

"No, no, no. Not at all." I still managed to hear his voice over the noise of the elevator and the machinery used by the workers, who were almost done with another day's work, but I could clearly see how he gestured with his thick hand from side to side to reinforce his words.

I liked the view that unfolded as I continued my ascent on the freight elevator at that time of the day. The blur of yellow, orange, and red which painted the twilight made me believe in the existence of some rather creative and tasteful God. The buildings of the great city took on a reddish tone making me think that, instead of wood and cement, they were made of pure, burning hot fire.

On the 19th floor, I opened the door of the small elevator and began to walk along the beams to do my usual inspection.

"Architect," said Oscar, one of the young Mexican construction workers, and I nodded back.

I felt my Blackberry vibrating and took it out of my pants pocket to answer the call. Since I was not wearing my reading glasses, I placed the device far enough away from my eyes to be able to see who was calling me, although I was almost certain it was my wife.

"Hello," I said, stopping and waving to Oscar, who was going to tell me something just as I took out my Blackberry.

"Hello, are you coming?" I heard my wife's sensual and authoritative voice over the phone.

"Almost, I'm just going to finish the checkup and I'll be right there."

"Call me when you're on your way, I need you to take care of some things."

"Okay, I'll call you in a bit." I ended the call and headed toward Oscar, who was still waiting.

"How is it that my wife always has something for me to take care of? Every day, before I get home, I have to go somewhere else to run some errands. It does not matter which country we are living in, or in which city I'm building something, she always thinks of something. How come she always thinks of something? Is that what all women are like?"

"I hope not architect because I'm getting married in two months," he replied with a slight laugh. I laughed, too.

"What's going on? Were you going to tell me something?" I asked.

"Yes. This is all set to start early in the morning tomorrow. I called the workers in at 7 a.m. so we would not have to make up time, but I think we're doing well and we should be finished assembling the structure of this floor in two days at most."

"All right, Oscar, thank you very much. I'm just going to do the routine inspection. I'll see you here tomorrow around 8 a.m." My Blackberry vibrated again.

"All right, architect, see you tomorrow."

I took the device out and saw it was a text message. I took my reading glasses out of my shirt pocket and put them on to read it:

"My mother-in-law just passed away in the hospital. I cannot get any calls here, but I'll call you later. I thought I should let you know that she asked to speak to me a few minutes ago; she told me to take care of her daughter and granddaughters, and she also said your name. She remembered you in her last moments, you bastard. I'll call you later."

The shock of the news must have reflected on my face because Oscar came to my side in an instant. "Are you okay, architect?" he asked with concern.

"Yes. Yes, thank you." I answered and kept on walking along the construction area of the 19th floor. But he followed along and grabbed my arm.

"Come architect, sit down." He took me to a safer place where there was no risk of falling into the void and helped me sit on a stack of beams in a corner. I was trying to process the news.

I thought it was funny that I found out while I was up here.

"You look pale, architect. Do you want me to call for help?"

"No, no. I'm fine, thank you." I reread the message. *My mother-in-law just passed away in the hospital...* Those words echoed in my head and the memories returned to me as intense as the passion that enveloped us when I was 18 years old. So profound was the recollection of those moments that, sitting there, 19 stories high, at 53 years of age and with the sky a color that reminded me of the fire of my youth, I felt the slight fruity taste in my mouth again.

CHAPTER 1

"Unlucky at cards, lucky in love," the old saying goes. And, by the time I turned 18, I had been unlucky at cards, and worse at love. I had only had one girlfriend and an almost sexual experience with that same girlfriend. I think it was a quick and traumatic act for both of us. She was just 15 years old and I was 16. Neither of us had the slightest experience in the matters of love, much less in those of the *Kama Sutra*.

My parents had gone away for the weekend and my brother Tavo, who was two years older than me, had gone out with his girlfriend. So, taking advantage of the situation, I took her to my room with the excuse of showing her my *Rocky* poster.

Her name was Martha; she was as shy as me and as thin as a bamboo stick. She did not have a single curve; she was as tall as my shoulder, and she wore glasses so old it seemed as if they had been passed down from generation to generation from her grandmother. She was milky white and wore braces on her teeth. She was a very lovely person, well, at least until that day.

While she was staring at my poster, I took the opportunity to take off my T-shirt and remain in a tank top, just like the one Silvester Stallone wore in the film. "It's very hot," I said, throwing the shirt over the bed. Then I went to the door with the intention of having her follow me, which she did. I stopped at the frame of the door, turned to her, and lifted my arms to hold the top frame in order to show off my nonexistent biceps, just as Rocky Balboa did when he was trying to seduce Adrian.

Unfortunately, my scrawny arms did not impress her very much, but as she was just as shy as Adrian; perhaps she identified a bit with the character, and when I took off her glasses, she let herself be seduced.

We began to kiss, rather clumsily, and awkward caresses followed, but despite our ineptitude we became very passionate and began to undress, or half undress, because I never unbuttoned her bra. I just pulled down her straps so she could pull out her arms and have her small, pale, young breasts exposed for me to squeeze like I'd seen in porn movies. But she subtly took my hands off her breasts after she unleashed three or four discreet yelps of pain. Which, of course, I knew translated to, "idiot, you're hurting me!" So, I totally forgot about the squeezing and we kept kissing and touching each other until the moment of truth came. I prepared to penetrate her and she, excitedly, arched her back to bring her pelvic region closer to my penis as she muttered my name: "Eddy. Eddy," and I became even more aroused. As soon as I felt the contact of her thin pubic hair on the tip of my penis, I started to ejaculate on top of her. Her face immediately became the spitting image of panic and that image remained etched in my mind for years. And I'll never forget what she said as long as I live.

"Did you pee, Edgar?" she asked me with a look of disgust on her face. "Are you peeing on me?" I was speechless and prayed to God to send an earthquake at that moment so that the house would fall on me.

When she lifted her head to look at the white, viscous liquid that was still shooting out of my member, as if it were some completely independent part of me, dripping all over her pubic hair and abdomen, she threw me off and pushed me away with such disgust that I felt like I was a leper or a repugnant monster with some contagious disease.

"What is that?!" she shouted again, standing up, and staring at her belly with disgust. She covered her mouth to keep from vomiting and ran to the bathroom where she did vomit. In 1977 there was no sex education in schools, and, within families, it was taboo. As a result, all the information came from friends and it seemed as if her friends had not given her enough guidance about this situation.

They say that you never forget your first time, and it is true. No matter how hard I tried, I could never erase the memory of that evening which has been engraved on my mind forever. After that experience, I did not feel like trying again and became an expert in solo pleasure. Meanwhile, my friends changed girlfriends every month and talked about their sexual exploits in front of me.

I became shyer and shyer and to top it all off, my face was covered with acne, making things worse.

I was never good looking, but I was not terrible either, rather I was what you'd call a normal guy. My features were ordinary. I mean, neither attractive nor ugly. In fact, I was the opposite of my friend Francisco Castillo, whom we all knew as Frank. He had light, almost blond hair and I had black hair. He had big, olive-shaped eyes and I had small, beady eyes. His eyelashes were long and curled, and mine were short and straight. He had no pimples on his face, while I had what he lacked in that department. I was as thin as a spike, and he was strong and robust despite being almost a year younger than me. He was nice and charismatic, while I was clumsy and shyer than a pangolin. He was the one who scored the goals during soccer matches, while I was the water boy. I never excelled at anything before I was 18, except school, because I was always a nerd. In general, I was just an ordinary guy. A completely ordinary guy. He was my friend, and although I gave him many reasons to stop being my friend after my 18th birthday, he remained my friend and not just any friend. We were the best of friends.

We were at an age where even slightly beautiful woman seemed remarkably attractive to us. We liked to go to the supermarkets near the Colonia Industrial, where we lived in Mexico City, or to very crowded places, just to see the women passing by. It was our lucky day when we met, *la señora*[1] Margarita.

---

1 Mrs. in Spanish.

Chapter 2

Mrs. Margarita was 36 years old, with a magnificent body and a face so beautiful it seemed to have been carved by God's hand itself. Her smile, with white, perfectly aligned teeth, was almost timeless. Her large eyes, framed by thick, lined eyebrows, had such a special glow they seemed to smile as well and were as black as her obsidian hair. She used to be the life of the party, and in our neighborhood, the star of the film in every teenager's mind, when we locked ourselves in the bathroom or in our wet dreams.

My friend Frank and I both stopped to admire the movement of her hips and the swoosh that her long skirt made at every step she took in the supermarket. Her firm bust looked great with the tight-fitting shirt she wore, which also highlighted her slim waist. Next to her were her two teenage daughters and, pushing the shopping cart, her husband.

This guy was the envy of every man in the neighborhood, and every time his wife threw a party at their house, Mr. Samuel had many more friends than he could remember. Some of them he was sure he had never seen before, but they had come with some other guy, with a sort of familiar face, whom he vaguely remembered. Samuel Montes was of medium height, but robust, with dark, curly hair and almost always wore a suit. His personality was opposite to that of his wife. He was taciturn and calm, and she was cheerful and full of energy. He was very serious, and she always smiled. He would go to bed early at his wife's parties, while she danced and had fun until the early hours of the morning. He was a little apathetic and insignificant, while she was charismatic, beautiful, sensual, erotic. It was inevitable to turn to her, whether you were a man or a woman, you turned to look at her.

"Just look at that body," said Frank.

I gawked as I watched her, without saying anything, and my imagination ran wilder.

Once she disappeared from our sight, Frank and I kept walking and I knew what he was going to tell me. Every time we saw Mrs. Margarita somewhere, he would showcase his great knowledge, the legend of old. Frank began to recite, "They say that at one of her famous parties, a very rich guy who had been invited by someone, apparently a cousin of hers, after a few drinks and already kind of drunk, managed to get her away from the others and offered her five hundred thousand pesos, bro! Five-hundred thousand pesos! For just one night of sex. No fucking way!"

As always, he paused to let me soak in the significance he had placed on those words. "No one heard the offer the rich loser had made to her, but everyone watched as she slapped him in the face and kicked him out of the house. Everybody was surprised, and even her husband was confused."

I had heard that story hundreds of times before because soon after it happened, it made its way all over the neighborhood and eventually became a myth. The real offer was never known and there was talk of sums of up to a million dollars, and by that time Demi Moore's movie, *Indecent Proposal*, was still not released.

I, like everyone else, had a crush on *La Señora* Margarita even though she was twice my age, and even though every day I entangled myself with her in some devilish erotic sessions in the solitude of my bathroom and in the boundless universe of my imagination. I never thought that dreams, let alone those kinds of dreams, could come true.

Chapter 3

A few months before my 18th birthday, Frank and I went to a get together at his cousin Laura's house.

"Look," said Laura in her shrilly fifteen-year-old voice, "this is Marisol and Maribel."

"Marisol Montes Luna," she greeted formally, holding out her hand with a sweet smile.

"Hi. Maribel," said the sister.

"You're Mrs. Margarita's daughters, aren't you?" Frank asked naturally as my hands began to sweat. They both nodded.

"We've all met before," he said to Maribel, "but we had not had a chance to talk." Marisol was 16 and Maribel was 15, and both had inherited their mother's beauty. However, Marisol was tall and thin, with almost brown hair and honey-colored eyes, and Maribel was shorter, with black hair and a curvier body like her mother's as well as having a slight resemblance to her father. Marisol did not really look anything like him.

Within a month, the youngest sister became my friend's girlfriend and I was trying to muster the courage to express my feelings to Marisol, the oldest. But despite the help that Frank and Maribel provided to get her interested in me, and the assurance they gave me that she was only waiting for me to take the first step, whenever I was about to do so, my mind would freeze. My hands would sweat, and my mouth would close with an invisible lock that did not allow me to speak even half a word.

"Were you going to tell me something?" she would ask me when we were alone on the sofa in her living room or when we were walking down the street after picking them up from school. My hands would get damp, and then I would get silly.

"Have you seen *Saturday Night Fever* yet?" I nervously asked. She grimaced in despair and sighed a long, loud sigh, as I had already asked her about 20 times.

Marisol had another suitor besieging her: Manolo. He was a guy with the latest fancy car, who was dressed in the latest fashion and even had a white suit just like John Travolta's. He was a jerk who had already tried to get at her twice, without success, because Frank and Maribel told me that she was waiting for me to muster the courage.

One day, when her daughters were busy doing homework, and Frank and I were waiting for them to finish, Mrs. Margarita, or "Assgarita," as we called her in honor of her round, well-proportioned buttocks, was with us.

"C'mon Eddy!" she said to me. "Just go for it already, I know she's gonna say yes."

"Isn't that right, ma'am?" Frank encouraged.

"Yes, do not be shy. I do not like Manolo as my son-in-law. I like you," she said endearingly.

Every time I tried, I became speechless or my words became pure nonsense, so I missed the opportunity. Manolo tried it for the third time and as they say, "third time's the charm." Marisol said "yes," and I ended up making a fool of myself.

"You are a fucking idiot!" Frank said to me.

"I did not like her much anyway," I said trying to show as much indifference as possible.

He shook his head to the side and grimaced. "An idiot, and a liar as well!"

A week before my 18th birthday and two days after being replaced by Manolo, I went to visit them to help Maribel with her biology homework. Not that biology was my strong suit, but like I said, I was a real nerd and always got good grades in every subject. When Maribel finished, she started watching TV with Frank, and Manolo sat down next to Marisol, hugging her with both arms and turning to me with his small, shortsighted eyes as if telling me, "She's mine, I beat you to it for being a dumbass." I was not interested in seeing my defeat rubbed in my face any longer, and so I began to say my goodbyes, but, somehow, I ended up talking to Mrs. Margarita on the couch.

She reproached me for letting stupid Manolo win and told me that this was still like my home and that I could go and visit them as many times as I liked. During the conversation, the topic of my birthday came up.

"You're turning 18?" She asked enthusiastically with her beautiful and timeless smile.

"Yes," I shyly admitted.

"Are they throwing you a party?"

"No," I replied somewhat sadly. My parents are going to have to go to the United States for a psychology conference and they're going to be gone all weekend. I think I'll just be at home.

"Oh, poor thing!" she added in a very maternal tone while hugging me, causing a huge erection in my pants. The arousal was so strong that the simple contact with her skin was enough to excite anyone. I turned red and she smiled at me and gently stroked my cheek. I almost fainted.

I did not see Señora Margarita and her daughters again until November 26th, my birthday. It was that day when I came of age and my life changed completely and forever.

CHAPTER 4

"Do not make plans for tonight. We're going to have some tacos at Susy's, and I'll buy you a beer to celebrate since you can legally have it now," Frank told me on the phone the day I turned 18. I could not figure out if he was making fun of me or if he was serious. First, he knew better than anyone that I had no one to make plans with. Second, he was the one who still could not drink, although they already knew us at Susy's and they never asked us for an ID.

At about 7 p.m., on the night of my boring birthday, he asked me to go with him to Maribel's house to pick up some things and from there we would go to Susy's taqueria on Fortuna Street. Maribel had already called me in the morning to wish me a happy birthday, and so did Mom and Dad from Texas. My brother also wished me a happy birthday before he left for wherever he was going. "Happy birthday, fucker," he said, giving me a hug and messing up my hair, which had taken me half an hour to prepare with the hairdryer.

I did not get many calls that day except from some cousins and aunts. Since I was not very good at making friends, and since I finished high school, I had taken a gap year because I did not know what I wanted to study. I had been stuck in my house for four months, completely bored and watching the days go by so slowly while living in a constant and deep state of depression.

When we arrived at Maribel's house, she opened the door for us, and I noticed that the house was a little dark. I was disappointed. I thought that at least they would say happy birthday to me. I was excited about Mrs. Margarita's hug and even Marisol's. It was my birthday, so even if it was just out of sheer obligation, she was going to give me a hug. I let my imagination run wild as we were walking toward their house, thinking that if Manolo was not there, Marisol would realize I was the one she wanted while saying happy birthday, and then she'd leave him.

Also stuck in my head was a scene where she told me she was not really Manolo's girlfriend, that I was the one she wanted, and that she had planned it all to surprise me precisely on my birthday. The silly scenes in my head changed as we walked and Frank told me about god knows what, because I was not paying attention.

"Happy birthday!" Maribel's hug was sincere and her smile was kind. "How are you doing, and how has your day been so far?"

"Alright," I lied.

"Come in," she invited, closing the door behind us and leading us through the garage into the house.

"I'll give you that in a minute," she added, addressing Frank.

"Are you alone?" I asked curiously.

"Just the housemaids up there watching *Siempre en Domingo*. The others went to Mass and then they're going to dinner, but I stayed because I have a lot of homework. I've been slacking off all weekend and now it's all catching up with me." We passed through the garage and she opened the door of the house, which was dark. She walked in and Frank let me walk in before Maribel turned on the light. The first thing I saw was Mrs. Margarita with her indelible smile, rising from behind the sofa at the same time that some friends and acquaintances from the neighborhood, my neighbors and many others that I never remembered seeing, all began to come out of their respective hiding places screaming in unison, "Surprise!"

And it sure was. I'd never had a surprise party before. Of course, I had parties before, but never a surprise one. A whole crowd had gathered since Mrs. Margarita basically threw a party for the whole neighborhood. Naturally, I did not know half of the people there.

Marisol gave me a cold hug, I think because Manolo was there with his sour face, in his enviable white John Travolta suit. He also congratulated me with a sarcastic tone and I thanked him in the same way. What surprised me the most was that Mrs. Margarita's husband was not there and all the wolves were on the hunt.

"Do not leave my side so all these men won't bother me," she pleaded to me when she came to sit next to me to ask me why I was there alone. Not even at my own party could I be brave enough to socialize with people. I explained that I was watching the others and resting a bit.

"Have you danced yet?" she asked me, pointing to the people who were dancing to the beat of the Bee Gees' disco music.

"Yes," I replied in a tone that indicated it was obvious, although I had not gotten up since I sat down an hour earlier.

"Have you danced with Sonya yet?" she asked, pointing to a corner where about 10 or more teenagers and a few dirty old men surrounded a beautiful seventeen-year-old blonde who was quite popular in the neighborhood, as she decided who would be the next lucky guy to share the dance floor with. I shrugged my shoulders in a gesture that clearly said, "I do not like her very much." In reality, that kind of beauty was light years away from any realm of possibility in my world.

Mrs. Margarita was about to say something when she saw a guy with thick Coke bottle glasses approaching us perhaps to ask her to dance. She grabbed my hand and said, "Get up. Let's dance."

I was going to tell her that I did not know how to but I did not have enough time to open my mouth. The next thing I knew, we were already on the dance floor and she was starting to move like a sensual goddess. I had no choice but to try and mimic Frank's moves, who was dancing with Maribel, but I was not sure I was doing it all that well. Little by little, I became more confident and began to loosen up and imitate the steps I had seen John Travolta doing in *Saturday Night Fever*. And for a moment, I thought of doing the famous little Travolta step, raising the index finger to the right, as if pointing to infinity.

Right next to me, Manolo was moving much better than I in his white suit and trying to impress Marisol, but when I did the sexy dance move, I accidentally poked his eye and knocked out his contact lens.

"Hold on! Hold on!" Manolo said extending his arms out at his sides to indicate that he did not want anyone to come near the area because he needed to look for the lens I had just poked out. "My contact, my contact! He just poked out my contact lens," he kept repeating.

We all went looking for his contacts while mostly everyone laughed their heads off. I did not know if they were laughing at me or at him, but it was very embarrassing. I won't deny that it was also fun to see him lying there, patting the floor to see if he could feel the lens. Finally, someone saw it, so he picked it up and went to the bathroom to wash it and put it back on while people kept laughing and cheered me on my little Travolta step.

After most of the guests had left, Mrs. Margarita and I sat down to talk and I thanked her for organizing my first surprise party. "I was so sad that you were not going to celebrate your birthday." Her soft hand gave me an affectionate caress on the cheek and it made me nervous.

When I asked her about her husband I realized her eyes became saddened, but it was only a moment, and she immediately recovered her timeless smile. "He had things to do," she replied, changing the conversation, adding "Can you bring me a soda from the kitchen? I'm gonna save what's left of the cake for you to take home." I got up and went to the kitchen. I took the Coke and was about to leave when I saw her come in.

"Do you think you could come with me tomorrow to buy some jeans?" she said to me.

"Yes, of course," I replied surprised.

"I do not want you to say anything to anyone so there won't be any misunderstandings, okay?" I nodded silently trying to analyze whether what was happening was real or whether I was imagining some innuendo in her gaze. So, I just shook my head in affirmation.

"I'll call you tomorrow at 9 a.m.; you answer the phone, otherwise I'll hang up and not call again." She smiled at me as she winked and left the kitchen. I stood there with the soda in my hand for a long time without understanding what had happened.

Did she wink at me? She doesn't want me to tell anyone? Is she serious or is she playing a birthday joke on me? I said to myself.

I had already gotten used to letting my imagination run wild when it came to women, but this time it seemed like my imagination was going too far. After all, she was the goddess La Señora Margarita, and I was, well, me.

That night, I could not sleep because, as we said goodbye, she gave me the customary hug and quickly whispered in my ear "I'll call you."

CHAPTER 5

I made love to her like a savage in my dreams, and let my imagination go as far as it pleased, without restraint, and without repression. I let it fly freely thinking of that beautiful and sensual woman's smile, her kiss when she said goodbye, her voice whispering in my ear, and the tremendous eroticism that her skin, her body, and her gaze gave off.

I took an early bath and had breakfast. At about 8 a.m. I stood by the phone stupidly because there was no one else in the house who could answer. My brother had already gone off to college and I was alone. At that moment, I had no idea, but this action of standing by the phone for hours, waiting for Mrs. Margarita's call, would repeat itself in the future, becoming a living hell.

At 9 a.m. I was still standing by the phone and kept staring at it as if my eyes had magical powers that could make it ring, but it did not. At 9:15 it still did not ring; at 9:45 nothing happened. I was already beginning to wake from my dream, thinking I had misunderstood everything as usual, and that that damn phone would never ring. Then, at 9:55 the morning after my 18th birthday, the phone rang. I jumped up and down and answered before it even finished making the first sound.

"I'll pick you up in 20 minutes at the corner of Montevideo and Insurgentes."

"Okay," I answered, trying not to make my voice sound too excited but before I could even think she had already hung up.

About 20 minutes was how long it would take me to walk from my house to the corner of Montevideo and Insurgentes Avenues. I took my keys to the house and went outside. *She just wants you to go with her,* I said to myself as I walked. *But why did she ask me and not someone else or one of her daughters? Or why not ask her son-in-law?* And so, question by question and without an answer, I arrived at the corner where Mrs. Margarita was already waiting for me in her blue Caprice.

***

"I want you to help me pick out a good pair of jeans because I like the ones you and Frank wear," she said after we greeted each other.

At that time, in the neighborhood of Tepito in Mexico City, they sold (and still sell) all kinds of electronic goods smuggled into the country at the U.S. border, perhaps by the airport as well, and therefore at a much more affordable price for most people, since there are no import tax expenses. Not only can you find illegally imported appliances, but it is also possible to find almost anything, from sweets to a beer served as a Michelada, which is sold halfway down the street by a guy with a supermarket cart who has everything you need at a bar: lemons, salt, Tabasco sauce, plastic glasses, a knife to cut the lemons, and, of course, a clever way to keep the beers very cold even in the middle of summer.

It was also very common to walk through the crowded streets of the fierce neighborhood of Tepito and find guys who barked at the passersby announcing, "magazines," "Chinese ink," and "films." They referred to pornographic magazines and films and an ointment that supposedly made you last longer during sex, or even get an erection if you were impotent. It was called "Chinese ink," but it was actually Pond's cream. I know that because I had already met a friend who sold them before and I helped him a couple of times to fill the small amber glass containers with the magical and wonderful "Chinese ink," with the very common Pond's face cream.

It was also possible to find extremely fine and expensive bottles of wine at a reasonable price. Though, you ran the risk that when you arrived home and opened the bottle to impress your guests, you would find you were serving them tap water dyed red and not the fine wine you were expecting.

Not everything is fake in Tepito. Some things were worthwhile, and, at that time, you could find fashion influenced by the success of the recently released film *Grease*. There were also jeans made in Mexico that fit the body very well and were made of a resistant fabric. Those were the kind of jeans that Mrs. Margarita wanted me to go buy with her.

"I'm afraid to go to Tepito; you know how dangerous it is. That's why I wanted you to come with me," she confessed.

You see, genius? She only wanted you to go with her because she did not want to come alone. She was not trying to have sex you fool, I said to myself, a little disappointed.

When we got to Tepito we went straight to the jeans stand and as we walked, people looked at us. Well, more like they were looking at her. Some were yelling at me, "damn, who's your friend bro?"

"Well, at least they think I'm your friend and not your mother," she said, showing her perfect white teeth as she smiled while holding my arm, perhaps instinctively as a sign to others that she was not alone. My mind started to run wild again, and I had to bring it back to Earth with a, *She just wanted you to go with her because she did not want to come alone! Not because of your spotty face.* The simple touch of her fingers on my skin was like an electric shock of pure eroticism, so keeping my hormones at ease was not easy.

I thought it would take forever to decide what to buy. I had heard that women took hours and hours to buy pants. They tried on hundreds or more and ended up buying the first one they had tried on. Mrs. Margarita was different. Mrs. Margarita took one of her size, measured it by taking it by the waist and putting it on her own, and said, "This one is fine."

She paid for it and we went back to where she had parked her car. It all happened so fast. "Will you come somewhere with me?" She asked me when we were in the car.

"Yes, of course," I answered nervously. *Somewhere?*

"Have you ever had your fortune told?"

"No, I have not."

"Do you want to try it?" she asked with a very mischievous smile. I just nodded, and we headed for the Avenida Reforma, heading toward La Zona Rosa.

***

We entered a rather dark place that had a giant Buddha statue about four feet tall, sitting on a table with his legs crossed. There were three or four small round tables with two chairs facing each other. On one table there was a lady dressed as a gypsy, and in front of her in the other chair, a very fat lady with a bag hanging on her arm. Like the kind used to go to the market to buy food. It was made of green plastic and had a big red cow painted in the middle and forming an arch over the cow, the words, "Butcher shop Robles."

I did not imagine Mrs. Margarita would believe in tarot cards and the future and all that, but I did not really care. Another gypsy woman received us. I didn't know if they were really gypsies or if they were only dressed as gypsies but this one asked us how she could help. Mrs. Margarita explained that we wanted to try a tarot reading, so they moved her to one of the tables with two empty chairs and asked me to sit in a chair away from them, where I could not hear what they were talking about. Though, I could still hear a few whispers.

When they finished "telling" Mrs. Margarita's future, it was my turn. I don't quite remember what the gypsy woman told me because I was a little skeptical, but I do remember her mentioning that a very passionate relationship was knocking on my door.

Wait a minute! A very passionate relationship? Me?

"You're going to fall in love with a woman."

That made me interested, but she did not tell me with whom or when. Well, she told me very soon, but not with whom. And I wanted to know with whom. I wanted a name, a phone number, an address, and all the details, but it seemed that this did not appear in the gypsy's cards.

As we headed toward Mrs. Margarita's car, she asked me what the fortune teller had said, but I was embarrassed to tell her, and I just shrugged shyly.

"She told me that a new love was coming into my life very soon," Mrs. Margarita said, smiling mischievously at me while blushing. "She said it was going to be a very passionate relationship." She told me all that while looking at me directly in the eye. I felt my blood rushing to my face.

"She said something similar to me," I started to say and realized my voice sounded a little nervous. I regained my composure and added, "Maybe she says the same thing to everyone, right?"

"You think so?"

"Probably," I told her. And I'll never forget the way she smiled and looked at me at that moment. That smile, that look, or maybe the combination of both, caused a strange feeling in me. It was like a revelation that lasted a few seconds, but at that moment I knew for sure that, regardless of whether the gypsy had lied to us or not, I was going to be that kind of passion for her and she would represent my greatest madness.

***

"I'm very hungry," she said when we were going down Reforma Avenue again. "Are you?" Shrugging my shoulders, I whispered something that was neither a yes nor a no, but rather something that indicated, "whatever; I'm too broke to pay for you." Luckily, she understood my indecipherable murmur.

"Let's go get something to eat. I'll treat you."

"Thank you very much," I muttered again. This time with more clarity, but without daring to look at her.

She turned around at the next roundabout on the avenue and took the road back toward Chapultepec. "I know of a restaurant where you can eat great food and they sell a delicious clericot wine. Do you drink?" she asked me with a smile that had mischief written all over it.

"Yes, sometimes," I said feeling self-important. Although the most I'd ever had was two beers with Frank at Susy's taqueria.

"Have you ever tried clericot?"

"Uh," I said, as if I were brainstorming the huge wine list I had tasted in my "hectic" social life; finally I added, "I do not remember, but I think so." Even though I didn't have the faintest idea what clericot was.

We took the road to Toluca and I thought, "Where is she taking me?" We passed a lot of motels and in each of them I got my hopes up that she was going to pull me into one and take advantage of me, but, no, nothing like that happened. We arrived at a restaurant that I thought was quite luxurious and I prayed to God that she would not ask me to pay half the bill. It was just after noon and the place was empty. We were met by a waiter and assigned a table in the corner.

She asked for a pitcher of clericot and when the waiter left we began to examine the menu.

Shit! With the cost of a steak here, I can buy a whole wardrobe.

"What will you have?" She asked me.

"I don't know. I'm not very hungry," I said, trying to hide my surprise at the prices.

"Do you like seafood?

"I do."

"Shall we order a grilled seafood platter?

"Sure," I said casually trying to look like a worldly man. When the waiter came again with the pitcher of clericot, I realized that I had never seen any-thing like it in my entire life. It was a glass pitcher with red wine and fruit. She ordered the grilled seafood, and once the waiter walked away, she handed me her glass. I took the pitcher to serve her some, then I served myself and with a beautiful smile, she lifted her glass, clinked it with mine, and said, "Cheers."

"Cheers," I replied. And, for the first time, I tasted clericot. It was delicious.

The conversation we had over lunch revolved around my future, whether I was thinking of going back to school, what career I would like to study and so on. After three glasses of clericot she asked me how many girlfriends I had, and I was stupid enough to tell her that I had already lost count. She was unable to hold back her laughter. She could be heard all throughout the restaurant, which fortunately was still empty. After two more clericots and half a platter of seafood, I found out why her husband had not been to my birthday party.

"My husband has a mistress," she told me as she raised her glass of clericot looking at it carefully at the level of her eyesight, probably a little blurry because of the alcohol, as if inside the glass was her husband with the mistress. Then she took a big swig and emptied her glass and placed it in front of me on the table, clearly indicating, "Pour me another one." I did not know what to say, so I took the pitcher and poured what was left.

"Ask for another pitcher," she ordered. I gestured to the waiter pointing to the empty pitcher and he understood immediately. She stared at me with what I thought was a half-dazed look, but I couldn't be sure.

"What do you think?" she asked without taking her eyes off mine.

"Now?" I asked playing dumb. I think she noticed I was playing coy.

"No, silly!" she said bluntly. "Of what I told you."

Fortunately, the waiter arrived with a full pitcher of clericot, put it on the table, took the empty one, and left after asking us if everything was all right.

"Yes, thank you," I said without turning while holding Mrs. Margarita's gaze. The clericot was giving me courage.

"Yesterday, he was not at your party because he left with his lover and did not even come back to sleep." I did not know what to say. Tears began to stream from her beautiful, dark eyes as she waited for me to tell her something, anything. I did not know what to say to her, but I remember I took the pitcher to pour myself another glass, stared at it, and without thinking, said the first thing that came to my mind. And the result was magnificent.

"Some people just don't know how to value what they have." She raised her eyebrows slightly in surprise. She did not expect me to say to that and neither did I, to be honest. "You…" I began to waver and took another sip of wine to give me courage. "Apart from being a very beautiful woman, which I'm sure you're aware of, and it's unnecessary for me or anyone else to tell you, you are a woman who is worth a lot. If he does not appreciate what he has, I think that's his problem and not yours. If your husband made that decision, it does not have to affect you, because it does not diminish your value as a person and especially as a woman."

She looked at me in amazement and I leaned back in my chair, trying to remember more parts of the book I had just read, clearly using my newfound knowledge to impress Señora Margarita. *Your Erroneous Zones* was a self-help bestseller by Dr. Wayne W. Dyer and I had finished reading it two days earlier. I liked to read those kinds of books to try to overcome my shyness, but they did not really help me much. I had to actually practice what I learned to get the most out of them which was precisely the problem laid, but in theory, I was quite an expert.

Because I was not handsome, clever, brave, or anything admirable by society's standards, I was a reader and a student, and at least I excelled at that. It was true that I never knew what to say when I was in front of a woman, but that holy clericot was calming my nerves. Or perhaps, seeing that woman, whom I imagined so vital and so full of joy, who was now showing her true self to me, her vulnerability, was what was giving me courage.

At that moment, I forgot about the allure of her sexuality and I only felt a great tenderness toward her. She was sitting across from me, her head slightly down and looking at her glass, her eyes hopeless, as the tears kept running down her cheeks. She raised her head and smiled at me again, wiping away her tears.

"I'm already a little drunk," she said, laughing like a girl. I noticed there was a struggle within her, like a feeling pushing her one way and a thought another way. She breathed out a long sigh and began to speak. I kept silent, staring at her. I realized she needed to let off some steam and I let her do it. "It's not the first time he's done it. He's been doing it since we got married. I had already gotten used to his infidelities, but yesterday he told me he wants a divorce because he is going to go live with her." She paused to restrain herself. "She's young, and I'm old now." The surprise on my face must have been obvious because she immediately added, to justify her words, "I'm thirty-six years old now! I'm not going to compete with a twenty-four-year-old girl. Can you believe it? She's twenty-four!"

I wanted to tell her that she could compete with any woman on planet Earth, but I preferred not to interrupt her. Once again, I felt that inner struggle that was becoming more and more evident. More tears streamed from her eyes; she was having a hard time controlling them. She breathed deeply and loudly, trying to restrain herself. I was going to say something, but she waved me away telling me not to talk and to give her some time to recover. "Let's go" she snapped once when she composed herself. She turned around looking for the waiter, but she did not see him. She went into deep thought again and after another sigh, she looked me straight in the eye. I was surprised at her sudden change in demeanor. "I want to offer you an apology. And I want to give you an explanation."

Explanation?

"You're going to hate me, but you have the right to know. I've never been unfaithful to my husband and I'm never going to be. I had this all planned out. I wanted to feel young, I wanted to feel alive and think I was giving my husband a taste of his own medicine, without actually doing it." Tears began to flow again. "I wanted to deceive myself into thinking I was doing it, but without doing it, you know what I mean?" I was going to say no, but I did not have time. "You're very cute and above all you're innocent." She paused, and I thought, *Sure, you're basically saying I'm an idiot, right?*

"I wanted to do all this with you because I knew that I was in no danger."

What the fuck! That's it. That's enough!

I rolled around on my chair uncomfortably. Enough for her to notice.

"I mean I knew you would respect me and…" she stopped and put her elbows on the table to cover her face with her hands in a desperate gesture, like when one realizes they have screwed up and wants to hide away, perhaps in shame.

I looked away and took a long sip at my clericot. More than angry, I was offended. I saw her wiping away her tears and trying to find the words to make amends for what she had already said. Then I found empathy her. It was obvious; she wanted to feel like a young woman again, to overcome all those insecurities that, perhaps because of her husband's infidelities, had built up in her, even though she had hundreds of men throwing themselves at her. And I was there; she had chosen me because she knew she was in no danger with me and it was the truth. She wanted to put on the little act of infidelity, of revenge, but without really doing it or risking another, cleverer wolf taking advantage of her emotional state. It made sense and I could not be bothered by the truth. I was harmless. She wanted to remain true to her principles and just pretend a little adventure. There I was, feeling offended by something true and in front of a woman who needed support, and I was denying it to her.

"Do not worry," I said smiling sincerely. "I understand, and I appreciate you telling me. Sometimes you need to think about what you're not, or what you don't do." She smiled at me. "Really, do not worry, ma'am, I understand, and if you need my help, do not hesitate to ask." She looked at me with surprise for a moment and then called the waiter who was passing by us at that moment. She asked for the bill waving her arm, pretending to write in the air. She looked at me again and took my hand in hers.

"Thank you. And do not call me ma'am, please. It makes me feel old." It was at that moment when she took my hand and I saw in front of me a woman who was not only beautiful, but also intelligent, vulnerable, tender, passionate, and faithful to her principles, that I made what would perhaps be the greatest mistake or the greatest success of my life. I fell in love.

***

We left the restaurant and as we were walking to the car she gave me the keys.

"You drive," she said, laughing and wobbling a little as she walked, so she grabbed my arm to hold on. "If I drive, we're going to crash."

What makes her think I am safe to drive as well? I took the keys, opened the passenger door and before she got in the car she gave me one of her irresistible smiles. "Thank you very much, gentleman," she said solemnly, but still smiling. I could feel my hormones stir within me. Her sexual energy was captivating.

I turned around and got on the driver's side and asked God for nothing to happen to us because I was seeing everything double. I started the engine and headed for the road. I had barely made it a few yards when there was a clap of thunder that made us both jump, and at least for me, it sobered me up a little. She screamed and after a few seconds she yelped, "A tire!" She started laughing as if she had just been told the best joke she had ever heard. It was the front tire on the left side. I stepped to the side of the road and drove toward a lonely, uninhabited road so we wouldn't be hit by a car or have any other kind of misfortune on the highway. She kept laughing and laughing.

"Do you want me to help you?" she asked.

"No, I'll do it. Don't worry," I said trying to impress her.

"If you need help, let me know," she said very enthusiastically. I took out the tools and started to change the tire.

It took me a while to unscrew the bolts because everything was still a little blurry and moving from one side to the other. I turned to look at her sitting inside the car. She was still in the passenger seat with her head back, looking at the ceiling in deep thought. Beautiful.

I finished changing the tire and put everything away in the trunk. I noticed that I had left my cross-shaped key wrench next to the tire and set out to pick it up when I saw two dangerous-looking guys coming toward the car. They were turning around as if they were making sure no one else was around. *We are going to get mugged*, I thought. *There was not a worse, more hidden place we could have chosen to change a flat tire.*

"What's up, pal?" The first goon asked me. You could tell they were both on more drugs than Jim Morrison during his prime.

"You need some help, brother?" the other one said.

Mrs. Margarita straightened up in her seat and peered out trying to see who was talking through the driver's open door. Goon number one approached me while the other peered inside the car. His face lit up when he saw Mrs. Margarita alone.

Everything happened so fast. The first guy pulled out a gun and pointed it at me while I kept turning sideways as if to make sure no one was watching.

"Look at what we have here," said the second goon, pulling out a knife and getting into the car through the driver's seat to grab Mrs. Margarita's arm just as she was trying to open the door to get out. I could see the panic on her face when the bastard stopped her inside the car.

"Give me all the fucking money, you son of a bitch, or I'll fuck you up, you shithead!" The first goon let go but kept pointing the gun at me.

At that moment, the other goon who was inside the car pointed the knife at Señora Margarita's face and grabbed her breasts. My drunkenness subsided due to the situation at hand. Señora Margarita, pale in fright, began to scream in desperation, "Help!" She wanted to scream a second time, but her scream was drowned out by the hollow sound of a loud slap in the face that the mugger. There was no time to think.

I remember the first robber saying something to me as he moved the gun in front of my nose, but I bent down, picked up the wrench, and hit him with all my might as the wrench crashed into his head. I waited to hear the bullet, but it did not come. I saw the guy fall to the ground on his knees and the gun on one side of him. I smacked him a second time, this time on his face, and he fell on his back with his head and face bleeding. I could hear Señora Margarita screaming, but I could not understand a word.

I concentrated on the second goon who was coming at me with the knife and I also threw a blow at him with the wrench, but not a very good one. Even though he was as high as a kite, he was still able to lean backward to avoid being hit. The truth is that I had never fought anyone; not at school or anywhere else, so I had no experience with that either. I did not hesitate to confront the bastard who came after me again with the knife. I leaned backward, but at the same time, I made the mistake of raising my arm to protect myself and felt a slight burning sensation, like a slight sting. I heard Mrs. Margarita shouting something again, but I still did not understand what she was saying.

The guy tried to stab me once more, but this time I did not raise my arm when I leaned back. Without missing the opportunity, I threw a second blow with the wrench, and this time it worked. It struck him in the head. I hit him once more and he fell to the ground. I thought he was unconscious like his partner.

I stepped over him and got in the car. I threw the wrench into the back seat, but I did it with such force and desperation that I hit the rear wind-shield, smashing it. *Shit!* There was no time for apologies, and it was not the time. I started the engine, threw it in reverse, and hit the road with my foot on the gas pedal as if I were in an action movie. A car passed us on one side honking and shouting more swear words than the first goon when he had first approached me.

Señora Margarita craned her neck to see if anyone was following us. I turned to look at her and make sure she was okay. Then I realized she was terrified, just like me. I could also see the finger marks the bastard had left on her swollen cheek.

"You're bleeding!" she screamed at me. I saw my arm and saw a small cut between my elbow and wrist. It was not serious, but at the time I thought I saw more blood than if I had been attacked by a shark. "Stop!" she shouted again. "Stop right there!" She insisted, pointing to a rest area on the road.

I looked in the rearview mirror to confirm that no one was following us, but it was more out of instinct. I knew the drug addicts were lying on the ground but I hoped I had not killed either of them. I imagined the burden of someone's death had to be difficult to face.

"Pull over!" she repeated.

"What for?!" I finally shouted at her, forgetting all about respect and good manners. "What the fuck for?!"

"Pull over!"

I suddenly ran off the road and stopped at a rest area.

"You're bleeding," she said worriedly.

"I'm fine."

She looked for something in her purse but I don't think she found it. Maybe she didn't even know what she was looking for. Then she started laughing. I didn't understand why. Then she started crying and stared at me while crying and laughing at the same time. I looked back at her. We stared at each other for a few seconds or maybe a few minutes. I do not know. I had no idea, but I know that her gaze changed at that moment and the panic disappeared. She also stopped crying and laughing.

Maybe it was the alcohol, the adrenaline, the strong feelings, the hormones, the fear, and so many emotions coming to the surface all at once, but I felt a fire in my belly that started to burn as if a volcano was about to erupt. I felt like I wanted to release it. A lifetime of repression and insecurity swelled within me and melted into the fire of the volcano. Her gaze burned, her breathing was restless, and her lips narrowed. We found ourselves in silence for one more moment, wondering what we each wanted to do, and it was she who broke the silence, "Kiss me."

Chapter 6

We did not throw ourselves at each other like in the movies where the main characters go to kiss so hard they practically break each other's teeth. Although the passion was consuming us, I approached her slowly, savoring the moment, trying to enjoy it with all my senses, watching her lips come closer to mine, and her eyes close little by little. I felt her hand rest on my cheek almost at the same time our lips joined together. I took her lower lip between mine very slowly, as if I wanted to make time stop and that moment become eternal. Our tongues searched for one other and I felt a slightly fruity taste perhaps because of the clericot we drank. It was the most delicious thing I had ever tasted.

We kept kissing and exploring each other's mouths for several minutes. I stroked her face, gently kissed the part where she had been hit, and my hands began to run over her body as if they had a life of their own. Then she moved away. We were both breathing heavily. Her eyes were burning; her skin was flushed, and she was sweating.

"No," she said, panting. "No, this is wrong." Her words and her face contradicted each other. She was silent for a moment as she looked at me like no one had ever done before, not even in my most erotic dreams. She came closer to kiss me again, but she instantly repented and moved away from me. "No, no, no, no, no!" she said, moving her hands in the air as if she was cutting something with every syllable. She straightened up in her seat, and trying to catch her breath she continued, "Let's go!"

"No," I said, surprised at my courage. I grabbed her by the shoulders and turned her toward me, kissing her again. She kissed me back with even more passion. I felt her hand on my pants near my crotch. She let out a moan when she noticed that my throbbing eighteen-year-old hormones responded to her kisses and caresses. I pulled her toward me hard and her hand explored everything just below my waist; squeezing, stroking, and squeezing again. I felt all the hormonal lava from the boiling volcano inside me was about to erupt but she stopped again. She pushed me, and I could feel a huge struggle going on inside her.

"No, no, no, no, no, no!" she said again. "No! You wanted to be my daughter's boyfriend. No! This is not okay. Let's go, please." Her last words were more like a plea. I wanted to say something, but she spoke again, "Please, let's go." I stood there looking at her with my heart about to come out of my chest and my virile member about to rip through my pants. I tried to control my breathing. I wanted to protest, but she spoke again, "Please." And tears began to roll from her cheeks again. I straightened up in my seat, started the engine, and took off furiously.

"Please understand," she said with her head down, looking at the palms of her hands as if the answer to her internal conflict was there somewhere.

I was about to get on the freeway. "It's crazy; it's silly." She paused before continuing with absolute determination, raising her head and staring at me, her gaze still burning. "I want this as bad as you do. You have no idea." I looked her straight in the eyes and knew she was telling the truth. "But it's not okay. I'm not going to make love to my daughter's boyfriend."

"I'm not your daughter's boyfriend, Ma'am!" I protested in a tone of voice louder than normal.

She smiled and turned her eyes back to the road. "See?" She said, unable to stop smiling. "You cannot even stop yourself from calling me, Ma'am."

"Yes, I can Ma'am!" I claimed as laughter proceeded to break the tension.

"Yes, I can see that," she told me with a laugh.

I had no choice but to join in. "I'm not your daughter's boyfriend."

"But you wanted to be. Besides, I could be your mother."

"You are not my mother, nor am I your daughter's boyfriend."

"But you wanted to be," she said again, making her tone of voice a little higher. "You like my daughter, and she likes you."

And she likes me? I said to myself silently, but I felt nothing. Maybe if she had told me a few hours earlier I would have been moved, but at that moment I felt nothing but anger, helplessness, and the desire not to have met her through Marisol. It was true that she was twice my age. It was true that she was the mother of the girl I liked the day before, but I was no longer interested. I was interested in her now. I wanted to continue kissing her all day long if possible. Caressing her and melting into her body as I had so often done in my fantasies where she was the protagonist. I wanted to tell her, yell it out, but I could not. I could not because as I turned to her I saw the tears running down her cheeks and her gaze lost in the void. A terrible struggle was still going on inside her. She was suffering, and it was my fault.

I decided not to say anything; to remain silent until she spoke, but she kept quiet for the rest of the trip back to the corner of Montevideo and Insurgentes avenues, where she had picked me up that morning.

"Thank you," she said in a quiet voice. It was like a sexual symphony to my ears. I came closer to kiss her, but she stopped me by putting her hand on my chest.

"No, please. Do not make this any harder for me. Let me think about everything that's happened."

You are so beautiful, I thought as I watched her in silence. *Such eyes! Such lips! God, how beautiful this woman is!*

I'm sure she could not hear my thoughts, but maybe by the way I looked at her she knew what was going on in my head because she blushed and looked even more beautiful. She was the mixture of a mature, beautiful, and erotic woman combined with a tender, sweet, helpless, and, yes, sensual young girl. I got out of the car and she moved into the driver's seat.

I put my hands on the door near the window and felt a slight pain in the wound that had already stopped bleeding. She looked at my arm and then looked up at me. "Thank you," I said when our eyes met.

"No, thank you," she replied with a smile that made even my legs tremble. "Please take care of that arm and do not tell anyone what happened, especially Frank."

"Do not worry," I said, shaking my head to the side. "And I'm sorry about the glass in the back."

"Do not worry about it. Thanks again for saving my life," she added with a slight chuckle.

"Later, Ma'am." I regretted it, but it was too late. *I called her ma'am again.*

She smiled again, and I turned around and started to walk. I heard the car's engine as it drove away, but I did not want to turn around. I kept walking. I had a lot on my mind too. *Her husband had a mistress. What an idiot! Seriously, what an idiot! How can anyone have a lover with a woman like that by your side! What an idiot!* I realized I was not thinking anymore, but instead, talking to myself because a lady in her 70s passing by jumped up and almost ran away from me looking at me as if I were crazy.

That night I could not sleep, not because of the wound on my arm that turned out to be just a slight cut, but because I could not get Señora Margarita out of my head. I had the taste of her kiss in my mouth, a fruity taste. I remembered her gaze, her caresses, her kisses, her girly and womanly face, her smile, her tears. I had kissed La Señora Margarita! My stomach felt funny and I wanted to shout it out, not only to Frank, who was my friend, but to the whole world.

I was not sleepy at all; I tossed and turned in my bed. *Enough dumbass, you are acting like a girl,* I said to myself. *Go to sleep!* Then, I became worried about what had happened and thought that she would never speak to me again, I kept turning, smiling again, butterflies filling my stomach with worry.

That's how the dawn found me. Amidst butterflies, worries, and silly smiles. *Now, stop acting like a girl; do not get so excited!* which I told myself every time my stomach swelled with butterflies.

Mom and Dad were coming back that day from their conference in Texas. But for the first time in my life, I was not excited about whatever souvenir they were going to bring me. Before I got up, I looked at all the buildings and houses I had built with my Legos since I was four years old, and how they were everywhere in my room and even in other parts of the house on shelves, on top of my bureau, and even on the floor. For a long time, I had wanted to build a nineteen-story building that I had designed myself. For whatever reason, I had not started it yet and there was no special reason why it would have been nineteen stories. Right then and there, I decided to start it. I took out my big boxes of Legos and started to build the base of the building.

An hour later I took a bath, put on my jeans and a blue, short-sleeved shirt with buttons on the front, and made myself some eggs for breakfast. As I ate, I thought, *she's never going to want to see me again, she was drunk and she's sorry for what happened. But I kissed her. And I touched her, and...* The phone rang, and I jumped. I thought it would be Mom to give me the time the plane arrived.

"Hello?" I answered a bit lifelessly.

"Can we see each other? I'll pick you up at the same place as yesterday in 20 minutes; is that okay?

Chapter 7

"Yes!" I almost screamed as I recognized the voice, but instantly tried to remain calm and cool. "Yes, I can. I'll be right there." She hung up and I put on my Adidas sneakers, took my keys to the house, and ran out without a jacket or anything.

As I was going to the corner of Montevideo and Insurgentes, my mind raced at a thousand miles an hour with sharp images like scenes from a movie changing in rapid succession. *I've been thinking about you all night and I realized that you're the love of my life,* she'd say to me and I'd take her in my arms as I kissed her.

My husband saw us, and he is going to kill you, she'd warn me.

I do not care if he kills me in your arms, I'd say. Then I'd hug her and kiss her.

What happened yesterday was really stupid and I do not want you to talk to me again. Can you imagine a woman like me with a silly, pimply little boy like you? It was all because of the alcohol. Then I'd hug her.

A car almost ran me over as I crossed the street because I was lost in my imaginary movie with so much hugging and kissing. The uncertainty had me on edge. *What does she want to tell me? Why does she want to see me?* An avalanche of questions came loose in my brain and I had no answer to any of them. My heart was pounding and my hands were sweating so much they felt as if I had just washed them and had forgotten to wipe them off.

Then I saw the blue Caprice and unconsciously stopped and put my hands on my chest as if wanting to stop my heart from beating even harder.

***

I got to the corner and noticed she had changed the back glass. I got on the passenger's side and she greeted me with a smile and a flushed face, "Hello."

"Hello," I replied. She headed down Montevideo Avenue. There was a slight silence, but even though it was small, it was quite uncomfortable. "You changed the windshield, didn't you?" I said to break the silence. She looked at me and squinted her eyes. I then realized she did not know what the windshield was. "The glass in the back window," I explained with a smile.

"Oh! Yes. my husband took it to Peralvillo's roundabout yesterday. They fix windows and stuff." She paused for a moment to see my reaction, but I kept looking straight ahead. "I told him someone had broken it where I had parked it."

I didn't know why, but when she said, "my husband," I felt a knot in my stomach.

"How's your cheek?" I asked.

"Better," she said, showing me her cheek covered with a light layer of makeup. "It's hardly noticeable and I can cover it well. My husband did not even notice."

And what the fuck do I care if your husband notices it or not! More silence.

"I was thinking last night," she finally said. "And I concluded that I also have a right to enjoy my life." *Good..., we're doing well.* "If my husband wants to leave with his mistress then he can go, but I still think that anything between you and I is not a good idea." *Ok, now this is heading in the wrong direction.* "You cannot deny that you like my daughter, that I'm exactly twice your age." I made a slight gesture of disagreement with my lips.

"Yeah, even if it bothers you. But it's also true that I really liked what happened yesterday." She blushed again and replied, "It's true that I really like you. A lot."

Wait. What? She likes me a lot? Me?!

If I had been told at the time that I had just won the lottery, I would not have been as happy. Nothing would have made me happier at the time than what I was hearing from those fruity lips. I did not know what to say and I do not think she did either because we kept quiet again.

We took 100 Metros Avenue and pointing with her finger, she said, "There's a restaurant over there; shall we have some breakfast?

"Okay," I said a little worried since I did not have any money. When I left school, my parents took away my allowance and my savings were already depleted. Arriving at the restaurant, she went into the parking lot and…

Well, I want to take a little time to explain here. I have never believed in fate, fortune, or higher forces that guide our lives. But it seems as though some things simply have to happen and everything in the universe conspires together for the prediction to come true, and that is precisely what happened at that moment.

She slowed down to enter the parking lot, but it turned out that this restaurant was part of the Del Dorado motel, and where she had accidentally driven into was the motel. When she saw the place, she stopped in her tracks and turned around as if trying to comprehend where she had gone. "This is not the parking lot!" She almost screamed in fear. I saw a valet starting to signal us to follow him. She listened to him but stopped again. She tried to back up when the motel clerk told us to go into what seemed to me to be an individual parking lot, like the ones in American houses with those big garage doors that open. She kept slowing down and starting the car as if she could not decide if she was going into the parking spot or if she was going in reverse.

"Oh no, no, no, no, no! This is not the parking lot," she kept repeating. She finally entered the place that the desperate valet had led us to. He kept pointing with exaggerated movements as if he was directing a plane at the airport. I noticed that when we passed him, he discreetly turned away, so he would not see us. I still did not know what that garage was and when I looked at her and saw she looked as red as a tomato, something inside me became suspicious.

"You do not have any money with you, do you?" she questioned.

"Uhm," I mumbled.

"Go out there and ask how much it is," she told me getting even redder. I got out and went over to the discreet gentleman. Once he gave me the price, I came back, gave her the information and she stared at me with a smile that said something like, "how embarrassing!" She asked me again if I had any money and I said "no." Now I was the one who was ashamed. Then she opened her purse and gave me some bills. "You're going to pay me back for this, right?" she said blushing even more and smiling nervously.

"Yes, of course," I assured. I took the money and went to pay the discreet man who immediately lowered the big American style garage door and locked us in. She was still inside the car, so I went back inside through the passenger's side.

"I thought it was the parking lot for the restaurant," she said, her face still flushed with a nervous smile. I just stared at her and did not know what to say. "You know where we are, don't you?" I nodded, although to be honest, I was not entirely sure. I had my suspicions, but I preferred not to speak in case I was wrong. "It's a motel!" she exclaimed.

"Yes, I know," I said in a tone that sounded like this was not my first time going to one. Of course, I had gone to hotels when I was on vacation with my family, but I had never stayed in a motel. My friends had told me about their adventures in those kinds of places, but they had not given me details of what they were like, only of their exploits inside the room. I had never dared to ask to avoid being made fun of.

"We're not going to do anything, okay?" she warned, pointing her index finger at me.

"All right," I said, feeling suddenly relieved. It was one thing to make love to her wildly in my imagination or to kiss and caress her in the car seat in broad daylight, but it was another to have her in a room with a bed and with all the responsibility of behaving like a man is supposed to. Again, the only experience I had was quite traumatic, and besides, since there was no penetration, technically I was still a virgin. Yes, I know, at eighteen, another embarrassment.

It is okay for me if we do nothing, because if you remotely say 'are you peeing on me?' I'll kill myself right now, I thought.

"Oh, this cannot be happening!" she said, covering her face with both hands, partially concealing her beautiful yet nervous smile. After a few seconds, she finally added, "Let's go inside. But we're not going to do anything!" She warned again as she opened the car door to get out. I, too, left the car while wondering what was going on.

The space we were in was only enough for a car to open its doors and for the occupants to get out. On the wall in front of us, in the left corner, there was a small space about one meter by one meter. That space was lit by a light bulb, but from where I stood I could not see what it was, so when she said, "let's go inside" and I did not see any doors leading inside, I went to the one the "discreet gentleman" had so kindly closed. When I was about to open it, I heard what I thought was a desperate scream.

"What are you doing?!"

I let go of the door handle and turned to see Señora Margarita who was beginning to laugh.

"Not that way," she said. Then pointing to the hole in the wall she added, "That way." She kept laughing and shaking her head.

I followed her and noticed that in that little cubicle stairs were leading upward where a carpeted room with a huge bed, a small table in the corner, an armchair, a sofa, and a modern TV were waiting for us under a dim light with thick, flowery curtains. There was also a large bathroom with a tub as well as shampoo, body wash, and even bubbles.

Visibly startled, she put her purse on the little table and gave me a timid glance. "I did not have this planned; I swear. I thought it was the parking lot." I approached her and then she stopped talking. I don't know how it happened, but at that moment I felt very confident. I touched her face and moved closer to kiss her gently. "I wanted to tell you so many things before," she said in a whisper.

I kissed her again. "I did want this to happen, but not so soon, not today." She looked me in the eye, then at my lips, and she kissed me with passion. I felt her taste again; the taste of fruit. I drew her to me and held her as if I were afraid she was going to run away or maybe disappear.

Chapter 8

Like bursts of images, the scenes of my first time began to come to my mind, but I tried to push them away. I started to lose the confidence I had gained, and I got nervous. I separated myself a little but continued kissing her. I did not know what to do with my hands so I clumsily put them on her shoulders, on her face, lowered them down to her legs, and put them back on her shoulders. She separated herself from me with a sweet smile and led me to the huge bed where she gently pushed me onto it. Her pupils were dilated, her lips half-open and she was breathing heavily. She slid over my body and kissed me. Our tongues were intertwined, and our lips were engrossed in an erotic dance that caused that volcano below my waist to boil again, seemingly demanding it be allowed to erupt.

She sat on me and felt my erection. She let out a long sigh and closed her eyes for a couple of seconds. When she opened them, she looked at me with a fiery gaze. She started rubbing on the hard bump on my pants with undulating movements, and very slowly she moved her face close to mine to kiss me. But this time she did it slowly as if she wanted to devour my lips, savoring, licking, nibbling without ever stopping her grinding on me. The swell of her movements intensified, and her kisses became more passionate. Suddenly her body tightened; she let out a long moan that sounded like a muffled scream. She closed her eyes tightly, bit my lower lip violently, and convulsed a bit for a few seconds. Gradually she opened her eyes again, smiled at me with passion and satisfaction, and kissed me sensually. All her movements became very seductive and sexy.

She knelt beside me and began to unbutton my shirt. When I was about to get up to take it off by myself, she stopped me with her hand and pushed me back onto the bed. Very slowly she began to kiss my chest as she stroked my entire erect member trapped under my jeans. She ran up and down my skin with her kisses. When she reached my abdomen she straightened up a little to unbuckle my trousers. She got out of bed, took them by the waist with her two hands, and pulled out my erect penis. I raised my hips a little to help her, but I fixed my eyes on the ceiling because I was dying of shame. I was going to be naked and she was fully clothed!

I was left in my underwear and my shirt was unbuttoned. She moved her face closer to mine and kissed me again. Then she straightened up and started to take off her blouse. Of course, I stopped looking at the ceiling. The fire inside me started to burn so badly that I felt my boxers choking my desperate erection. She took off her pants and kept her bra and panties on. She looked more beautiful than ever in her white bra decorated with beautiful strawberries and sexy bikini underwear of the same color with some tasty-looking cherries. *No wonder she tastes like fruit,* I thought innocently.

Her arduous discipline with diet and exercise was clear in the symmetrical perfection of the sensual contours of her curves. With the delay of a slow-motion film, she put her hands behind her back and unbuttoned her strawberry bra while still looking me in the eye. Her breasts were exposed and were nothing compared to anything I had ever seen in magazines or movies. They were beautiful, sensual, erotic, and exciting. There they were, live, and in full color, firm, round, and sexy. Golden areolas framed her erect nipples; they were inciting and provocative. Then she grabbed my underwear by the waist, and I knew what she was going to do as she pulled. I looked back at the ceiling. As soon as my virile member was released, she let out a slight sigh, went on top of the bed, knelt again beside me, took it in her hand, and began to caress it as she kissed my chest and slowly made her way down toward my abdomen. She kept going lower and lower. I felt her wet and warm mouth. My breathing grew heavy; my heart was racing, and I immediately realized that I was approaching an orgasm. I wanted to push her away. I remembered my previous experience and thought, *If I finish in her mouth she'll kill me!* I put my hands on her head to move her away, but she began to suck and moan harder, which brought me to the brink of climax. My body began to convulse as she continued to suck and the volcano inside me exploded. A swelling energy rose from my pelvis to my head and burst in my brain. The convulsions continued, and the orgasmic waves ran through every cell of my being like an atomic explosion.

Once the storm inside me had subsided, I realized the volcano had not expelled a drop of lava. I had not ejaculated. She moved away and stood there looking at my swollen, shiny member which still looked like it was about to explode. Then she looked up to gaze into my eyes. I still felt like I was in a dream, half-asleep, but also confused. "What happened?" She said straightening up. I stared at her and did not know what to say because I had no answer. She smiled sweetly at me, got out of bed, and began to remove her cherry decorated panties, revealing a beautiful, perfect triangle of pubic hair between the two pillars that supported such a magnificent structure.

Once she was completely naked, she came back to me with her knees on both sides of my hips. Then as if we were made for each other with exact measurements that fit one another, she put herself so perfectly on top of me, and I simply slipped inside her. She groaned again, and her eyes widened in surprise. I felt the heat and humidity of her womanhood and I could not help but let out a grunt of pleasure. She leaned toward me as she began to move very slowly, with a fixed cadence, up and down, rubbing. "You can come inside me; do not worry," she whispered in my ear. I only mustered a slight groan.

She straightened up again and I had the opportunity to admire such a magnificent monument to eroticism on top of me moving, moaning, enjoying herself. I put my hands on her breasts and began to caress them with a little trepidation, but she placed hers on the back of mine telling me to do it harder. She then lifted my head and directed it toward her breasts. I began to kiss and suck on them as we kept moving faster and faster and she groaned and groaned until she started screaming, pressing my head against her chest. "Suck them, suck them!" she shouted at me, clutching at me tightly. She closed her eyes again, her pelvic movements accelerated, and she started yelling, "Come with me, come with me!"

She let out a prolonged scream, arched her back backward, and I could feel the contractions of her vaginal muscles, clinging rhythmically to my penis. I felt myself explode and I gave a choked scream. My whole body tightened, blood was flowing through every cell of my being like a torrent and my head was about to burst. Finally, she fell on me and I stopped moving. My testicles started to hurt, and I was panting and sweating and so I started to worry. I had not ejaculated again.

"What's going on?" She asked me again trying to catch her breath and I could hear the concern in her voice. "Do I not turn you on?" she added sadly.

Moving me to the side, she settled down to the side. I leaped almost in one movement, leaning my body over my forearm and stroking her face with my other hand. "Yes, of course you do! Of course, you turn me on!"

"Then, why did not you come? Has this happened to you before?"

Fucking hell! How do I tell her there has not been a before? My testicles hurt more and more as if I had been kicked a hundred times, but I tried to hide it so as not to make things worse.

I stroked her silky skin and kissed her on the lips. I hugged her, squeezed her against me and went back into the innermost part of her body, wrapped my arm around her waist as I inhaled the scent of her strawberries and sucked her hardened nipples, moving my hips slowly, softly and firmly. Again, she began to moan, holding my head, lifting it fiercely, to bring my tongue into her mouth. I made love to her four more times, but the volcano still did not emit a single drop of lava and my testicles tortured me like never before in my life. Again, I felt like a failure.

CHAPTER 9

I could not get any sleep that night either. My parents had brought me an Atari 2600 from Texas, which I had asked for since it came out in the United States the year before. But I did not play with it for long; I did not feel like doing anything.

Lying on my bed, I was going over what happened during the day at the 100 Meter Avenue motel. The clear, crisp images crossed my mind even sharper than those of the film *Grease* with John Travolta, which had been released three weeks earlier at the Futurama cinema, the largest in the country. The year prior, John Travolta had lost his girlfriend to cancer; a girlfriend 18 years older than him, the exact age difference between Mrs. Margarita and me. There I was, lying on my bed with my hands crossed behind my head, feeling like John Travolta.

The pain in my testicles had gone away, but it lasted about three hours and my erection lasted about another hour after I left the motel.

But it had not all been a failure. Mrs. Margarita, with her face gleaming, drenched in sweat just like me and panting like a racehorse after the Kentucky Derby, told me at the end of my last attempt to finish like a normal man. "I've never felt so many orgasms before, if you're like this at eighteen, how will you be at twenty-five!" I was not sure, but I believed her, and my ego swelled like a Cantolla balloon. It's amazing how a lifetime of insecurities and low self-esteem can be destroyed in just a few hours of good sex. I wasn't able to ejaculate, of course, but it was still good sex.

Before I went to bed I called Frank with the excuse that I was not feeling well. Although I did not tell him what had happened, I did ask him to get me an appointment with his cousin Juan. I needed to find out what was wrong with me.

Juan was twenty-six years old. He was a doctor, just like his father and Frank's father.

***

"Please come in," said the pretty nurse as she walked out of Juan's office and held the door open for me to come in. I got up from the seat quickly and almost ran to her.

Once inside, I saw Juan sitting on top of his desk, with one foot touching the floor, waiting for me.

"What's up, dude?" He greeted me, stood up, and walked toward me with his hand outstretched. I shook his hand and he invited me to take a seat.

"What can I do for you today?" He asked me very formally, which was a bit disconcerting because I had never seen him that way. Not even there in his office, which I had already visited twice because of a few bouts with the flu to which and he just prescribed a lot of rest and a lot of water. "Sike! Got you there for a second, didn't I?" he said, laughing out loud. "What's wrong? You do not look like you have the flu or anything. What's the matter with you? Did you get a canker or something?" It was not going to be easy to confess to Juan. I was regretting going to him, but it was the only option I could think of. I explained the situation and my past sexual experience as well.

After questioning me to find out who the woman I had been with the previous day was and the fact that I didn't leave out a single detail, he concluded, "It's all in your head. You do not have priapism, or retrograde ejaculation, or anything like that. You just have a serious fear of coming and you can solve that by forgetting about your fear and your previous experience. You did have an orgasm, didn't you? I mean, you felt everything that you're meant to feel in an orgasm; you just did not ejaculate, right?"

"Yes," I replied. "In fact, several times," I muttered while blushing.

"Well, if it were not for the pain in your balls, your trauma would be a blessing," He laughed out loud. "Any dude would want the same thing to happen to him but without the blue balls." Juan had not really been much help, but he did serve a purpose.

***

When I returned home I asked if anybody had called me. "No," said Mom who had not gone to work that day. "But it's like the fourth time they called and hang up." I went to my room and sat on the bed by the phone. I knew who it was. "I'll call you tomorrow as soon as I can," Mrs. Margarita told me, but I had not told her I was going to the doctor to find out what happened to me.

I do not know how many hours I spent glued to the phone.

I did not even want to go to the bathroom, in case it rang, so it wouldn't catch me by surprise like Santa Julia's tiger. To pass the time, I would take a book, leave it, take my brother's guitar and strum it (I never learned to play it), leave it, stand up and walk around the room and sit down again, play Atari and then turn it off. I finally decided to continue the building I had started with Legos and that calmed my nerves a bit.

"Eddy, come and eat," Mom said later.

I sat at the table but paying attention to the phone.

"What's wrong with you?" my mother asked. Ever the psychologist, her inquisitive gaze was uncomfortable but effective. I could not hide my nervousness.

"Nothing."

She grimaced. "Oh, honey! I'm your mother and I know you very well.

"Are you on drugs or something?" my brother intervened.

"Tavo!" Mom protested. "Do not be ridiculous."

"Mom, it's possible, look at him. It seems to me that in every one of those pimples he keeps cocaine. Squeeze one of them and you'll see something white come out.

"Do not be disgusting, we're eating!" Mom shouted. After eating, I went back to my room and sat by the phone again. I waited… and waited. It finally rang when it was getting dark. I picked up the speaker in a hurry.

"Hello?" There was a silence for a few seconds. "Hello?" I repeated.

"Hello," said Mrs. Margarita's voice on the other side. "Can we meet?"

"Of course!"

***

We met again at the corner of Montevideo and Insurgentes and when I got into the car I noticed she was worried. "What happened?" She asked in anguish.

"With what?" I asked without understanding.

"Why didn't you want to answer my phone calls? You do not want to see me anymore?" I looked at her bewildered. "I thought after yesterday you would not want to see me anymore."

"After what happened yesterday, I want to see you even more," I said. She smiled at me, drove to a small street and parked. She turned off the engine and kissed me with what seemed to me to be a small amount of despair.

"I do not have much time because I said I was going out to buy some things for the girls' school," she kissed me again and suddenly she said. "Why were not you answering your phone? Did you go out?" I explained that I had gone to see Juan and that he had told me that it was just fear of ejaculating. I told her nothing regarding the cause of that fear, so she came to her own conclusions. "Are you afraid of getting me pregnant? Do not worry, I've had surgery. After Maribel was born, I asked to have my tubes removed because my husband had been fooling around and I did not want to have any more children."

Suddenly her face turned pale and her eyes were as big as saucers as she looked out of the window on my side. I turned and saw a man coming out of the house where we had parked, and his face looked familiar. She straightened up, started the car's engine, and drove. The guy crouched down a little bit trying to recognize the driver of the car who had flown off.

"Shit, shit, shit!" she shouted as she hit the steering wheel with one hand. I was confused, although I could imagine that it was some acquaintance of hers who had seen us. "I had to go park right outside his house! He's a friend of my husband's. He was at your party with his wife, don't you remember?" I did remember. I had seen him undressing her with his eyes as his wife danced very close with another guy to *How Deep Is Your Love* by the Bee Gees.

I do not remember what street she drove to, but we ended up at the National Polytechnic Institute, a rather lonely and dark place. A few meters away from us, there was another car parked with the windows fogged up and I thought it was moving as if someone was jumping inside. I did not pay attention because when she parked the car she stared at me. This time it was a cold, determined look. "We're not seeing each other anymore. This is crazy! It's crazy!"

I was mute, I did not know what to say. I had to wait a moment before I could speak again. "But why? Because that guy saw us talking? He did not even see us do anything. Besides, I do not think he even recognized you."

"He knows my car! And how do you know he did not see us kissing?" She lowered her head worryingly and hit the steering wheel again. "Oh, no, no, no, no! If he tells my husband."

That was enough for me. I did not let her finish and interrupted her. "If he tells your husband, isn't he the one who's with another woman?"

"But he's a man!"

I could not believe she said that.

"So what? Because he's a man, he has the right to have a mistress and you do not?" She looked at me like she was with a kid who did not understand what was so obvious to an adult.

"You do not understand. You're still too young."

"What am I supposed to understand?!" I almost shouted. "That he can do what he wants because he's a man and you cannot because you're a woman? You have as much fucking right as him, or I, or anyone else to do whatever the fuck you want and enjoy your fucking life!" This time, I raised my voice until I ended in a rather impetuous and somewhat insolent scream.

She fixed her eyes on me with her mouth open in surprise and I could see how her pupils were dilating and her breathing began to intensify. Her nostrils widened and she rushed at me, kissing me hard. Since the lever of the automatic car was next to the steering wheel and not on the floor, the front seat shifted, and it was not difficult for her to be right next to me in a matter of seconds. She put her hands under her white dress and took off her panties while still kissing me a little wildly. Quickly after, she unbuttoned my pants, freeing my member that was already more than ready for what was fast-approaching.

Without even noticing if anyone saw us, she climbed up, fitting me inside her with a single, perfect, and forceful movement. She began to swing up and down with slow but steady movements, biting and kissing my lips as she ran her fingers through my hair. I squeezed her buttocks with both hands, helping her slide while increasing the up and down movement. Our breathing accelerated and our mouths were united in a continuous kiss. Our moans became grunts that tried to quell the screams, blocked in our throats, unable to release them. The climax came like a tidal wave that wipes out everything in its path. Our bodies became a rigid mass of muscles, with a torrent of blood flowing through them, but it only lasted a few seconds.

Suddenly we were freed, and a great relaxation took hold of us as we tried to steady our breathing, but again, not a drop of lava from the volcano. Apparently, that was the last thing she cared about, because she did not even mention it. She did not even think twice about what she said next and it was worse than the pain in my testicles. "We're not seeing each other anymore, I'm serious. This was the last time."

Chapter 10

The next day I thought she'd call me, but she did not. By the third day, I was desperate, so I went with Frank to see Maribel with the excuse that I needed a biology book.

"What do you want it for if you do not even go to school?" he questioned.

"I just want to shake off a doubt that I have." I insisted.

"If you want, I'll bring you the book," Frank insisted.

"No, I also want to say hi to her; it's been a while since I've seen her."

"You're full of shit," he said, "the one you want to see is Marisol." I smiled and consented. "All right steal her from that sucker, Manolo."

When we arrived, Maribel greeted me with an effusive embrace. Marisol only shook my hand just like Manolo. I did not see Mrs. Margarita anywhere, so I asked, "Where's your mom?"

"She went out with my dad," Maribel said, and I felt the blood rushing to my head. I tried to hide my anger as much as I could.

"Is this the book you wanted?" Maribel said to me.

"Yes, thank you."

"What do you want to see?"

"Uh…" *Shit!* I had not even thought about that, and as pissed off as I was, I could not think of anything to say. "Some stuff," I said like an idiot.

Marisol bowed her head a little flushed and Frank and Maribel smiled at me while Manolo looked bitter. I opened the book and made a fool of myself for a few seconds, returned it to Maribel, and said goodbye.

"You're leaving already? So soon?" She said to me.

"Yeah, already. I have some things to do," I lied. Then we heard someone opening the front door.

"They're here," said Marisol. My blood ran cold, and I froze. The front door opened and Mrs. Margarita came in, followed by her husband. I could see her surprise but it lasted only a second because she immediately regained her composure and smiled at me.

"Hello! What a surprise!" She said to me, greeting me with a kiss on the cheek.

Judas!

"Hi, how are you doing?" Mr. Samuel said to me, dressed in a suit as always and holding out his hand for me to shake.

"Very well, thank you," I said with difficulty. "What about you?"

"Good," her husband said. "We went out to eat," he added as he greeted Frank and Manolo. "Excuse me, young men, I have to go." He headed for the stairs and disappeared.

They went out to eat!

"How have you been?" Mrs. Margarita asked me after greeting Frank and Manolo with their respective kisses on the cheek. I noticed that she did not dare look at me and that she was blushing.

"All right," I answered as convincingly as I could and added as stupidly as I could, "Happy with my new girlfriend." Then she turned to look at me, her eyes wide in complete shock. Marisol, Maribel, and Manolo were surprised as well. But not Frank. He looked at me like, "What are you talking about?!" But there was no time to fix things and take it all back.

"Really?" Maribel asked enthusiastically. "Who?"

"You do not know her," making myself seem important. "She's older than me by quite a bit." In a matter of seconds, I noticed that Mrs. Margarita's face was turning an almost transparent white, the same amount of time it took for my stupidity to increase by ten-fold.

What are you doing? I said to myself, but this time I did not have any answers, just some good insults like *idiot, animal, piece of shit!* and things of that nature. Mrs. Margarita said goodbye like the polite lady she was and disappeared down the stairs without even turning around to look at me.

"How many years older?" Maribel asked with great interest.

"Well, not many really. But I must go now. I'll tell you about it later," I said, kissing her on the cheek and saying goodbye to the others with a slight wave of my hand as I walked to the door as if I was suddenly in a hurry.

Before I left, I heard Maribel asking Frank, "Did you know?"

"Not at all," replied Frank.

***

I was sitting on my bed thinking about the stupidity I had just committed when the phone rang. I did not want to answer because I knew who it was. On the third ring, I picked it up, "Hello?"

"I just wanted to say thank you," said the familiar voice.

"Thank me?" I asked without understanding.

"Yes, for opening my eyes. I just want you to know that we went to lunch because we were going to agree on how we would explain to the girls that he was going to leave the house, but we did not want them to be there, so we went out to eat. I was very relieved and the first thing I wanted to do when I arrived was to talk to you on the phone to tell you that I did not care what he did anymore, that it did not even hurt me and that I wanted to see you. But you made me see that I was going to make a mistake by being with someone so…" She paused and continued with a somewhat sarcastic tone. "As young as you." There was a small pause which I could not take advantage of because I did not know what to say. "Thank you for everything," she added, and I could hear some sadness in her voice, but I could not be sure, because she immediately hung up. *How stupid I am! It's over; it's all over!*

CHAPTER 11

She did not call me the next day or the day after that, And I kept spinning in circles like a caged beast, unable to sleep or eat or do anything. On Monday morning before my brother went off to school, I knocked on his door, so as not to wake up my parents, and beckoned, "Tavo."

"Come in."

I went in and found him putting the finishing touches on his Barry Gibb hairstyle from the Bee Gees. "Can I borrow some money?"

"Fuck no! You never pay me back, dude."

"Then go fuck yourself!" I left and went back to my bedroom very upset. A few minutes later, he came in and gave me a few bills.

"Calm the fuck down. You've been in such a shitty ass mood these days that no one can put up with you, you dumb fuck." He was right; I could not even stand myself.

After my bath, I went to look for Mrs. Margarita knowing her daughters were in school and her husband had gone to work. I stood in the corner of her house waiting for her to come out. I saw the two housekeepers leave and after a few minutes, they came back. I kept waiting until she finally came out. When she saw me approaching her, she stood paralyzed. "What are you doing here?" She asked looking around to make sure no one saw us.

"I want to talk to you."

"Well, I don't. Let's leave everything as it was and forget about what happened."

I interrupted her with total determination. "I'm not going to forget anything, and I want to talk to you. Please." She stared at me for a few seconds in silence.

"Wait for me at the usual place. I do not want anyone to see you get in the car. I'll pick you up in 20 minutes." I turned around and went to the corner of Montevideo and Insurgentes Avenues.

"I want to offer you an apology," I said inside the car as she drove somewhere far away from our neighborhoods.

"Do not worry," she replied in a cold voice. "Everything was wrong from the beginning and it should have never happened. But it's over now and we still have time."

"Time for what?"

"To forget," she said, staring at me. "It's barely been a week and you'll soon forget it."

"And you?" I asked with some fear of the answer.

"Me, what?"

"Are you going to forget it soon too?"

She looked at me again and her eyes began to cloud over. "I'm in a bad place, a very bad place right now. This should not have happened and I'm going to have to pay the consequences. You are very young and in a few days it will pass, and it will pass for me too. I do not know when, but it will pass." She wiped away a few tears that had run down her cheek. "Plus, we're making a storm in a teacup. I had never been with anyone but my husband and it was something new. An adventure. The feeling of being alive and young again, but it was also stupid to want to do it with someone who wanted to be my daughter's boyfriend. That's the worst part; how could I do that?"

"I already told you that I am not, and I was not."

"But you wanted to be!" She yelled, interrupting me.

I looked at her for a moment and a whole storm of emotions began to build up inside me. We remained silent, with our eyes fixed on the road, not talking, not looking at each other, but feeling a wave of passion that was slowly beginning to permeate the atmosphere. Suddenly I felt an enormous need to have her, to kiss her, to make love to her. "Let's go to the motel, please. I have money," I told her. I did not turn to look at her, I only heard her breathe a loud sigh and we headed for the 100 Meter Avenue motel.

***

We kissed as if we were never going to be able to do so ever again. Our mouths met in a battle of pure and wild eroticism; our tongues challenged each other, searched for one another, and interlocked in a fierce battle. We were two bodies that wanted to merge into one. Our collective breathing was agitated and heavy, our hands were like warriors, ripping and tearing away the clothing that stood between us and our skin.

In a few seconds, we were completely naked. I laid her down on the bed, slid into her, and instantly felt the vaginal contractions that indicated orgasm. I kissed, sucked, and bit her breasts as she screamed and convulsed. My heart was pounding, my brain stopped thinking, and I became immersed in sensation and rhythmic movement, a volcano about to erupt. My movements were slow at first, but deep and impetuous. Then, they grew as if my hips had their own life separate from my mind. I was pushing fast and hard; the nectar from the depths of her body was pouring down on my genitals and thighs. Her face was a mass of contorted muscles contracting with her head tilted backward and her back forming an arch as if she had adopted that position forever. The vaginal contractions continued unabated. Screams emitted from her throat, drowning in muffled grunts only to become increasingly intense screams once again. Tears began to stream from her eyes.

I was lunging harder and harder and I began to bellow an unusual energy that flowed from me, increasing in intensity, originating in my genitals and rising to the brain. A primal scream arose from my throat. She kept on crying and her body convulsed in unbridled pleasure, then the volcano inside me erupted and I felt the torrent of liquid gushing out like a stream of hot lava. She opened her eyes in surprise and pressed me tightly against her body as if she did not want to let me escape. Both of us shouted as if possessed by other-worldly forces while convulsing uncontrollably as the lava from the volcano, which had awakened with an imposing explosion of sensuality, continued to flow from within me. All the muscles in my body remained in endless tension for a time that seemed eternal.

It took us a few minutes to recover from such a singular erotic explosion. Our bodies were shaking in intermittent involuntary spasms. Grunts resembling those of a wild beast burst from my throat and sweat poured from our bodies as if we had just submerged ourselves in the sea. Slowly, our breathing returned to normal. She would not stop crying. She hugged me tightly, kissed me on the lips, and then it happened; the two of us spoke in unison, "I love you!" We both said it and tears began to flow from my eyes as I held her tightly against me. It was as if I wanted to melt her into my body, into my being. There was no turning back; we were completely swept away by each other and the world was turned upside down.

CHAPTER 12

"When are we going to celebrate our anniversary?" Mrs. Margarita asked a week before Christmas. "The day we kissed or made love for the first time?"

"Well, it's only one day apart," I told her, placing a curl of her hair behind her ear as we recovered from another sensual and erotic session in the motel room as we had been doing almost every day for about a month.

"Well, that day makes a big difference. Either we celebrate the 27th or we celebrate the 28th."

"On the 27th," I told her.

"The day we first kissed?" She gently turned my face toward her to give me a sweet kiss on the lips, and then rested her head on my arm. "Why?" She wanted to know.

"Because it's sooner," I said smiling and kissing her back.

So, two days after Christmas, we were at the restaurant La Escondida, on the road to Toluca, in the State of Mexico. She was not as uncomfortable there as she used to be when people would stare at us in such a public place. The restaurant was full of young women with older men and a few older women with good looking men.

We had ordered a pitcher of clericot to celebrate our first month together. In a month many things had happened: I had changed considerably and not only my personality, but also physically. The pimples on my face had almost completely disappeared. After having been as thin as a spike all my life, my body had begun to strengthen. I had also changed on the inside. Now I was confident, not like James Bond of course, but I was not so introverted anymore, and people seemed to notice because Mom kept asking me when I was going to introduce them to the girl who had changed me so much. Also, some girls from the neighborhood who never said hello to me now stopped to talk to me, asked me for my phone number, or gave me theirs. Even Marisol saw me differently. But it was not all rosy. Her husband was beginning to suspect that she was seeing someone because she was constantly sneaking out and he did not like it at all.

"His friend told him that he had seen me outside his house with someone he thought looked like you," Mrs. Margarita told me one afternoon while we waited for the movie *Jaws* to start, "but he totally ruled out that possibility," she added with a smile, "and so he asked me who it was. I said to him, 'Do you think that if I had a lover, I would go to the door of your friend's house?'"

"He has no right to say anything to you and he was going to leave the house, wasn't he?" I questioned.

"Yes, but I do not know why he has not left. I have not asked him either." We had been doing this for a month now, giving of ourselves almost every day as an offering to the god Eros, like newlyweds on their honeymoon; living in the moment, forgetting about the past, and not worrying about the future.

On days when we didn't go out, I went to her house with the excuse of accompanying Frank to see Maribel, with whom I was beginning to have a very fraternal relationship. One day she said to me, "I wish I had had a brother like you," then, turning to her mother, she added, "Mom, can we adopt him as our brother?" She nodded with a smile and that moment came back to my mind like a knife stuck in my heart later, when she and her dad discovered us. That was one of the things that hurt me the most, to let Maribel down like that.

Many times, I was tempted to tell Frank about everything, but I could not. He was her daughter's boyfriend, so I did not know how he was going to take it. Of course, he already suspected I was seeing someone.

"Who is it dude?" he asked me once, his eyes fixed on mine with great curiosity. "Where did you meet her?"

"You do not know her. She's not from around here," I replied airily. "I met her one day at Sanborns, around the books."

"In Sanborns? What do you mean?"

"I saw her and asked her for her phone number."

He interrupted me in great surprise, "You?! You came up to her and asked for her phone number? What the fuck! How is that possible if you are even embarrassed to talk to your own mother." That's how I'd spend my time. I had been lying to my friend, my family, hiding from everyone, and not remembering what I had said to whom and when. But anyway, there was no need to worry about the lies for much longer, the bomb would soon explode, and the truth, as always, would come into the light.

Mrs. Margarita's beauty was augmented further by the charm of La Escondida, which looked like a huge cabin in the middle of an impressive and splendid forest. "As soon as the next year comes by I'm going to look for a job to pay you back for all the money you've lent me," I said to her before taking another sip of my clericot.

She smiled, "That's fine, but what I'm most interested in is getting you into school."

"I'll likely start at UNAM in January, but I do not know yet. My dad was going to talk to a friend to see if I could still make it this semester, but it's not certain. In any case, I can start next August."

"Are you going to study architecture?"

"Yes."

"Perfect! That's your thing. You have the talent and you like it. I do not know why you had doubts about architecture or psychology."

"My mom and dad are psychologists and my brother is studying that career too," I responded.

"That does not matter. You have your own vocation and I'm sure you're going to be a great architect maybe someday. You'll build a more beautiful house than this place," she said smiling and looking around at the spectacle that nature offered us through the huge windows.

"Where, of course, we will live together," I added.

She burst out one of her loud laughs. "We'll see, we'll see," she replied.

I liked that we made plans, even though I did not really know if we had a future. After eating and drinking we went to a motel on the road until it started to get dark, then she dropped me off. It had become a habit to be picked up and left in the same place, the corner of Insurgentes and Montevideo, which, as we later found out, was a big mistake. It was very close to where we lived and someone happened to see us and told her husband, who after putting things together came to the correct conclusion: his wife had a lover.

***

On New Year's Day, I went to visit them. "Happy New Year," I said to her husband, and his look made me freeze. He did not answer me; he just looked at me very seriously and shook his head up and down gently, then turned around and left me standing there.

"Excuse him," Maribel begged, very embarrassed. "He's just had a bad day." I should have listened to that red light that came on to tell me DANGER, but I was so stupid that I did not notice it.

"My husband is no longer moving out," said Mrs. Margarita two weeks after that incident, as she drove to the usual motel on 100 Meters Avenue.

"Why?"

"Last night he wanted to touch me and I turned him down. He started yelling at me that he already knew you were my lover. I denied it and claimed that it was he who had a lover who he was going to live with and that I did not care. Then he told me that he had ended that relationship and that he wanted to make things right with me for the girls' sake."

"And what did you tell him?"

"That I did not care about what he did and I was not interested in fixing anything."

"But what did you tell him when he told you he already knew I was your lover? How did he know?"

"He says that every time you do not go home, I go out and he's already been told that you've been seen getting in my car."

"You did not say I was?"

"That you *are* my lover?" she asked almost with a scream of surprise. "What do you think?!"

"Why not? Let him know already."

She looked at me, her eyes huge with surprise, "You're crazy! You want me to tell my daughters, too?" she added in a sarcastic tone. "Marisol, since you did not want him, I went for him, okay? But everything is fine because we love each other very much and we have amazing sex. How can you think I'm going to tell them?"

"So, they'll never know? Are we going to hide forever?"

Again, her gaze was one of disbelief. "No," she finally said more calmly. "We're not going to hide for the rest of our lives. We're going to hide until you get tired of me and leave me."

"I do not have to get tired."

She did not let me finish. "Understand, you're 18 years old and you've just started to live. I am aware of that."

"But I know what I want!" I shouted exasperatedly. "And no, I'm never leaving you."

"You say that now but let time pass." That day we had our first big argument. We did not go to the motel, we did not go out to eat, we did not go anywhere. She parked on a street where we argued for hours about whether I was going to leave her, whether she was twice my age, whether everything was pure sex for me, and whether she was going to tell her husband or not. We did not reach an agreement, but it was not necessary either, at least not as far as her husband was concerned. It would not take long for him to find out. The same with Maribel, Marisol, Frank, and Manolo. In fact, the whole neighborhood found out.

Perhaps because we were so exasperated, we did not remember we had agreed she would no longer pick me up or drop me off at the corner of Montevideo and Insurgentes Avenues, but it was precisely there where she left me that night and neither one of us noticed that in the other corner, Maribel, with a broken heart, and her father, blinded by rage and with a gun under his belt, saw me get out of the car and confirmed what they had already suspected. I was the hypocrite. The traitor. The lover.

CHAPTER 13

The next day, I was surprised that she did not call me like she did whenever her daughters went to school and her husband went to work. I thought she was still angry about the argument we had had. But I kept waiting since, sometimes, her husband would leave later for work, although he was almost always very disciplined in that sense. I went into the bathroom and heard the phone. *Shoot, of course, it's ringing now!* My mom answered and I heard her waving to someone, so I figured it was not the call I was expecting and it was just one of her friends.

I came out of the bathroom and went to my room. From there, I could hear mom talking to her friend perfectly. "No way!" Mom said very surprised. "The one with the pretty house?" When I heard her last words, I was petrified. Ever since I was a child, we knew Mrs. Margarita's family as "the ones with the pretty house" because it was the prettiest house in the neighborhood.

She and her husband had gift shops downtown in a very popular area called La Lagunilla. There you could find very cheap furniture among many other things, but above all, you could find shops that sell everything you needed to look elegant without spending a lot on any kind of special party like a baptism, first communion, wedding, or quinceañera. In these shops, you could also find all the necessary arrangements to decorate the place where the celebration would be held and even gifts for guests. Since they owned 7 of these establishments, their financial situation was quite good, and their house was the most beautiful in the neighborhood.

When the neighborhood children of my generation grew up to become lustful teenagers with hormones full raging, we changed the name from "the pretty house" to "La Señora Assgarita's house," but our parents still referred to "pretty house." Sitting on my bed and totally still so as not to make any noise, I listened in carefully.

"Really?" My mother added with a carefree laugh, like when you get really good, interesting gossip. "A lover?!" I felt the blood rushing out of my body and my heart started to beat fast. I heard my mother's laughter cut out quickly; then I did not hear anything. I could not tell if they were still talking or not. I could only hear the beating of my heart, like the drums of a cannibal tribe preparing for a banquet of human flesh. Then I saw my mother standing at the threshold of my door, and from the look on her face I imagined she was the great leader of the cannibal tribe, ready to light the fire under the pot where I was to be cooked alive.

"Is it true?" Mom asked, inspecting me with her expert psychologist's eyes to detect any sign of a lie.

"What?" I asked, visibly nervously.

"It's true!" she pointed with a gesture of desperation. The downside of living with two psychologists for parents is that they can guess your answers even before you can answer the question yourself.

"Her husband was seeing a woman," I started to say.

"What does that have to do with you!" she interrupted. "Who told you, you could comfort her?" She paused for just a second and continued, "The problem is not that you are sleeping with her, to which I must admit you have good taste, you son of a gun." I thought I detected some motherly pride, but I was not sure. "But the husband wants to kill you! That's the problem!"

I did not know what to say. I was silent for a moment and so was she. I finally got a chance to talk, "How did you find out?"

"Someone saw you last night and by now everyone in the neighborhood knows. He told his sisters or cousins; I do not know. The point is everybody already knows."

She looked at me for a moment and I realized she was worried about me. "You're not going out today. You stay in here, and tonight when I get back from the office, we'll talk." She turned around and left. *We've been caught! It's all fucked up now!* I thought, lying on my bed suddenly. *I hope that bastard did not do anything to her.* The doorbell rang, and I felt my heart beating again.

I could see myself opening the door and seeing her husband standing there, unloading his gun on me.

"I'll open the door," Mom shouted. "I'm leaving now, I'll see you tonight and do not go out." I heard her walking to the door and then I imagined the gun was being unloaded on her instead.

I jumped up, but I heard Frank's voice. "How are you, ma'am?"

"I'm okay I guess. I'm leaving, I'll talk to you later too. He is in his room." I heard the door close behind Mom and Frank's footsteps toward my bedroom. I sat on the bed waiting for Frank to beat the crap out of me.

I'm not going to defend myself, I thought. *I deserve it.* "Fuck off!" Frank yelled at me from my bedroom door. "Fuck off! Are you really fucking that cougar? You lucky son of a bitch! How did you do that? Fuck off, I cannot believe it! You're my idol, you fucking bastard!" He began to bow to me with his arms stretched out as if he were praising Allah in the mosque. "You were so fucking quiet about it. Why didn't you tell me anything, asshole?" He concluded by smacking me around.

After I'd explained part of the situation to him, I asked him if he knew anything about Señora Margarita. "Well, just that you're fucking her," he replied with laughter.

"Fuck off!" I told him in a low voice and without entertaining his joke. "I'm serious about this. You don't know if she's okay?"

"I do not know," he said more seriously. "I did not go over there. I'm just going to school, but I'll be back in the afternoon. I have not talked to Maribel either, but I'm sure she must be pretty pissed at you, and at her mom, too." When Frank left, I was even more worried, not only for Mrs. Margarita but also for Maribel.

I wandered around the house and ran to answer the phone every time it rang, but it was not her. It seemed as if all my mom's friends had agreed to look for her at home, even though they knew she was at her office. Strangely enough, they all ended up asking me, "So, how have you been? What's up?" I'd apologize, claiming I was in a hurry and would hang up on them.

Just after noon, someone opened the front door. "Is anyone home?" my brother shouted.

"I am," I answered from my room while I heard his footsteps as he rushed into my bedroom.

"Is it true, buddy?" he asked with a huge smile from ear to ear.

I rolled my eyes. *Not you, too!*

He lunged at me with playful punches while making a big fuss. "And I thought you were a faggot." He said very entertained and kept hitting me. At last, he stopped and sat down beside me on the bed, adjusting his hair which had fallen apart.

"Looks like the problem is that the cuckold wants to kill you. You have not talked to your woman?" I shook my head. "If that bastard does something to you, you let me know and we'll kick his ass; and if you want, I'll gather my buddies and we'll give him a beating." I, of course, did not agree with his plans.

He left a little later and I was alone and desperate again but about an hour later the phone rang again. I answered and heard a man's voice, "Edgar?"

"Yes."

"I want to talk to you," he said, and I recognized the voice in an instant. "Come to my house right now or I'll come and get you by beating the crap out of you." He hung up and for a moment I was left paralyzed with the phone in my hand. I put it back and left the house, despite Mom's warning.

***

"Come in, punk," said her husband when he opened the door for me.

He was wearing a gray suit as usual. Although he was not wearing a tie; he was still wearing a blazer. I did not know if he had just arrived, if he was about to leave, or if he slept and perhaps even bathed in his suits.

As I walked in I tried to hide my legs shaking from fear. He then shouted at Mrs. Margarita, ordering her to come down; then he told me to sit down.

When she came down and saw me, she turned pale. "Why did you call him here?" she asked her husband. "I told you I was going to talk to him."

They began to discuss many things I did not pay attention to; whether he was at fault for being a womanizer, whether it'd been her or fate; whether I had betrayed her trust, or whether I had used Marisol as a pretext. The point is that there were only two things that were very much on my mind during the whole discussion. While her husband was asking her questions and she was under pressure, she looked him in the eye and said, "Do you want to know? Do you really want to know?" She paused for a dramatic, soap opera-like moment and stood up. "Yes, I do love him. Very much!"

He was dumbfounded and pale for a moment, but he regained his composure and turned to me with a wry smile.

"I have a question for you."

I was already getting ready to tell him, "I love her too." I felt like the character in a great love novel, passionate and intense.

"Do you know that it's not the first time she has cheated on me?"

What?! "Shut up!" she screamed at him.

He looked at her. "Ah, you did not tell him?" he added, smiling with a hint of irony that bothered the hell out of me. Then he looked at me again. "You know she's been unfaithful to me before?" It was as if a bomb was put in my chest and had just blown me to pieces.

She lied, I thought, feeling everything explode inside me. *She lied to me. Why?*

Chapter 14

She turned to see me with a slight hint of sadness in her eyes. I longed to hear, "It is not true," or, "he is lying," but she said nothing. She was silent and looked down.

Anger and disillusionment began to take over my insides, a slight buzzing sound began to ring in my ears, and I felt as if I was going through a tunnel or falling into a well. "That's all," I got to hear like an echo in the distance. "I never want to see you around any member of my family again for your sake. And for your sake, do not ever see her again." I thought I saw him pointing his finger at Mrs. Margarita. "Not even if she goes looking for you."

I started walking toward the door like a zombie. When I arrived, I stopped and turned to them. My brain wanted to insult her, but my heart wanted to run to her and embrace her. Within a microsecond, mind and heart were engaged in a rapid battle, in which the left hemisphere of my brain was crushed and defeated. "Me too," I said with my head still dazed.

"You too, what?" Asked the surprised husband.

"I love her too," I said.

Mrs. Margarita opened her eyes wide and covered her mouth. Her husband closed his eyes as if he had received an unexpected shock, and I turned to leave that house to which I never returned. With each step the peace and quiet of that house collapsed behind me, leaving in the rubble the memory of the words I had heard just a few weeks prior, "Mom, can we adopt him as our brother?"

I felt betrayed and a traitor at the same time.

***

I laid on my bed looking at the ceiling. Thinking. Meditating. *She lied to me*, the rational side of my brain said.

There must be an explanation, replied the emotional one.

There's nothing to talk about, it's all very clear. She's a damn liar! She said she loved me. I'm sure there's an explanation! I wanted to see her and embrace her, but I also wanted to shout at her and demand an explanation. I wanted to get away, and I wanted to stay; to tell her how much I loved her, and how much I hated her; that I forgave her, and that I would never forget her betrayal.

My mind was filled with so many thoughts. Moments of intense passion came to me from when we were in the motel room, kissing, hugging us as tightly as if we were trying to melt our bodies into one. At that moment, when we said, "I love you," to each other, an unknown body and face took my place and I imagined it was that other person she had whispered words of love to. It was that stranger she gave herself to as she had done with me, and to another, and another.

I thought about Maribel. I had betrayed her. Disappointed her. Like a nuclear bomb, this passion had begun to destroy everything in its path. Of course! It was the price I had to pay for being a traitor. I hated myself…and her, Mrs. Margarita. Maybe I even affected Frank with all this. I was a bad friend, the worst of them all. And I was also naïve and a fool. How could I have fallen for her game? How could I have believed she loved me? She chose me because I was the biggest idiot of all. My conscience was happy to punish me, to torture me.

Mom and Dad arrived that night and they both talked to me, but I did not pay attention or remember what they said. I just told them they were right whenever I thought they wanted to be right and after God knows how many hours I spent alternating between their respective monologues, I went to sleep after they made me promise never to see her again. It was strange, but oddly enough I slept like a log that night. Maybe I was emotionally and physically exhausted.

The next day I woke up hoping that everything had been a dream, but as I stirred in bed I came to terms with reality. I looked at the phone next to my bed and picked up the speaker to check if it had a dial tone. Once I heard the buzzing, I put it back in its place. She had not called me, which meant it was all over.

***

Dad went to say goodbye to me before he left for work. "Take care of yourself," he said like a worried father would. "Do not come out until we're sure you're not in danger. Did that lady call you?"

"No," I lied. I did not tell him I had been at her house the day before and had disobeyed Mom's orders.

"Well, I'll see you tonight."

A half-an-hour later it was Mom's turn. Before she left for her office, she gave me the same order, and then I stayed home alone. My brother went to college early in the morning, so he was always the first one out.

After my bath, the phone rang, I subconsciously wanted to hear Mrs. Margarita's voice, but it did not happen. It was Sonya, the blonde who was surrounded by boys at my birthday party. Sonya lived a few blocks from my house on Larin Street. She was seventeen years old, with green eyes, blonde hair, and a body of a movie star, of course I had always seen her as one of the most distant stars in my universe. Her older sister, Lety, had been Frank's cousin Juan's girlfriend,

The longest conversation I'd had with her had been "hello" and "bye."

"I was worried about you," she said in a mellow voice, trying to be very sexy.

"Worried?" I asked unable to hide my amazement, thinking maybe she had the wrong number and was confusing me with someone else. *But she asked for me*, I thought, still intrigued.

"Yes," she continued with her sweet voice. "There has been a lot of people talking about you and I do not want anything bad happening to you," she said as if we were great friends. "Are you doing anything on Saturday?"

"On Saturday?"

"Yes. Do you want to go out? We can go to the movies or to the disco or wherever you want," the latter seemed very suggestive to me.

A new battle started in my brain between the left and right hemispheres, but it did not last long. "Yes, of course."

"So, I'll see you on Saturday. But if you want to talk to me before then, that's fine too. Take care. I do not want anything happening to you."

After I hung up I pinched myself. *I really did it!* I could not understand how she suddenly became interested in me. However, I felt even more treacherous.

"She deceived me. She is to blame," I said to myself in self-defense.

And although I kept thinking about Mrs. Margarita, a part of me did not miss the chance for revenge. With Sonya! I could not believe it. Again, I could not sleep that night because, in my already frequent internal battles, a third contender intervened, and it was Mrs. Conscience.

That morning I woke up more confused than ever. It was Thursday. Mrs. Margarita had not called me, and in two days I would see Sonya. That morning I picked up the phone three times to see if it had a dial tone. Yes, it did. It was a fact; Mrs. Margarita and I were done. It hurt a lot, but Sonya would probably be a good balm for the wound.

Before she left, Mom gave me her protective orders, and I just said, "I'm going out on Saturday." She was going to protest, but I went on. "With Sonya." She stood there for a couple of seconds with her bewildered gaze fixed on me as if trying to decipher what I had just said.

"Sonya?" she squinted, confused. "Larin's Street Sonya?" I nodded my head and could see the surprise on her face. "Oh," was all she said. I spent the rest of the morning building a tower with my Legos. That's how I tried to stop thinking about Mrs. Margarita, but without success.

Early Friday morning, after my bath, the phone rang. I figured it was Sonya because she'd been talking to me every day.

"Hello?" I answered.

"Hi, I want to talk to you. Can we get together?" Mrs. Margarita's voice sounded grieved.

My heart began to beat rapidly as if trying to stun the brain with its thunderous throbbing. "Where?"

"Outside of Sanborns. In half an hour."

"Okay." I hung up and got dressed at lightning speed. I was about to leave when the phone rang again, and I thought she'd forgotten to tell me something. "Hello?"

"Hello."

It was Sonya!

CHAPTER 15

"Hi," I said, and she started talking, and talking, and talking, and talking. Doesn't this girl go to school? Although I had already changed a lot in a month, I had not changed enough to get up the courage to tell her I had to leave, so I kept listening to her, but without actually listening to her. I stood there with the speaker in my ear and babbled when I thought it was necessary, thinking that Mrs. Margarita would be waiting for me outside of Sanborns.

My watch hands seemed to be moving as if one was chasing the other and Sonya, meanwhile, was talking, and talking, "Remember I told you that I had not been to school all week because I had been sick on Monday and Tuesday?"

"Oh, yes. That's right."

"Then why are you asking me again? Don't you pay attention to what I'm saying?

"Yes, yes. Of course." *Did she tell me? When? At what time? Fucking hell, she won't stop talking!* When she finally said goodbye with a sensual, "See you tomorrow," I ran out of the house on my way to Sanborns, but she was already gone. And it was for obvious reasons. I was an hour late. I thought about going to get her, but I remembered her husband's warning. I looked for a payphone and ventured off to call her, but no one answered.

Confused, disappointed, and terribly worried, I went home hoping she would call me. I sat by the phone, waiting and waiting for I don't know how many hours until I decided to dial again. "Hello?" I heard her seductive voice.

"Can you talk?" I asked cautiously.

"What do you want?" I realized the seductive tone was natural; it would not disappear even when she was angry.

"I'm sorry, I could not get out because…" She hung up. I kept the head-set in my hand and felt the rage and fear began to invade my bones. I dialed again.

"Hello?" she said wearily.

"Do not hang up on me!"

"What do you want?! I waited almost an hour for you."

"I could not get out," I almost begged. "My mom would not let me leave," now I was lying. "But she's gone now. Can we get together?" There was a long silence and I knew she had not hung up again because I could hear her breathing. Then I heard a deep sigh and she finally spoke, "My daughters are coming home from school now. If you want, tomorrow morning at 9 a.m. outside of Sanborns. If you're not there by 9, I'm leaving. And please do not call me again." *Why is she giving me an ultimatum? She was the one who lied to me; the one who had a lover!*

***

That night Frank came to my house. "Have you seen her?" I asked him as I continued to put the small plastic pieces of Lego, one on top of another.

"No. For the last few days, when I've gone to visit Maribel her mother has not even come down to say hello. But I did see her dad. He talked to me."

I let go of the piece I was about to put down and concentrated on Frank. "What did he say to you? When did you talk to him?"

"Today. He told me that he was not going to stop me from seeing Maribel, that what you did had nothing to do with me, even though we were friends, and that he liked me, but he did not want to know anything about you, and that I should absolutely not be exchanging messages between you two."

There was a short pause. "And what did Maribel tell you?

"Well, she does not want to see you. She is super disappointed in you." I felt like trash, like an insignificant bug. "She said that the day they saw you together, her dad was going to kill you, but she convinced him to stop and think." *On top of everything else, I owe her my life.* "She also told me that it seems that as soon as this school year is over, they will sell the stores and the house and move out of Mexico."

Even though I was sitting on my bed, it seemed like the floor was moving. "They are going to leave?" I asked without being able to hide the pain I suddenly felt in my chest.

"Yes." Very seldom had I seen Frank as serious as he was at that moment. "Apparently, love hit her so hard, they preferred to go somewhere far away from you." He paused again and was almost back to his usual self. "What the fuck did you to her? They say they've never seen her like this before. She even told her daughters how much she loved you and that it's going to be very difficult to forget about you. For fuck's sake! And you're crazy about her too."

When Frank left, only one thing occupied my mind. *She's going to leave. So, she wants to see me to say goodbye? Or to give me an explanation? She told her daughters she loved me, but it could have been just to justify herself, but she also told her husband in front of me. Though she also didn't deny she had a lover or maybe more than one. They're going to leave town! What if she wants me to leave too, on the sly? No, it's most likely over. We've already come a long way; everyone knows it and I was just another lover on her list. That's so fucked up!*

***

I arrived at Sanborns five minutes before the hour. I told my mom I was going to go downtown with Frank. I just hoped Frank would not think of looking for me since I had not said anything to him either. I was creating a world of so many lies that it would surely turn against me one day. At nine o'clock she arrived. I got in her car and saw that she was wearing big sunglasses, so big they reminded me of Elton John. Her skin, fresh and lush a few days prior, now looked pale and withered, her red nose revealing long hours of crying.

All the anger I felt was gone. The offensive monologue I had prepared along the way had completely vanished. I did not say anything on the way, and neither did she. After a few minutes, she parked in a secluded, distant street, turned off the car engine, took off the Elton John glasses, and looked me straight in the eyes with her red, swollen eyes. "I wanted to talk to you because I did not want us to end it like this."

"Is it true?" I interrupted her.

"Did I have a lover before you? Is that what you want to know?"

"What I need to know is whether you lied to me." *I also want to know if you're leaving, but let's go in order.* "Yes, it's true." I felt a bucket of cold water being thrown at me. "But if you're interested in whether I slept with him, no, I did not sleep with him." I looked at her with doubts. "That's why I did not tell you, because I did not think it too seriously, but okay, I'll tell you." She sat up in her seat and went on. "It was 10 years ago; my husband was with a young girl, as usual. The phone rang in the house one day when nobody was home. I had just returned from leaving the girls in Kindergarten and answered. It was a young man who had the wrong number and told me he liked my voice. I liked his personality and we started talking. I was very lonely, so we met and went out for coffee. His name was Arturo. We dated twice more but never made love. I did not feel good about doing it and although he was very handsome, I did not want to and would not have had the courage to go that far. So we never saw each other again." She just stared at me and I perceived some hesitation. "We did kiss." I felt my stomach shrink, "but we never slept together. One day, arguing with my husband about another lover I had discovered him with, I shouted at him and told him I too had gone out with someone, that I had had a lover." She took another short pause and looked down at her hands. "That's the story. It was 10 years ago and that's why I did not care. I've never slept with anyone after Samuel. You're the only one." Tears began to roll down her cheeks. "And it was a terrible mistake." Now she was sobbing. "Because I cannot leave you. I do not know what to do! It's an obsession! I'm out of my mind! I came to tell you that we were not going to see each other anymore and I cannot." I hugged her and she cried on my shoulder.

How could I be so stupid! I should have listened to her before I judged her.

I could not leave her either, but I knew what to do. At that moment, I decided we would go ahead, no matter what happened, no matter who or what may fall. I kissed her on the lips and drank the tears that soaked her face, "Is it true that you're going to leave?"

She looked at me for a moment without understanding. "Oh," she said, understanding what I meant. "Frank told you?" I nodded. "It's a plan." She looked down. "Maybe. I do not know." She fixed her eyes back on mine. "But I cannot leave you. I do not know. I do not know what to do!" She started crying like a young girl who had experienced the worst tragedy ever, and I hugged her, consoled her. Even though she was twice my age, I felt in my arms that other part of her that I loved so much. The sweet, helpless little girl who needed protection, and above all, sympathy.

***

Inside the motel, I laid her down slowly on the bed and started kissing her very slowly. I started with her face and went down to her neck, slowly. I stripped her of her blouse and bra by kissing her skin, sucking her breasts and stroking them with my hands. I walked the silky road to the navel and paused to strip her of the clothes that still covered her body until I stripped her of everything other than her skin.

I kissed her feet and headed north with soft and slow touches, going around her thighs with my lips, my teeth, and my tongue; going up to the portal of the sanctuary between her two columns, where I could sense the most exciting fragrance. I noticed how my skin was bristling with its scent, as well as hers, at the touch of my lips. I eagerly explored the temple of pleasure, gently sucking up the little cherry that stood to be devoured, and thought, if paradise had a taste, this would be it, no doubt. I drank the ambrosia of her being with as much eagerness as anyone who drinks water after days in the desert. She was bending her back experiencing a prolonged orgasm and clinging to my hair, squeezing me against her pelvis.

After a few minutes, I continued ascending with my kisses until I reached her mouth again, where our tongues were frolicking like children in a forbidden forest. Bold, daring, fearless, but with stealth, with caution. I barged in with total determination, down the well-known road inside her and began the slow movements, in the way I knew she liked. Pushing fast and deep, backing up slowly. The rhythm was gradually accelerated, enjoying, feeling, noticing every movement, accessing nirvana gradually, creating an energetic field full of eroticism, which invariably ended in an explosion of orgasmic bliss that ran through every cell of our bodies. Our encounters had become almost a religious experience, a path toward divinity.

As I stroked her head on my chest, I did not care about her husband, Maribel, Frank, or anything that might happen. And much less about Sonya, but it was a mistake to forget about Sonya. The Sonya effect would not take long to develop consequences. "My daughters are angry with me and my husband gave me an ultimatum; he wants me to leave you and go to a marriage retreat where they can help us," she said, stroking my abdomen with the edge of her fingernails. "He already ended the relationship with that girl and made me promise never to see you again."

"He made you promise?" I asked in surprise. "So, you promised him we'd never see each other again?"

She raised her head to fix her eyes on mine. "I had to," she replied worriedly. "He can easily put me on the streets. The stores are under his name; the house is under his name. He could even take the girls away from me."

"But…" I started to say before she interrupted me.

"It's the only way. We can see each other in secret. I'm not going to risk my whole life, my daughters and everything for you to leave me in a month."

"Again with that?"

"Yes, again. You're 18 years old and have a lifetime ahead of you." I was going to say something, but she would not let me. "Please," she practically begged. "Let's live in the moment. Let's enjoy it to the fullest and forget about everything else."

***

After noon I returned to the house and started to build my small nineteen-story building with Legos. I already had, of course, the classics like the Latin American Tower, the Empire State Building, and many others I had built over the years, both with the Lego and the Mecanno which had the metal pieces, but this building, although not as tall as the previous ones, had a special meaning for me, because it was the first one I designed myself.

The sun was already setting when the phone rang. "I'll answer it!" I yelled automatically. I'd already made it a habit to scream out that exact sentence every time the phone rang, and at home, they had become familiar with it as well.

"Hello?"

"Hi, my mom's lending us her Caribbean, so you do not need to get a car. I asked my dad for his Le Baron, but he did not want to lend it to me since it's new. He does not want us to scratch it or do anything to it. I'll pick you up at 8 p.m. because I have permission to stay out only until midnight. Is that okay?"

Sonya! I had completely forgotten about her. "Yeah, okay," I said like a fool because I should have said no.

"Ok. Ciao! I'll see you later."

Dumbass! Now how do I get out of this one?

Chapter 16

While I was getting ready I began to imagine fantastical stories, *Sonya came to pick me up at 8 o'clock and there was an ambulance outside my house. She ran in and Mom, crying, told her, "He slipped in the bathroom and is unconscious. We're taking him to the hospital right now." "Sonya, you guys won't be able to go out today," mom said. "The witch's husband shot him when he was going to buy you some flowers and he's in intensive care at the hospital. We do not know if he'll live! But if he lives, he'll call you. Do not look for him, he will probably not remember anyone when he comes out. Not me. Not even his dad. Not even you."*

Someone rang the bell and I, dressed and groomed like Travolta in Saturday Night Fever opened the door and a policeman said to me, "Do you know a pretty young girl with green eyes and blonde hair who came in an orange Caribbean?"

I said, "Yes, it was Sonya."

"She just crashed into the corner and she's in pretty bad shape."

***

"Are you going to need the car?" Mom helped snap me out of my fantasy.

"No, she's picking me up." If I wasn't mistaken Mom's smile was one of pride.

"They all want what the most envied woman has, don't they?" She said with a smile on her face. "Lucky bastard!" I did not feel so lucky. More felt like I'd hit a dead end. Sonya was well known in the neighborhood, although not very well-thought of.

Perhaps even Mrs. Margarita's daughters will go out with us! I thought to myself as I turned on the blow dryer to do my hair, wishing something would happen to me at that moment because I did not have the courage to stand Sonya up.

At 8 p.m. I was still wishing she would not come, at 8:20 I was even glad she did not show up. At 8:30 I was breathing calmly and starting to feel relaxed. At 8:45 the doorbell rang. I opened the door and there she was dressed like Olivia Newton-John in *Grease* with black stretch pants, a black blouse, and a black jacket, high heels, and blonde hair combed like Ms. Newton-John. I must admit she looked hot, but I still felt the world coming down on me. I felt a bit old-fashioned because I had dressed like Travolta in *Saturday Night Fever* and not like in Grease, which was becoming more popular at the time. I thought I would change quickly but I decided not to when she told me, "Oh, how handsome!" I think I blushed.

*****

We went to the club and the whole way there she was telling me about her life and everyone else's. As we danced, she kept talking to me and whispered in my ear so I could hear her over music by the Bee Gees, Tavares, and Olivia Newton-John.

"They say you're very good in bed," she said when we had sat down for a while to rest. She said this as I was taking a sip from the rum and coke I ordered, which caused me to almost choke and start coughing. "Is it true?"

What kind of question is that? I thought. I just smiled at her very self-consciously as I moved around my seat trying to get comfortable. Without taking her eyes off me, she took a sip from her second vodka with orange juice. Even though she was a minor, she knew everyone in the club, and they gave her anything she wanted. We did not even have to line up to get in. "They say you've already slept with a lot of ladies in the neighborhood, and that they pay you for it." I looked at her with my eyes wide in shock and without knowing what to say. "Is it true?"

"Is that what they say?" I finally was able to talk. The rum and coke were starting to make me feel a little loose and her words were boosting my ego. I crossed my left leg over my right leg while leaning back against the chair. I fiddled with my glass of rum and coke, created what I thought would be my sexiest look, and talked in what I thought would be my deepest, most sensual, and manliest of voices, "What do you think?"

"I do not know," she said with a very sexy smile. "I'll have to find out."

I think that was all I managed to say the entire night, she kept on talking and talking and talking until it was time to leave. "Let's go, it's nearly 12 o'clock." We left the club quite dizzy due to all the rum and vodka drinks.

"I'll take you home and then I'll walk to mine," I told her, trying to enunciate every word before we got in the car.

"No, I'll take you home and then I'll go home because I do not want you to get mugged or let her husband do something to you." *She reminded me of Mrs. Margarita!*

I did not have time to react. I felt her breath very close to me, her hands on my neck, her body attached to mine, and her lips on my lips. I admit I liked her kiss, but it did not have that taste of fruit. It tasted of alcohol and betrayal. My betrayal. We got home and she kissed me again, and I reciprocated. "I'll call you tomorrow," she said before taking off.

I just stood there for a moment. Even though I could blame it on the rum and cokes, I felt very badly about myself. I remembered Margarita's tear-stained face and her sobbing voice telling me she could not leave me. While she faced a dilemma for loving me, risking her future, her family, and even her life, I made out with Sonya. *I'm such a son of bitch!* I felt awful.

***

The next morning, I had a headache and still felt terrible, physically and emotionally. I had not slept well because, although I was not drunk enough to throw up, I was drunk enough that when I lay down on the bed, it was as if God was spinning the world around like I did with the little globe my father had on his office desk when I was a child turning it as hard as I could and stopping it with my finger to, supposedly, see where I was going to go.

"We're going to the market for breakfast. Get ready, we're leaving in half an hour," Mom said, tapping on the door. It sounded like cannonballs to me. Sometimes, we would go on Sundays to have breakfast with the family at the Colonia Industrial market with their famous *memelas*.

I took a quick bath so they would not see the terrible state I was in. Even though I had only had about three or four rums, it seemed as if I had drunk the entire bottle. I had never really been good with hard alcohol. When I was putting the finishing touches on my hair, the phone rang. "Hello?" I said still with a terrible headache, and I could hear something strange in Mrs. Margarita's voice when she said, "Is it true you're Sonya's boyfriend?" My hangover instantly went away.

CHAPTER 17

We met at night in a park in Tlatelolco, where Paseo de la Reforma Avenue began, so I could explain the situation. We'd already spoken on the phone three times that day and she'd hung up on me twice. The day was torture. Sonya called me and I told her I was on my way out with my parents and would call her when I got back. I did not call her. From my mind, a torrent of wild thoughts and ideas, lies, truths, forgiveness, excuses, guilt, accusations, and terrible regret flowed.

I saw Frank in the afternoon. "Now you're Sonya's boyfriend, you bastard? I cannot believe it! What the fuck is wrong with you?" I told him what had happened with Sonya and that I was afraid that now I had lost Mrs. Margarita. He looked me in the eye with a very serious look, something extremely rare for him. "So, you two thought you were still going to see each other despite all the trouble?" I was silent because I did not know what to say. After slowly moving his head sideways, he continued, "Look, I do not give a fuck what you guys do. If you want to stay with her and she wants to stay with you, that's on you, but do not be an ass. If you're going to go out with Sonya then do not fuck up the lady's life, dude. You've got nothing to lose and she does…she's got a lot to lose. I thought you were into her too, but if you just want to keep banging her, and Sonya too, and be a fuckboy, then leave her alone. Sonya is also really fucking hot and free. She has no children, no husband, and no issues. And she is our age." He paused again before continuing. "Think about it carefully, man. Looks like Maribel's mom does love you a lot, but if you do not, then go and fuck Sonya all you want. Leave the lady alone and do not fuck around man."

I had never cried in front of Frank before, but the conflict of emotions was so intense that I could not stop a couple of tears from slipping from my eyes. I thought he was going to start teasing me, but he put his hand on my shoulder and said, "You know I'm with you, brother. I do not care about her fucking husband, even if he's my girl's father. But think about what you're doing; do not act like a fucking idiot." I wiped my cheeks with my fingers and smiled gratefully at him as I was quite surprised by the way he was acting. We had known each other since we were four-years-old and had always been best friends, but very rarely had I seen him so serious. He usually made jokes and made fun of everything and everyone. "And no crying dude. Do not be a faggot!" and with that, he went back to being his normal self. When Frank left, I just sat on the floor by my bedside meditating. The storm of contradictory thoughts turned into a damn hurricane! I was getting more and more confused.

***

I arrived at the park when it was almost dark. A couple who were on the bench next to us got up and walked away. I think they were looking for a more serene place not to disturb their romance. I saw her arrive a few minutes later dressed in a thick pink wool sweater, and although it was a little chilly, her long, loose white skirt; the one she wore when we made love in her car that made her look as sensual as the goddess Aphrodite. Her look was so cold, it froze my blood. She sat next to me on the bench and her gaze was like ice. She did not say anything; she just waited for me to talk. At that moment, I decided to take responsibility for my actions and assume the consequences. I told her everything. There was a moment when I noticed her jaw clenching with rage and the tears of disappointment began to roll, but she let me finish talking without interrupting. When I finished, I could tell that anger, sadness, and disappointment were all mixed up inside her.

"Well, somehow I'm glad this happened," she was able to articulate at last. "And that it happened now that I still have time to save my marriage." Her gaze turned hard, her jaw tightened, and I thought she was going to hit me. "You're just like everyone else! Worse!" She got up, turned around to leave and I got up too, going after her. I managed to grab her by the arm and turn her around with some force.

"No," I said, hugging her by the waist and holding her tight against me.

"Let go of me!" She said while crying. She struck me with a well-deserved slap. However, her tears hurt me more than the blow because the remorse burned me, and the risk of losing her overwhelmed me.

"No!" I repeated, holding her tighter. "I swear it won't happen again."

"It will happen again, and many times because you are a man and because you are still a child. All men are the same!"

"Not me. Please, let me show you." I tried to kiss her, but she resisted.

"Let me go!" she said again as we tussled around.

"No, not until you forgive me." I looked her right in the eyes and from the bottom of my soul the following words came out, "I love you."

"That's not true!" she shouted trying to get away from me. "Hypocrite!"

When I saw her so determined, I could not help it, the tears began to flow. "I swear I love you. I swear!"

She stopped resisting, stared at mine for a moment, and with a glare told me that she loved me as much as I did. She did it in such a way that it was etched in my mind like an indelible tattoo. Even now, I can see her eyes fixed on mine, her lips half-open, her pupils dilated, and her kiss passionately devouring my lips, squeezing me tightly toward her, pushing me down to the grass, and then tearing off her panties, freeing my member and perching on top of me to make love in the middle of the public park, hidden in the darkness of the night.

We were beginning to approach climaxing when suddenly, she stopped moving, took my face with both hands, and looked me in the eyes with a burning, fiery stare. "Did you sleep with her?"

"No."

"Do you swear?"

"I swear to God," I said as I tried to continue thrusting but she squeezed her hip tightly, rendering me immobile.

Her gaze became wild, primitive, erotic. Without letting go of my face, she said to me, "Don't you dare! Ever!" She started to move again while clenching her teeth tightly, and saying "Did you hear me, asshole? Never!" We both climaxed in a few seconds with a burst of wild, obsessive passion and, yes, no doubt, love. A sickly love, some said, but a love so intense that I had the privilege of feeling, of living, a love that left its mark on us forever.

After we both orgasmed, we got up and put on our clothes on before a policeman could arrive or someone could see us. We stayed a little longer in each other's arms, sitting on the bench, kissing. "Do not ever do that to me again," she said with her lips rubbing against mine.

"Never!" I kissed her tenderly and looked her straight in the eye. "I love you."

She hugged me tightly as if she were afraid I was going to run away. "What's going to happen? My God, what's going to happen?" I could hear the anguish in her voice. She went home on the Caprice and I took the bus. When I arrived at my street, I could see an orange Caribbean parked outside my house. With arms folded over her prominent chest, leaning against the car, and with a sour look on her face; it was Sonya!

***

"Hello," I said trying to give myself courage, but determined to do what I had to do.

"Where were you? I've been here for almost an hour waiting for you, freezing."

"You could have gotten in the car," I said, realizing too late that I had made a stupid comment.

"You said you'd call me when you got back from I do not know where with your parents, and your parents have been home for a while. Where did you go?" she demanded of me.

"I need to talk to you."

"Well, that's what we're doing, isn't it?"

I was silent for a moment trying to gather my words, but in the end, all I could muster was, "We're not seeing each other anymore."

The pain and anger contorted on her face was more about wounded pride than a wounded heart. "Are you out of your mind? Everyone already knows we're together."

I stood in front of her not knowing what to say. It was a lot of work to fix this situation, but I had to do it. "We're not, actually."

"No? Then what are we?"

I felt my hands sweating. "We're friends."

"Friends who kiss. Are you telling me that I'm a whore?"

"No! Of course not. I just," I could not tell her the real reason, of course. "I'm not ready to have a girlfriend."

"Do not give me that! You're with that lady, Margarita and she will not let you be with me, right?"

"No, it's not that."

"I can go talk to her and tell her to stay away from us."

"No, no, no!" I knew she was capable of it. Sonya had a reputation for not beating about the bush, and she was also quite impetuous. One time she saw Santiago, who was her boyfriend at the time, hugging a girl as they walked quietly down the street. Sonya approached with a furious look on her face, went berserk on the girl and almost ripped her hair off, who turned out to be Santiago's cousin, and when she found out, she just said, "Oh, I'm sorry."

Although her fame as a fierce, hard to tame woman was well known, there were many guys trying to get with her because of her beauty and perhaps also because of her reputation. But in reality she had only had a couple of boyfriends. Many friends, of course, but she was very demanding when it came to courtship, so I should have been flattered by the distinction, and she quite hurt by me daring to refuse.

"Why do not you want me to talk to her?"

"It's no use. She had nothing to do with it."

She came up to me, put her hands on my neck and pulled me toward her to kiss me. Her thick, sensual lips were truly appetizing, but I was not willing to make the same mistake twice. "No, Sonya" I said, holding her hands and removing them from the back of my neck as I pulled back.

I felt my left cheek burning and I heard a loud noise in my ear as if something had exploded inside it. The slap she gave me left me stunned for a couple of seconds. She started yelling at me at the top of her lungs, but I could not quite understand her screams because of the loud buzzing inside my head which still had me dazed.

Suddenly the door to my house opened and I saw my mother. "What's going on?" she asked as she approached us.

"It just so happens that your little boy is just playing with me. But you're gonna regret it. You're gonna regret it!" she shouted at me in tears of rage. Then she went straight into the Caribbean and left, while I just stood there speechless.

Mom looked at me for a moment with that psychologist's look trying to uncover my most intimate secrets and then told me, "Get in the house." As I walked inside the house, I was thinking about how less than two months ago I'd been complaining about how my life was boring and monotonous. I was depressed all the time, and now I could not even sleep from all the drama. In one night, two women had slapped me on the same cheek, the two most beautiful women in the neighborhood. I had to choose between them. A few weeks before not even the housemaids had noticed me, not even Gloria, who had worked with us and had gone back to her village three months earlier with two of my mother's watches, some golden cuff links from my father, and my Sheaffer fountain pen.

Gloria was 20 years old, with monumental breasts and hips, and had slept with a couple of guys from the neighborhood, not counting my brother. One day, when I got home early, I saw her running out of his room, trying to cover her nakedness with her own underwear in her hands. Later, my brother, all sweaty and flushed, begged me not to say anything to my parents. Two days later, she said she had to go back to her village urgently for a week and she did not come back. It was precisely the week she was supposed to come back when Mom realized that the watches, the cuff links, and my Sheaffer were missing and that she wouldn't be coming back.

"What's the matter with you?" Mom asked.

"Nothing," I answered in a whisper, like a scolded child.

She waved me to sit on the couch. "Are you still with that lady?"

"No."

"Then why don't you want to hang out with Sonya?" I shrugged without saying a word. "Don't you realize her husband's going to kill you if you don't leave her alone?" I remained silent. "Sonya is your age. She is beautiful and all the boys in the neighborhood would beg her to go out with them. And you have the luxury of turning her down." I looked down, picking at nonexistent fluff from my jeans on my knee. Mom was silent for a moment and I kept looking for lint on my pants. She moved onto the sofa to get closer to me, took me by the hand, and looked me in the eye revealing great concern. "I'm not going to tell you to leave her because I know you're not going to." She caressed my face like she did when I was a kid, stroking my hair backward. She got a little misty-eyed. "I just want to ask you one favor. Take care of yourself. Take very good care of yourself." Tears fell down her cheeks. She kissed me on the forehead and I got a lump in my throat. Neither of us said anything. It wasn't necessary.

She got up and went to the kitchen. I followed her with my eyes and then I realized that Dad was watching us in the doorway. He stepped aside and looked at me, walked toward me, lovingly tossed my hair around, and smiled at me. There was love in his smile as well as understanding and perhaps even some pride. He bent down and kissed me on the head, tapped me on the cheek twice, and went back to the kitchen with Mom.

I didn't understand it at the time, but now I realize how much I loved them and miss them both. They taught me how much one can love and suffer in silence for their children. I can also understand what a torment it was for them every time I went out, and how difficult it must have been for Mrs. Margarita when she did what she did for me. It was crazy, I know, but we were blind, totally in love, passionate, and lost. We had already fallen into an abyss of obsession and delirium and we would not stop until we hit rock bottom. And everything and everyone in our path would be collateral damage.

CHAPTER 18

On Saturday, Frank wanted us to go to the Road of Guadalupe, a 3.5-kilometer-long avenue that connects downtown Mexico City with the Village of Guadalupe; the road that pilgrims take to the Basilica. Pope John Paul II was about to take this route to celebrate his first Mass for the Mexican people, but also on that day Mrs. Margarita and I had our two-month anniversary. The problem was our meeting place. Almost all the main roads leading to and from the Basilica would be closed and could only be accessed by foot. A lot of people would be on the streets and it would be dangerous for us, so we decided to meet in the afternoon at the Hidalgo subway station.

She had a friend Annie who was helping her out. Annie would pick her up and then go off with her own lover. Despite being short and plump, she had a primary lover and several part-time ones; aside from her husband, of course. But for her everything was much easier. Her main lover was her husband's best friend and although they had been lovers for more than 10 years, the husband did not suspect a thing. When she wanted to go dancing, she asked her husband to take her, but since he did not like to dance or go out or anything and preferred to stay at home all the time, he'd tell her, "Go with Pancho; he likes all that kind of stuff. I do not like it."

If we were out every day, Samuel would become suspicious, but Annie came up with a great idea that would allow us to spend evenings together. She had long since taken a course in vegetarianism at the Roma district with Shaya Michán. The course was in the afternoons and lasted about four hours each day. Annie had all the notes and recipes. "You register for the course," Annie told Mrs. Margarita the day after my well-deserved series of slaps, while we were having coffee at Vips on Tonalá Street, near the roundabout in Los Insurgentes. "And with that, you can show Samuel that you go to the class. I'll pass you the recipes, notes, and everything you need while you go somewhere else."

"Well, that's a very good idea," said Mrs. Margarita turning to me. "What do you think, babe?"

"That's fine with me. When does the course start?" I asked.

We both turned to look at Annie, waiting for an answer. "A new one starts next week; that's why I'm proposing it. You can register now if you want. It's here on Tabasco Street."

"Well, let's go," Mrs. Margarita said decisively.

Annie gave us the address, and after one last sip of her coffee, she got up to leave. "I'm leaving because I have a date with a really hot guy."

"You are hilarious! Are you going with Pancho?" asked Mrs. Margarita.

"No, another one I met yesterday," she replied with a cynical but pleasant smile.

Mrs. Margarita laughed out loud. "No way!"

"If Pancho finds out, he'll kill me."

I looked at Annie a little confused.

"Pancho is your husband?" I asked.

"No, he's my husband's friend," she said laughing and kissing me good-bye on the cheek.

***

One day before Pope John Paul II's arrival in Mexico City for the first time, Mrs. Margarita and I went on a tour of the Road of Guadalupe. Many people, walking and even on their knees, had been traveling all week on the newly remodeled roadway, which was worthy of admiration. On our way, we passed in front of the modest Villa of Madrid hotel and rented a room for about twenty pesos. "It is no longer so easy for me to go out to see you. He asks me where I am going and with whom. Next week we'll have the vegetarian course excuse, but we won't always be able to say the same thing," Mrs. Margarita told me as we recovered from our usual erotic encounter while I stroked her lush hair as she laid her head on my chest.

"But why do you have to explain yourself to him?"

She was silent for a moment as if deciding whether to tell me something. "Because he's my husband."

I was stunned. "So, you two are okay now?"

"No, it's not that!" she straightened up in bed and sat down next to me with her legs crossed. "We're not okay in the sense you mean." She paused again and gave me the impression that she was hiding something. "It's just there are things you do not know." I really liked her face after making love. Her skin was pink and very smooth, her gaze was even brighter, and her lips were redder and more sensual. Even though the conversation was beginning to bother me, I still wanted her. It seemed like I could never get enough of her.

"And if you don't explain them to me how will I know?" She was silent again and those suspicious pauses were beginning to make me desperate. I straightened up a bit in bed and sat down, leaning my back on the headboard, and could not help but feel attracted by the firmness of her breasts. *God, I like this woman so much!* "I love you very much and you know it," she began to say, "but this is the only way we can see each other. I do not want to, and I cannot leave you, but I'm not going to leave him and my daughters.

"But you can leave with your daughters," I interrupted her, confident in what I was saying.

"I'm not going to do that to him either. I cannot do it. Understand it, please!" I realized there was a great conflict taking place inside her. "There are things you do not know about and which I cannot tell you."

"Why?" I began to grow impatient and at the same time, I began to caress the skin on her thighs. I could not help it.

"Because I can't! Because it's not just about him and me; it involves other people and I cannot tell you anything. Period!" she added exasperatedly. "If you want us to continue seeing each other it has to be like this. Me living in my house with him and my daughters, pretending that I do not have a lover and that I no longer have anything to do with you." She looked down at her hands and then continued in a calmer voice. "He asked me to leave you and go to a marriage retreat. I do not want to leave you and I've put off the retreat and I'll keep on doing it as long as I can. If he thinks I'm not going out with you anymore, he might forget, but unfortunately for us, he's already finished his relationship with that girl and I'm not going to leave him until he leaves me." I felt the burden in her voice again. "And please do not ask me anything anymore. Trust me and let's enjoy our relationship for as long as it lasts. I do not want to fight with you." She came up to me and kissed me, placing her lips on mine and her burning gaze. "Please." She kissed me again. "I love you." I kissed her luring her back to me to make love to her again.

That contradictory pattern in our relationship was becoming habitual. Even when we argued, I wanted her. If we were doing well, I wanted her. If we did not see each other one day, I wanted her. As soon as I saw her, I wanted her. There was no way to be satisfied with her smell, her fruity taste, her fire while making love, her intensity. It was becoming an obsession. When we got caught up in an argument where we could not reach an agreement, we made love.

Many of the problems that arose, we did not solve, we simply transformed that intensity into sexual energy and took it to bed…or to the park, or to the bathroom of a restaurant, or to a dark and lonely street, or even to a subway car just to try it out.

That night, I stayed up thinking about what she was hiding from me. Why can't she tell me? Does it involve other people? Whom? Why can't she leave him unless he leaves her? All of that bothered me; I wanted to know. I did not keep any secrets from her, and it did not seem fair that she should keep any from me. But there was no way to get anything out of her, and every time I brought it up she got very nervous and exasperated. One day I finally found out, but not from her. From her husband. I wished I'd never found out.

***

On Saturday afternoon, after the uproar in the northern part of the city calmed down over the visit of the Vatican City Head of State to the basilica, Mrs. Margarita left her home with Annie, and then picked me up outside the Hidalgo subway station, on the Avenida Reforma. "You're wearing a suit and tie," she told me.

"For what?" I asked her confused.

"Because I want to see you in a suit. I'm sure you're going to look very handsome," she replied, kissing me on the lips.

"Where are we going?" I was anxious to know as soon as I got in the Caprice, although I was sure that Eros was part of the plan.

"It's a surprise," she said, giving me that huge smile that made her lips look even more sensual. "You look so handsome in that suit!" I swelled up like a peacock. She was wearing a red dress that showed off her shoulders and a part of her left thigh, as it was open at midleg.

"You look… beautiful," I said, stroking her bare leg, on top of the silk tights, and smiling mischievously at her. She headed down Reforma and I thought we were going toward the road to Toluca to some motel there but when we got to the Periferico, she turned off to the right, went through some streets that I did not know, and we arrived at a very big and beautiful place that looked like a hacienda.

"What is this place?" I asked as we entered the parking lot.

"La Hacienda de los Morales," she said with a smile.

"Is this a hotel or what?" I asked, revealing my ignorance of high society.

"No!" She replied with a chuckle. "It is one of the best restaurants in Mexico. Do not be surprised if you run into the president."

"Lopez Portillo eats here?"

"Sometimes," she said, smiling with a certain amount of pride. "That's why I told you to wear a suit. They won't let you in if you're not wearing a suit and tie." We got out of the car and the valet froze when he saw her get out of the car in her red dress and her matching heels. I immediately took her fur coat from the back seat, went over to the other side around the car, and put the thick coat on her shoulders, kissing her on the lips. She looked beautiful.

As we walked through the place toward the table they were going to give us, everyone turned their heads to look at her. I also saw something I had already noticed on other occasions: when she entered a room, even people with their backs to us turned as if attracted by a magnet. Every ounce of her being exuded eroticism, charisma, and charm. She provoked the admiration of men and the envy of women.

The place was impressive, and as I later found out, the food was exquisite. "The chef here is one of the best in the world," she told me, sitting at an elegant table that we had been assigned with very fine table linen and glassware. "He was brought in from Italy. His name is Lorenzo Ponti and he cooks delicious food. I know one of his daughters. We used to go to school together."

She ordered a bottle of 1975 Dom Perignon champagne. "I recommend you try the cream of walnut soup. It is delicious and is one of the creations this place is known for." The waiter brought us the bottle of champagne and showed it to me. I made a face as if I were a wine connoisseur. Mrs. Margarita laughed at me when she realized I did not know what to do, but she did not tell me either. "This is an excellent year for Dom Perignon." She raised her glass to clink it with mine.

"Cheers, babe."

"Cheers."

We ate and drank our fill. We left the place buzzed from the alcohol and I thought we would go to a roadside motel. But instead, we headed inland to the neighborhood of Polanco, to Mariano Escobedo Avenue, where we entered the parking lot of a rather luxurious, expensive, and well-known hotel: El Camino Real.

"This is where we are going?" I asked impressed.

"Yes," she replied with a very seductive smile. "And we're going to be here all night." I did not know what to say. I was surprised by the luxurious celebration. It seemed as if we were celebrating a year instead of two months. We were greeted at the entrance in a very sumptuous manner and as we were led to the reception, the soft music of a piano, coming from the bar, permeated the atmosphere with the notes of "Somos Novios," by Armando Manzanero.

"Good evening, welcome to El Camino Real. Do you have a reservation?" the beautiful receptionist asked us when we arrived. At the enormous counter, there was also a tall, handsome boy, who was wearing his hotel uniform and he carried Mrs. Margarita's small suitcase.

"Yes, in the name of Margarita Luna," she replied giving the receptionist her maiden name. The young woman could not conceal her surprise when she saw the age difference and how we'd walked in holding each other. But she had no choice but to play dumb. She asked for Mrs. Margarita's credit card and did the registration administrative work. She then gave the key to the young man who was still standing next to us as if he were a soldier.

"Benjamin will take you to your room on the second floor. Capistrano Mission, room 2119. Do you have any other luggage?" she asked in what I thought was a bad mood. Mrs. Margarita thought so too.

"No, that's all," she replied, looking her in the eye with a smile that said, *Is there a problem with that you idiot?*

The handsome Benjamin came to the rescue immediately. "No problem, let me take you to your room." We followed Benjamin to the elevator and then to our luxurious room. After receiving his well-deserved tip, he set off and we were left alone.

From the moment we entered the room, I smelled fruit from the large bowl in the middle of a small table next to the balcony, on which there was also an elegant metal bucket with another bottle of Dom Perignon cooling on ice. I turned to the door where she had been sitting very quietly, leaning against the wall, watching me. I was mesmerized by so many surprises. "Do you like it?" she asked me, walking toward me, dripping with sensuality every step of the way. She hugged me by the waist and kissed me gently on the lips.

"Very much," I said, kissing her back.

"I hope we will have many more months to celebrate, but since I don't know I want us to enjoy each day as if it were our last. I want you to never forget this anniversary if it's the last one we ever celebrate." Her eyes began to blur. "I ask you to always remember me positively. No matter what happens, I wish that this be the memory you have of me, okay?"

I drank the tears that began to flow down her cheeks. "What, is something going to happen?" I asked worriedly.

"No. I do not know what's going to happen. But let's enjoy this day. Please, or rather this night." She caressed my face and smiled mischievously at me, "all night long."

"Are we going to stay all night?" I was very excited and at the same time a little worried because I had to make something up so my parents would know I was not coming back.

"Yes," she said, still smiling. "I told Samuel that I was going with Annie to some talks for married women who were having problems, and that they were in Puebla. Annie left with Pancho and I came with you." Her gaze turned a little bit naughty and she added as a double entendre, "well, not yet, but I'm sure very soon…and many times." She kissed me on the lips ardently and immediately turned me on. I hugged her tightly and responded to her kiss with equal passion, grabbed her by her round, prominent buttocks, and pulled her toward me, squeezing her against my throbbing erection. "Open the champagne," she requested, pulling away and leaving me with my blood boiling. "We've got all night and I plan to enjoy it to the fullest." She took the small suitcase that Benjamin had left on the huge bed and while looking at me very seductively, turned around and went to the bathroom. "I'll be right back," she said in a tone of voice very similar to the one Marilyn Monroe used to seduce in her films. "I'm going to get more comfortable." I was already so excited that I felt the lump under my pants was going to explode.

I took the champagne out of the ice and noticed that it was also from 1975. I opened it just like I had opened Christmas ciders at home, although it took me a little longer because I was afraid that the stopper was going to go off and break something that we'd be charged for later. Then I served it in the thin, tall glasses on the table. The fruit was so perfect, I thought perhaps it was all fake. I took a peach and bit into it. The juice immediately dripped down my chin. The strawberries were big, red, and shiny. I wanted to give them a bite, but what I wanted the most was what had reentered the room. "Hi," I heard a sexy voice from behind me. I turned, and with one hand on the wall and the other on her waist, was the most erotic being I had ever seen.

Dressed in a black silk negligee, garter, and stockings, and her hair a bit tousled, giving it a touch of primitive savagery, Mrs. Margarita looked at me with an indomitable desire. "Do you have a drink for me?" She began to walk toward where I was standing, slowly, emitting tantalizing sexuality from every pore in her body. "Or maybe you'd rather bite me? My strawberries?" She said subtly touching her breasts. "Or maybe my cherry?" She rubbed her pubic area gently. She stopped a few centimeters away from me and added in a quiet voice, "You have peach juice here." She brought her face closer to mine to lap up the juice still on my chin, licking me like a cat. Then she put her hand on my crotch. "Mmhmm! It seems the banana from this fruit bowl is ripe enough and ready to eat." I was already on the verge of an orgasm!

She started to unbuckle my belt, but suddenly stopped and grabbed one of the glasses. "Cheers," she said. It took me a moment to react before getting the drink. We drank and she left it on the table. I did the same thing. She took off my jacket and tie, then unbuttoned my shirt and stopped. "There in the suitcase," she said, pointing to the small piece of luggage she had left on the carpet outside the bathroom. "I have a tape recorder and a cassette. Could you pull it out, plug it in, and put the cassette on side A?" Her tone was extremely exciting and provocative. "I want to see you walking over there. It turns me on."

I went to the suitcase and did what she asked. Meanwhile, she sat on the chair by the table, her legs crossed, a glass of Dom Perignon 75 in her hand and a large, shiny strawberry in the other, watching me. I pressed the play button on the recorder and some sensual blues music began playing. "You Don't Have to Go," by Jimmy Reed. Beautiful and provocative, she drank a sip of champagne, then took the strawberry very slowly to her lips, biting it in a way that seemed to send it into ecstasy as she did. I walked back to where she was sitting, and when I stopped in front of her, she left the remaining piece of strawberry on the table and did the same with the glass.

"Take off your shirt," she ordered and I obeyed. She then unzipped my pants, undid the button, grabbed them by the sides, and pulled them down hard, just a little bit, just enough to free my erection. She kissed it and took it in her hands, got up, and without letting go, took the glass of Dom Perignon with her other hand and guided me to the bed, where she made me lay down. I took my shoes off, each foot helping the other. She placed the glass on the carpet and then removed my pants, including my underwear, leaving me completely naked and lying on the bed. She stroked my swollen member with her hands and took the glass with champagne again. "I think this beauty is thirsty," she whispered. Then she emptied some of the cold liquid onto my penis to immediately put it in her mouth, which I felt warm and in perfect contrast to the cold Champagne. I noticed the liquid had also fallen on my testicles and as if she had guessed my thoughts, she began to suck all the areas where the wine dripped, transporting me to the garden of Eden itself.

She repeated the maneuver four or five more times and I was on the verge of madness, feeling the cold champagne, her lips, her tongue, and the warmth of her mouth all over my genital area. She licked, sucked, and I squirmed with pleasure. "Do not cum yet," she ordered me in a very authoritative tone, like when you know you have total control of something or someone. "Not until I tell you to. Do you understand?"

"Yes," I muttered with difficulty, although I did not know if I would be able to keep my promise since after such a preamble I was too excited. Very slowly, she climbed up, kissing every inch of my skin until she reached my mouth, where our lips devoured each other like wild and hungry beasts. Our hands touched, squeezed, caressed. The contact of the silk on the negligee and the softness of her skin were like electric shocks at my fingertips, transmitting its excessive sexual energy to every cell of my body.

Between kisses, caresses, and groans there came a moment when I could not take it anymore and I lost control: I took the negligee with my hands and tore it with force. That excited her even more and she hugged me anxiously, encapsulating my body with her arms and legs and inviting me to penetrate it, putting me on top of her. She immediately gave a long, deep scream; I bit her breasts and she stuck her nails in my back and kept screaming and shaking.

We were mad. We bit and licked each other; we tightened our grip. We had entered a state of pure, wild, primitive eroticism. Our movements became more and more bestial and the orgasm could no longer wait. "Now!" She shouted at me, and at the same time, we felt the explosion of pleasure coming from the innermost part of our being. We both shouted rejoicing in the moment, feeling a wave of joy that seemed to have no end. Even though the lava from the volcano had been expelled, I continued with the now slower, more sensual movements, which helped me to not lose my erection. She was still feeling it and I was determined to please her as much as I could. I then separated myself, noting the astonishment on her gaze, and walked over to the table, grabbed the bottle of champagne, and returned to her.

I placed the bottle in the bureau by the bedside and she smiled knowingly at me. I kissed her on the abdomen and climbed up to her breasts as she wrapped her legs around my waist, luring me toward her so that I could penetrate her again, but instead I turned her upside down and lifted her hip, placing her on the bed on her knees and elbows. Very slowly, I went back into her body, took the bottle of Dom Perignon, and emptied some of the fine, cold liquor on her back. She screamed and I immediately began to drink the champagne from her skin as I moved my hip behind her in circles, rotating slowly to suddenly straighten up and penetrate hard and fast for a few seconds; then I would slow it down again, pour Dom Perignon on her back and repeat the process until I felt a strong orgasm coming inside of her. When she was on the verge of climax, I stopped, laid her down on her back, in a somewhat violent way, poured a good amount of champagne over her pubes, and drank the liquid I had poured out, combined with the liquid produced by her body. I also went into ecstasy while she had a strong orgasm that made her whole body tense and her hands clench onto my hair.

Meanwhile, Howlin' Wolf was singing "What a Woman!" on the tape recorder. Once the long orgasm had subsided and with her fingers stuck in my hair, she lifted me to her. Her eyes had that fierce look that excited me so much. "Now you," she gritted her teeth. She kissed me furiously and with a vigorous movement put me on my back in bed, standing on top of me. "You're going to come when I tell you to. And you're going to feel like you're dying," she ordered and she was right. She practically took advantage of me in such a sweet and wild way that I really felt like I was dying. And again, I was transported to paradise.

That night we did not sleep. We made love even on the balcony. We toured every corner of the room, the tub, and even the closet when she took out the leather jacket she gave me as a present which she had hidden because I never noticed it. There seemed to be no way to satisfy ourselves; even before we left the room we ended up wallowing in the carpet, hot and impetuous as if we had just arrived.

"I cannot get enough of you," I told her in the elevator of the hotel, where we almost did it again if it was not for the fact that it was only two floors. "Is it because you're only 18?" She told me when the doors opened. We then exited into the lobby.

"Isn't it because I love you?" I replied. She stopped and looked me in the eyes, kissed me sweetly on the lips, and I was sure that a glint of sadness was shining on them. I did not know why, but I was sure.

***

I arrived home almost at dusk, as Mrs. Margarita was supposed to return from Puebla at that time, so we still had time to eat and even go to the movies to watch *Superman*. When I called home the night before, I had said the truth, well, in part. I said I was going to sleep over with a friend. I did not say the friend's name when Mom asked me, but I guess my silence gave her the answer, and I guess there were not many options to consider. Reluctantly she said, "Okay, take care of yourself." I know she was about to say no. I felt it in the tone of her voice, but she immediately changed her mind. It was the first time I'd ever slept away from home.

When I walked in, they were all watching TV. Dad hid his smile, Tavo did not. "The look on your face," he said, smiling mischievously.

"How are you?" Mom said, almost not daring to even look at me.

"Good," I replied, and I stayed there for a while waiting to see if any conversation would arise, but the silence became uncomfortable. "I'm going to my room."

"Okay," Mom said. "Rest."

Dad just said "uh-huh" and my brother made a thumbs-up hand gesture.

I came to my room and lay in bed with my stare fixed on the ceiling. I realized things had changed at home. I felt like they were embarrassed to talk to me like they preferred not to talk to me directly to avoid the embarrassing subject. I was separating from my family at the same time as I was separating Mrs. Margarita from hers. We were creating a world apart, separate from the real world. Suddenly the memory came to my mind of something she had said to me at the hotel. "I want you never to forget this as if this were the last anniversary we were celebrating." I was trying to decipher her words, but I fell asleep. I was exhausted.

CHAPTER 19

I did not hear from Sonya for a week following the slap she gave me, but I did the week after my anniversary with Mrs. Margarita. "Hello," I heard her voice on the phone.

"Hello," I replied worried, but at the same time grateful that it was over the phone and not in person. Listening to her voice I could feel the burning on my cheek again.

"How are you doing?"

"Good," I replied, noticing that she was calling from a phone booth. "Where are you?"

"At school."

"At school?" It was 10 a.m. and she was supposed to be inside and not outside.

"Yes, but I wanted to talk to you, and I went out to find a phone that would work."

I was surprised because it was not customary for anyone to be allowed to leave during class. "And they let you?"

"I did not ask for permission," she told me with great confidence. "I told the teacher I was going to the bathroom and told the janitor to open the door for me because I had to make an urgent call." That was Sonya. She did what she wanted when she wanted to do it. I liked that; I admired her spirit. But at that time, for me, there was only Mrs. Margarita. "Hey, can we be friends?" she added, fresh as a daisy.

"Yes, of course," I replied in surprise. "Of course."

"Ok. Then we'll talk later. Oh! And don't even think I'm going to apologize for the slap. You deserved it. I was even going to kick you in the nuts, but your mom came out and I felt embarrassed."

Embarrassed? Really? You? "Do not worry," I said, unable to avoid smiling widely.

"Okay, then I'll talk to you later. Ciao!" And she hung up. I could not deny it. Her ways had overpowered me a bit.

***

"Sonya called me," I told Mrs. Margarita at the vegetarian restaurant Las Fuentes on Río Pánuco Street, in the Cuauhtémoc neighborhood. Even though she was not taking Shaya Michán's course, she was very interested in vegetarianism.

"When?" she asked me with interest, pausing with the fork halfway between the cheese-stuffed poblano chili dish and her thick, sensual lips.

"Yesterday."

"And what did she say?" her fork still frozen in mid-air.

"She asked if we could be friends."

"And what did you tell her?"

I shrugged. "Yes."

"You like her, don't you?"

"No, I only said yes because I'm not interested in having her as an enemy."

She looked at me for a moment. She left the fork still with the stuffed chili on the plate, and took a deep breath, then expelled it loudly. "Look, babe." She put her hands on the table, intertwining her fingers and leaning against the back of the seat. "I took Maribel to the doctor yesterday. She has not been able to sleep and her hair is falling out. The doctor says it's stress, and she's depressed about everything that's happened. Marisol is also sick; she has lost a lot of weight and has lost her appetite." She paused and sighed again. I looked at her expectantly. "You should try it out with Sonya. She's very pretty and she is also about your age. She's not old like me."

"You're not old."

"That does not matter," she interrupted. "The important thing is this weekend." She paused again, and I was getting desperate with the tension she was creating.

"This weekend what?"

"This weekend I'm going to a couples retreat with Samuel to get help. It's from Friday the 2nd to Sunday the 4th of February." She immediately changed her tone of voice, as if trying to be convincing, and leaned in my direction. "Maybe Sonya is the woman for you, and maybe you can be the man for her."

"Didn't you say you'd kill me or something if I slept with her?

She smiled as if she had said something foolish and leaned back against the seat again. "No, that day I was going to."

I did not let her finish. "You were lying?"

"No, not lying." She sighed deeply and the tears betrayed her. She looked at me with great sweetness and added, "I love you and you know it, but I also love my daughters, and this is affecting them a lot. You do not understand right now because you do not have children, but someday you will have them and you will understand me. This is crazy and we know it." She took my hand between hers. "That's why I wanted us to celebrate Saturday as if it was the last time." She began to sob louder and the three ladies next to us turned to us discreetly, mumbling to each other in amazement. "Because it was the last time." I took my hand away and pulled back, a bit pissed off. "I am destroying an 18-year old marriage, my family, and my daughters' peace of mind all for the love I have for you. They realize I've rejected their dad and they feel the tension between us. Although he has been a womanizer, Samuel is not a bad person, believe me," I noticed something strange in her eyes when she said that, but I could not figure out what it was. "He is not. He's also been a great father to my daughters and…"

"But he's been unfaithful to you many times. You told me yourself."

"All men are unfaithful," she said to me in a resigned tone of voice.

"I'm not," I replied, looking her in the eyes.

She smiled. "Maybe not now, but in the future?"

"Why do not you believe me?" I was getting irritated.

"Why don't we enjoy the time we have left together?" she added, nearly begging. "Please." She wiped the tears from her cheeks and gazed into my eyes. "I'll never forget you. I swear. Rest assured that until the last minute of my life, I will think of you, but please do not make it any harder. Let me go to that retreat to clear my head and decide."

"Make a decision? You mean you haven't made a decision yet?" I said with irony.

"No, and it's even harder now that I've seen what I've done to my daughters."

"Or maybe he has been nice to you and been saying nice things to you lately? That's why you're trying to get rid of me?"

"Look Eddy..." She started to say and I interrupted her taking offense.

"Oh! Now I'm Eddy, I'm not 'babe' anymore."

She looked up at the ceiling and tried to avoid the laughter that was beginning to take over the fight, and it did. "Oh, babe! You're worse than me!" She laughed. "I wanted us to enjoy this week and I was not going to tell you anything until Friday morning, but the Sonya thing came up. Think about it, babe. Think about it." Her eyes teared up again, but this time she stopped crying. "It's torture for me to picture you with someone else, but I have to accept that sooner or later it's going to happen. If I don't fix my life right now than when I do I'm going to be crushed under the rubble of what my family has become while you'll be calmly living your life. You have nothing to lose. Nothing at all. I do."

"Your husband?" I said, being ironic again.

"No, my daughters. I'm destroying their life forever just for a few months of joy." She took another short pause, looked at me very sweetly, and sighed deeply. "After Marisol and Maribel, you're the best thing that's ever happened to me, but if the price is the happiness of my daughters, I do not want to pay it. These have been the most wonderful two months of my entire life, but I have responsibilities to fulfill, please understand." When we left the restaurant we did it quietly, and so we continued in silence almost all the way back. The tension was building up as we traveled back along Reforma to be dropped off on Guadalupe Road, where I could take a bus home. Although I did not want to turn around and look at her, I knew she was crying.

When I reached the Peralvillo roundabout, where Guadalupe Road begins, and where I was supposed to get off, she kept driving. I turned my head to her, bewildered, and noticed the tension in her jaw, the tears on her cheeks, and the fire in her eyes. She stepped harder on the accelerator as if speed could help us escape from reality. The emotion within her began to boil like a steam kettle, reaching its highest point at that moment and exploding with a loud whistle, "No, no, no!" She shouted. "I cannot! I cannot!"

We were driving down the avenue at full speed as if we were running away from someone or something. When we arrived at the Villa de Madrid hotel, we went into the parking lot and we ended up facing one more problem the way we always did: without solving it. But loving each other passionately, obsessively, wildly. Inside the room, we cried, screamed, kissed, bit, and swore eternal love. However, once the passion, the obsession, the screams, and the tears had subsided, she did not allow her mind to stray from the task at hand; she would go to the marriage retreat with her husband and save her family.

Chapter 20

When I woke up, I realized I was in a hospital. My whole body hurt from head to toe. I was laying on a bed with white sheets. On my left side, there was a white wall and on the right side there was a blue curtain, closed only halfway, that separated me from an empty bed and next to that, one that was occupied. I could not see by whom because there was another curtain between us. Next to that last bed, there was a wall with large windows where light from the sunset entered. From a serum carrier hung a bottle with a plastic hose that ended in a needle stuck in my arm.

I could hear voices and people passing down the hall as well as some groans of pain. I remembered what happened. I was waiting for Mrs. Margarita to pick me up. It was September and I was returning from the university. I remembered the black car that stopped in front of me and the guys who got off. Again, I watched everything I could perceive while I was laying in that hospital bed: the ceiling, the incandescent light bulbs, the bottle of serum. I wanted to make sure it was not a dream. I did not know how long I'd been there or if my parents knew about it. I also remembered that my wallet had been taken away with my school ID and my license, so maybe no one knew I was in a hospital. I was probably at the Red Cross.

"So, you think you're a badass?," the guy told me that day. *Me? What did he mean?*

I was sleepy, but I did not want to fall asleep. I wanted to know how I got there, and how long it had been. I tried to get up, but severe pain on my left side indicated that it would be best to sit still. I began to do a mental scan of my body from head to toe. I felt something on my forehead. I slowly raised my right hand and touched a bandage around my entire head. Then I moved my neck and thought I might be paralyzed, so I started moving every part of myself to make sure I was not paralyzed. Everything hurt, but fortunately, I could move everything.

My left arm had a bandage; even my chest was wrapped in bandages. My face felt swollen. In fact, I could see the swelling in my mouth if I looked down to the left side, and I could also see my nose wide and purple if I squinted. I thought of my family again. Mom, Dad, and even my brother, but the strongest image that came to mind was that of Mrs. Margarita. And without knowing why, I remembered when she had gone to that marriage retreat with her husband in early February. It had been seven months since that Friday when we said goodbye thinking that we would never see each other again.

***

That farewell before going to the famous retreat had been very difficult for both of us, but she was determined to rescue her family from the shipwreck and I was not willing to lose her. But I had no choice but to let her go and try to learn to live without her. Saturday, February 3rd was the first day I spent without her. Of course, we had already spent some days not seeing each other, but it was very different to spend them knowing that I would see her the next morning or the one after that. It was difficult to live knowing that I would not enjoy her erotic beauty again. And knowing that she was with her husband, trying to fall in love again, and that surely many other things would happen, and I wished they didn't. But I did not want to think about it. I had not slept well that night, and in the morning after getting dressed and wearing the leather jacket she had given me for our anniversary, I went for a walk to clear my head and arrived at Sanborns. I went in and started looking at the books and leafing through the magazines.

"Hello, Edgar," I heard a voice behind me. I turned my head and saw small, bulging eyes glaring at me through a pair of Coke-bottle lenses. He had a flat nose and a mouth too big for his round face that was made more prominent by his rather large lips. The lower lip hung down, saliva disgustingly dripping from each corner of his mouth accentuated by twisted, yellow teeth. He wore a suit without a tie, and the neck of his collared shirt hung over the jacket lapel. He was tall and chubby and his smile was repulsive.

"Do you remember the guy who looked like a runover toad with Coke-bottle glasses who was going to ask me to dance at your birthday party?" Mrs. Margarita once asked me.

"A runover toad?" I laughed. *"Yes, I do remember."*

"Since the gossip about me hanging out with you has been going around, you cannot imagine how much he's been bothering me. I see him everywhere. I think he's following me around or something. He's a friend of Samuel's. He works at the police station but then calls Samuel at home when I'm sure he knows he's not home and just wants to talk to me. Sometimes I find him at the supermarket, and he stares at me with that morbid, perverted look, and he even asks me out. You would be surprised by how many suitors I've had since they discovered us. Now they must think I'm a whore."

I laughed. *"You've had suitors for as long as I can remember."*

"Exactly, so just a couple of months," she said with a big laugh.

"Hello," I replied to the runover toad, shaking his fat hand.

"How are you doing?" he said with some admiration. "Are you still... there?"

I did not quite understand what he meant. "Where?"

"Do not play dumb." He smiled at me as if we were great friends. "With the lady."

I looked at him stunned. "What?" I asked in shock.

"She's pretty hot, right?"

I think my face reflected so much shock, that he turned around and left. I'm not sure if he was embarrassed, but I was sure that I was left thinking he was the biggest idiot I'd ever met in my life. *What's wrong with this asshole?!*

I left Sanborns still furious about what that damn toad-looking asshole had said.

***

As I walked back I thought I saw Mrs. Margarita's car several times, but in reality, recently, I began noticing any blue Caprice I saw. I had her on my mind all the time; she had completely invaded my being and I could not get the images of her and her husband at that damn retreat out of my thoughts.

I did not know what they were doing there, but I imagined it and the mere imagery it made my stomach ache.

Before I got home, I went over to Frank's. "What's up?" I said greeting him.

"How are you doing?" He signaled me to come in and follow him to his room.

"Good," I replied indifferently.

"Well, you do not look so good. How did things end with Mrs. Margarita?"

"How did it end with what?"

"Will you still see each other when she comes back from the retreat or what?"

I shook my head.

"It's better this way," he said. "You were already going too far. Maribel is in a very bad place and so is Marisol." I knew what we were doing was not right and that our relationship was destroying everything in its path, but I also knew that I needed her. Her kisses, her body, her laughter, and every bit of her had become a drug for me. The more I had her, the more addicted I became. "Why don't you get a job so you can distract yourself a bit? I'm going to start working with my father-in-law at the shops."

"Really?"

"Yes. He offered me a job and I took it."

I sat down on his bed and started playing with his pillow which had the football club America's logo on it. I began throwing it up and catching it when it fell. "I can't. I'm going to college."

"Are you kidding me?! You're going in August and we're just starting February, you lazy fuck. That's why you're always thinking about bullshit because you don't have anything to do. And stop throwing my America pillow, it's autographed by the famous Borja and you'll fuck it up!" I put the stupid pillow aside before he told me the story (again) of how he got Borja's autograph. He had already told it to me so many times that I even dreamt of Enrique Borja once. "I went to watch America play at the Azteca Stadium," he told me every chance he got. "I was about 10 years old." He actually remembered exactly how old he was and the exact time of day, but I think he hoped when he told it that way it would become a more interesting story. "He had just finished the game against Atletico Español." He continued, "and my dad bought me the pillow with the America's logo, so we went to wait outside the stadium where the players came out to see if Enrique Borja would come out and give me his autograph." At this part, he always paused as if to add a certain amount of drama to the story. "We waited and waited until finally, after almost an hour, he drove out in his '71 red Mustang. I ran to him, but he just waved goodbye and continued driving. Then with all my might, I shouted at him, 'Borja, please!' and then there was a massive screech as he slammed on the brakes, squeaking and everything. I ran to the car and my dad came after me, worried. I arrived at the red Mustang and," he would also pause here for another dramatic break. "Enrique Borja himself! He rolled down his window and said, 'What's up, champ? Are you all right?' I said yes and that I wanted his autograph. So, he took out a marker and signed my pillow, shook my hand, and tousled my hair before he left." That was the famous story of Borja's autograph, but at that moment I wanted to get it out of my head because I had other, more important things to think about.

Maybe Frank was right; maybe that's why Mrs. Margarita had taken over every fiber of my being, every neuron in my brain; because I had nothing else to focus on. Maybe with a job, my mind would have something else to do. "Well, I think you are right," I said. "On Monday I'm going to buy the newspaper to look for a job."

"Look for something in a bank or something like that, or maybe even in an architect's office; drawing or as a fucking messenger but look for something you dummy. Start looking on Tuesday because Monday is February 5th and a holiday —Constitution Day— and no one works. Don't be an idiot." I went home thinking about the job and how happy Mrs. Margarita would be if I started working. I also remembered the runover toad. I wanted to tell her that I had seen him and what he had told me, but I realized it wasn't possible. She was starting a new life and I had to resign myself to never seeing her again.

✦✦✦

The second day I spent without her irresistible presence was Sunday, the day she returned from the retreat with her husband. I had already memorized every nook and cranny on the ceiling of my room and my mattress was only a couple of days away from absorbing the silhouette of my body forever. Maybe I was about to discover the memory foam that later made the Tempur-Pedic mattresses famous because even when the phone rang I could not stretch my arm to answer it. I knew it was not her. So, I kept looking at the ceiling, motionless, like a corpse, stamping the image of my body on the bed.

"Eddy! Phone," Mom announced.

For me? I went to great lengths to pick up the earpiece and said, "Hello?"

"Hello, friend," Sonya's voice sounded very cheerful and carefree.

"Hi."

"Hey, I'm exactly 17 years and 3 months old today. Buy me a cup of coffee? And do not even tell me you have plans because Mrs. Margarita is on a retreat with her husband, so you have nothing to do." I did not feel like going anywhere, but I was afraid that if I said no, she would come to my house and take me out by my hair, and even give me that kick she wanted to give me.

***

We were sitting at the Vips restaurant, located on the corner of Montevideo and Insurgentes Avenues, precisely where Mrs. Margarita used to pick me up before they found out about us. They gave us a table and once they brought us the drinks and the waitress left, Sonya started in without beating around the bush.

"How's your relationship with Mrs. Margarita going?"

"We are not together anymore," I replied a little nervously.

"You do not have to lie to me. We are friends, aren't we?"

I nodded my head. "How do you know she's on a retreat?" I wanted to know.

"She and my mom are friends. They are not best friends, but they know each other."

"And she told your mom?"

"No. Her husband. She has not talked to anyone since she's been with you, but the husband has taken it upon himself to tell his misfortune all over the neighborhood."

"But there's nothing between us anymore. That's why she's at the retreat."

"They say she's very much in love with you."

"Is that what they say? People say a lot of things," I tried to hide my joy, but I don't think I was able.

"That's true. They're very gossipy. And you love her too?" she asked me, putting her elbows on the table and her chin on her hands, very interested in what I was going to say.

"Why don't we talk about something else?" I said to her somewhat afraid of her reaction.

"Okay," she took her hands off her chin and put them on the table. "What do you want to talk about?"

"I don't know. Anything. I'm going to look for a job this week."

"And why don't you go back to school instead? You're not going to study anymore?"

"Yes, of course. But I'm going to college in August, next semester."

"What are you going to study?"

"Architecture."

"Really?!" she said with an honest smile. "Me too. But I still don't know where. Maybe I'll go to La Salle."

"Are you really going to study architecture?" I asked incredulously, thinking she was just messing with me.

"Yes, I've always liked architecture. So where are you going to work?" she added, changing the subject.

"I don't know yet. I'm just going to start looking for a job."

"Don't you want to work at the Camino Real Hotel?"

I was just sipping my soda and was almost shocked. *Does she know about the time Mrs. Margarita and I visited the hotel? This girl had a knack for surprising me.* "At the Camino Real?!

"Yes, great, isn't it? Are you interested? My aunt is the human resources manager and my cousin is a receptionist. I can talk to my aunt and tell her to give you a job." I was silent for a few seconds, unable to say anything at all. *What if her cousin was the pretty receptionist who took care of us? Shit!* "Do you want it or not?" she asked me impatiently.

"Yes, yes. Thank you."

"It's just that you were as surprised as if you were going to be given the manager's job. At most they'll put you in the front desk, so don't get too excited."

"That's okay," I said. "Thank you." Sonya was quite an enigma. To be honest, I thought that she'd tell me about what happened the last time Mrs. Margarita and I met, but she did not even mention it. She behaved like a friend and nothing more. Then I realized that this is what Sonya was like; she had a certain amount of admirable integrity. If she said something was red it was red, if she said it was blue, it was blue. She did not beat around the bush. She was who she was.

***

On Monday, beginning at first light I waited for the phone to ring and to hear Mrs. Margarita's voice, but she never called. The night before she had returned from the retreat and should have made up her mind by now. Maybe because it was a holiday her daughters didn't go to school and that's why she didn't call me.

On Tuesday morning I had no doubt about her decision. By 10 a.m. I was already at the Camino Real Hotel. "Get there at 10 o'clock sharp so you can make a good impression," Sonya told me on the phone. As soon as I arrived, the memories came back to me like a whirlwind. *How the fuck am I going to forget her if everything reminds me of her!* It was as if fate was playing with me and was having a blast doing it: first Sonya would ask to meet where

Mrs. Margarita picked me up, then I had my first work appointment where we celebrated our second month anniversary. And what a celebration! Fate was mocking me!

I walked into the Human Resources office and a beautiful young woman gave me a nice smile. *Do all the women here have to be pretty?*

"Good morning," she said.

"Good morning, I have an appointment with Emma Schultz."

"Edgar Portales?"

"Yes."

She gave me an application to fill out, then she gave it to Sonya's aunt, a beautiful and kind blonde who after interviewing me and realizing that I did not have the slightest experience in any job, told me, "All right, Edgar, let me see what I can do. There is an open spot in the reception area at the front desk" *Front desk!* "The problem is that you've never worked, but that does not matter. I had other people for that position, but Sonya called me and asked if I could give you a job." She smiled with admiration and pride. "More like she demanded that I give you one!" Now she laughed, shaking her head to the side like when you think of someone hopeless, but you still admire them. "How do you know my niece?"

"We live in the same neighborhood."

"I see. Well…" she stacked some papers on her desk and got up. I took that to mean goodbye. "I'll call you this week, but it's almost certain that you'll start next Monday." I was equal parts excited and tormented. I was sure that every day I stepped into that hotel would be an ordeal for me.

***

I returned home and still had no news of Mrs. Margarita. However, in the hope that she would call me, I didn't want to go out for the rest of the day and continued constructing my nineteen story Lego building. In the evening, Frank came over to say hi and I took the opportunity to ask him, "Have you seen her?"

"Yes," he replied, lying on my bed, taking my soccer ball that had never been kicked (I didn't even remember who had given it to me; probably someone who didn't know me well) and bounced it off the wall.

"And?" I said, beginning to despair.

"And, what?" he replied, throwing the ball back and hitting my old *Rocky* poster this time.

"Watch out! You're going to rip it," I warned him irritated.

"Take it easy bitch, or I'll tear you apart. Besides that poster is old as fuck. Take it off, you dumb fuck! Change it to Lucía Méndez from Viviana's, the one that shows her cleavage down to here," he took the ball with one hand so he could gesture with the other. "She's hot. Buy it at the newsstand. She's wearing the blue dress she wears on the soap opera; the one she's wearing on the river, and you can see her tits which look amazing."

"What's up with the lady?"

Now Frank was getting mad. "What's up with what?"

"So? Did you see her? Did she tell you anything?"

"I saw her and she did not say anything." I was quiet for a moment, disappointed. "Let it go, you fucking loser. Enough!" Perhaps my face showed the pain I felt because he immediately changed his tone. "She's fine with her husband now." I felt as if my friend had stabbed me in the chest. "Well, not that they're okay, but she's trying and so is he. You have nothing to lose, but they do. Stop messing around, leave her alone, do not look for her, and fuck Sonya instead. Do not be an idiot. Everybody wants Sonya, and you've got the chance and don't want it." He paused, "Are you stupid or what dude?!" *She's made up with her husband.* Those words burned me like I'd fallen in a pool of acid. I felt more and more desperate and unable to think clearly.

***

The next day I could not stand it anymore. It had been five days without seeing her and I could not restrain myself. I was like an addict who suddenly had his drugs taken away and they expected me to adapt just like that. I could not admit we'd come to the end. I had to do something about it. I had to go to her and tell her that I loved her, or something, but it had to be now. Then I remembered something she had said to me, "If you ever give me flowers, do not even think about giving me daisies. My favorite flower is the tulip. But no man has ever thought of giving me tulips, not even Samuel." I got up early and asked my brother Tavo to lend me money.

"More?" he said somewhat annoyed. "You already owe me a shit ton. When are you gonna pay me back?" I knew he was going to say that, but I also knew he'd end up letting me borrow the money. When they opened the flower shop, I was already outside.

I sent a beautiful arrangement of tulips to her house, of course, without a note, and I waited for the response which arrived in the afternoon, when she called me, "Annie, my friend!" I heard her seductive voice on the other end of the line. "Thank you so much for the flowers. You're the only person who sent me tulips and not daisies. Thank you very much."

Annie? I realized she could not talk. "You cannot talk right now, can you?" I whispered.

"No, my friend. I cannot go out right now. I'm fixing up some things in the stores with the accountant and Samuel. But what do you say we meet tomorrow?"

"You want to meet tomorrow?"

"Yes, Annie. How about we meet early?"

"You want to see me in the morning?" I began to get excited.

"Okay, my friend. I'll call you early to arrange the time and place." She hung up and I still had the phone in my hand, trying to figure out what she told me.

She wants to see me tomorrow. She'll call me early. She was with her husband and the accountant, so she could not talk, but she's going to call me early. I understood it correctly. Yes, I understood it!

***

When I got in her car the next morning, I was completely disconcerted.

"Hey, babe," she said with a smile.

Are all women this enigmatic and complicated? I asked myself without getting an answer. Although years later I did. *Yes, all of them are!* I looked at her a little confused, but I could not help but flutter with the simple, pure emotion I felt in my stomach, "Hey, how'd it go?"

"Very well," she added, smiling and driving to the Lindavista neighborhood.

Very well?

It all seemed so strange to me because I figured she would not call me anymore, so I asked her how everything had been, but she told me to wait until we got somewhere to eat something. We arrived at the Apache 14 restaurant, well-known at the time because the owners were two very famous singers in Mexico: Carmela and Rafael, a couple in both their personal and professional lives.

"So, well," she began by saying once that we had ordered a pitcher of clericot and a seafood platter. "The retreat is to remind couples why they fell in love, what their lives were like, and their feelings when they met and all that. They separate the men from the women and do exercises to remember and," she made a gesture with the index and middle fingers of both hands as if to indicate some quotation marks, "fall in love again."

The waiter arrived with the clericot. I poured her some, poured myself some, and she smiled at me while lifting her glass to "cheers," with that mischievous smile that made me boil with desire. We drank and she continued slowly, "I understood things I did not understand before. I know that Samuel is a very good person. I know that I have loved him."

What?

"In the 19 years I've known him, we've had some very happy moments."

Excuse me?

She took a short pause, as if hesitating to say the following, "I am eternally grateful to him for many things."

Hold on, hold on, am I missing something?

"I remembered good times," she went on, but the waiter arrived with the seafood, and she stopped.

So, we're done and you're staying with your husband? And what about the 'hi, babe' when I got in the car? What the hell is going on? I do not understand anything!

She took a shrimp, blew on it to cool it down a bit, and put it in my mouth. "C'mon, baby, eat," she said laughing. I ate the shrimp, but I did not know what to say or think. Everything seemed very confusing and contradictory. Then she continued, "at night they gave us exercises to meditate on why we had fallen in love with our partner and so on. Since the men were on one side of the convent and the women on the other, besides the fact that we slept in individual rooms, we had all night to do the exercises, to think and meditate." She stopped, took my hand, and fixed her gaze full of love on me. "During those exercises and meditations, it was you who came to mind. And all this week I've been thinking and thinking. I realized that I love you and that I do not want to leave you. And I decided I'm not leaving Samuel."

What? Well, either this woman is crazy or I don't understand a damn thing about what is going on. This woman is even more badass than she is pretty. "I felt bad while making this decision because I feel like I'm losing my integrity; that I'm going to live a double life, but I also know he has done that many times. He even wanted a divorce so he could go and live with a 24-year-old girl. Why should not I live my life and be happy for as long as it lasts? All this week I didn't call you because I wanted to think and clear my head. I also wanted to do everything I could to save my marriage, but I cannot be with him anymore. I feel like I'm betraying you and I cannot do it." I wasn't able to speak. I didn't know what to say. Tears began to fall from her cheeks and without thinking I raised my hand to wipe her tears with my thumb. Without knowing why I put my finger in my mouth to drink that tear. "Do you see that?" she said full of emotion. "That's one of the biggest differences." I looked at her without understanding. "I've always been a crybaby, and he always told me, 'You're going to start crying now!' You're so different." She paused and took the glass of clericot, looking at it again as she did the first time we went out as if what she was looking for was in the glass. "I don't want to make comparisons, but I can't help it either. I have such a grudge against him for all his infidelity for 17 years that I cannot fix it in one weekend. I missed you so much these past few days, but I didn't want to call you. I said to myself I'm going to wait for a sign that he really loves me. If I don't get it I'm not going to look for him. Yesterday I went with him to the stores and we went back home with the accountant to do the taxes. He wants me to get more involved in the business and all that. But when we were on our way, I thought that if I didn't get a message or proof of your love…" She paused again, blushing. "How corny am I?"

"No!" I told her right away.

"That if I did not get proof you loved me, I would do everything I could to forget you and never look for you again. So, yesterday was the day I set as the deadline. We were in the dining room working when the doorbell rang, and I went to open the door." I noticed how her eyes lit up. "Then I saw the tulip arrangement and almost fainted because I knew they were yours. At that moment I realized that I needed you as if I were addicted to you, and although I am aware that it will not last forever, I want to enjoy it as much as possible for as long as it lasts." She caressed my face and I felt the warmth of her touch like a detonator that ignited my blood. "I love you, babe," she said as she shed more tears and I began to drink them with my kisses, "I love you."

We began to kiss passionately but stopped almost instantly. We stared at each other, burning with desire. We did not say anything, but we knew what we wanted. Then she got up without taking that lustful look off of me and went to the bathroom. I waited a couple of minutes and took the same path she had taken.

I put the lock on the door, and we threw ourselves into each other's arms in a wild, obsessive way. We kissed and made love, reaching an intense orgasm in just two or three minutes, but we breathed as if we had been engaged for hours in the sexual act. I left the bathroom first because it was the ladies' room. Then she came out and caught up with me at the table. We realized that we had hardly touched the seafood platter and so we ate our meal while still looking at each other with some mischief for what we had done in the women's bathroom. We both knew it; it was one of the laws of physics: an object in motion will stay in motion until a contrary force stops it. And there was still no such force capable of stopping us.

***

The day I started working at the hotel I met the receptionist who had greeted us and I started blushing. "Hi," she said with a smile. "Are you Eddy?"

She is her cousin! Shit!

"Yes," I replied. I was a little self-conscious.

"I'm Elena, Sonya's cousin," she added with a mischievous smile. "She already told me about you. But do not blush," she told me laughing very amused while I longed for the earth to swallow me whole. "I'll give you your training. It's me you're covering because next week I'm starting as the reception manager, and you're taking my place." Elena turned out to be very nice. At 22 she worked in the mornings and studied tourism in the afternoons. She was already in her senior year at university and had worked in almost every area of the hotel.

"How do you feel about work?" she asked me one Easter day in April when she went to the employee cafeteria instead of the manager's cafeteria.

"Very well."

"You could have a good future here. You're a fast learner. In two months, you already know more than those who have been at the reception for almost a year."

I smiled at her, grateful. "And why are you eating here now?" I asked while taking a bite of my chicken taco.

"Because I love crispy tacos and they are serving meatballs in the manager's dining room," she replied with a cheeky smile. "Hey, do you like my cousin?" I was left with my half-eaten taco and she started laughing. "Why are you always blushing? It was just a question."

I shrugged.

She mimicked my shrugging somewhat exaggeratedly and added, "What does that mean? Do you like her or not?"

"Well, yes. She's very pretty."

"Then why don't you go for it? Why are you going out with the married lady?" It seemed like the women in my life had an extraordinary ability to shut me up. "Think of the future. When you're about 25 and you're in full swing, she's going to be how old? What's the age difference?"

"Eighteen."

"Eighteen! Look, when you're 30, she's going to be hitting 50."

And it's going be a hot 50, I said to myself.

"Yeah," I answered with a little bit of complacency.

"My cousin likes you and let me tell you one thing. You won't find another one like Sonya. My cousin is…" she started looking for the right words to describe her. "It's, well…Sonya is Sonya." And I totally agreed with her on that.

However, I was still in love with Mrs. Margarita. Although things had gotten complicated again because her husband wanted to be intimate with her and she rejected him which was creating a lot of tension between them again. He accused her of continuing with me and she denied it. He told her he was going to kill me and she insulted him. Days, weeks, and months passed and nothing had really changed. The bomb had been activated again and was ready to go off.

***

In August I quit the hotel and started college. Elena asked me to change my schedule so that I would not have to leave work, but that meant I would not have time to see Mrs. Margarita. So, I quit Camino Real. But during the last week I worked something strange happened. I had just checked in a guest and set out to look after the next one when I spotted a guy who seemed familiar to me. But when you work in a hotel, a lot of people seem familiar to you because a large majority of them travel for business, and they do it so often that their faces become extremely familiar. However, this one was not a regular customer of the hotel. "Hello," the runover toad said.

"Good morning," I said automatically.

"How are you doing?"

"I'm well, thank you," I replied, surprised and disgusted by the saliva peeking out between his huge lower lip and his twisted yellow teeth.

"Since when do you work here?

"It's been about half a year," I told him, "but it's my last week."

"Oh, yeah? Why?"

"I'm going to college. Do you have a reservation?" I added changing the subject.

"No, I was just passing by and I saw you. I said to myself, 'I'm going to stop by and say hello to my friend.' I'll let you get to work. I'll see you later."

***

That September afternoon, I was leaving the university as I had been since August and I took the long way home, stopping as I had been doing at the Insurgentes' roundabout, the famous and huge roundabout formed at the intersection of the Chapultepec and Insurgentes Avenues. I stopped, as always, outside the Insurgentes cinema waiting for Mrs. Margarita to pick me up, as I did every day but little did I know that afternoon we would not go out to eat as we had planned. But rather I'd end up in the Red Cross.

There I was waiting when in front of me a big, black car stopped and two guys exited and headed my way. They both wore jackets with their shirts open as low as the abdomen. The two also had a bulging belly, and it seemed that the buttons made every effort to stay attached to the eyelets of their tight, flowery shirts, whose fully opened collar rested on the flaps of the jacket.

Both wore a thick mustache and appeared to have been made of the same stock. The two of them even did the same backflip to their jackets at waist level to let me see their guns, and one of them pulled out a judicial police badge, which he showed me so quickly, I could not see the photo or what it really was. It could have been plastic but I couldn't tell.

"Judicial police," said the man with the badge and took my arm. "Your ID." But before I could say or do anything they both took me by the elbows and dragging me into the car. "Do not make a scene you bastard. Do not make a scene," said the guy who did not have a badge (or who at least didn't show it to me). They shoved me in the back of the four-door car and another guy was already waiting for me in the back by the door on the right side. He was just as fat as the others. The guy with the badge got in after me and the other one turned around and went in on the passenger side. I managed to see that the driver looked the same as the other three before I was bent over to lie on the floor of the car.

"So, you think you're a badass! Don't you motherfucker? You're fucked!" said one of the judicial officers, policemen, whatever they were! *Badass? What are they talking about!*

"How much you got, fuckboy?" asked one of the ones in the front.

"I do not have any money," I said. I was scared.

"You don't, motherfucker?" The one with the badge protested and then I felt a heavy blow to the head as if I had been hit very hard with metal or maybe with the pistol grip. I could not see them. The only thing I could see in that position was the floor and the black shoes that had been waiting for me when they got me in the car. I heard directions, but I did not quite understand. I had a headache from the blow and almost lost consciousness.

"I'm talking to you, you bastard!" I heard them yelling at me, but I was not sure I heard a question. I felt another blow but this time it was on the back of my hand since, after the first blow, I had covered my head with both hands, opening my fingers as wide as I could to protect most of my skull. I wailed in pain and I felt like crying. I was really scared. I do not know how long I was lying on the floor of the car with the four guys, but it felt like it went on forever. They took my wallet and my college ID. Suddenly they stopped. They opened the doors and I could see the gray floor of the street. The guy on the right side grabbed my hair, pushing my head down to prevent me from lifting it, which made it harder for me to get out of the car.

"Come here, you bastard," he said as he pulled me out. Then I saw that his black shoe was moving fast and I felt a tremendous punch in the nose. Everything became dark, like the sun had gone down, much like an eclipse.

"Quickly," they said as I continued to feel blows not only on my nose but on my whole body. On the head, abdomen, legs, face, arms, ribs, everything. Then I heard nothing and felt nothing. As if I had fallen asleep. At times I heard people talking and then silence again. I thought I heard a siren and again silence. Then there was only silence and nothing else.

****

I'd only been unconscious for a couple of hours in the hospital, but it was almost dark when Mom, Dad, and my brother arrived. "Just look at you!" Mom said to me, unable to hold back the tears. "Who did this to you?"

"I was mugged."

"If I find out it was that lady's husband, he's going to be sorry," added Dad, visibly shocked at my condition. He bent down to kiss me slowly on the bandage on my forehead. My brother only grimaced when he saw me lying there and smiled at me, but he wasn't making fun of me as usual. Instead, he wore a smile that indicated concern and affection.

"Look at yourself, son," Mom said again, crying while looking for an area of my body that she could caress without hurting me. She gave me sweet, motherly kisses on my forehead. "They called us to tell us you were at the Red Cross and we came right away."

The doctor came in and greeted my family with kindness. After his routine monologue, he explained the damage caused due to the beating I received.

"In addition to multiple contusions all over his body, he has a fractured nose and two ribs on his left side. There are no head fractures, but there are some severe contusions." Mom sobbed every time the doctor discussed some of the bruises or broken bones I had as if they were hurting her just by mentioning them. "I hope," continued the doctor, "that we can discharge him tomorrow or the day after, but most likely tomorrow. The boy is strong and recovering quickly," he smiled kindly at me. "But we'll leave him here for tonight to look after his recovery."

They would not let anyone stay with me, but because Mom and Dad had friends at the Red Cross, she wanted to spend the night with me. I convinced her that it was not necessary. I wanted to go home, but the doctor insisted that I should stay at least until the next morning. I was worried about Mrs. Margarita. I was sure she did not know anything, and I had no way of communicating with her. Frank might be my only solution. "Does Frank know I'm here?" I asked

Mom grimaced as if she knew that it was Mrs. Margarita I was really interested in speaking with but she immediately changed her attitude. "No, son. We did not have time to tell anyone."

"I'll call him now and let him know," my brother said, smile at me like we were in cahoots. He winked at me, showing me he knew what I wanted.

"Thank you."

Later, three doctors came in and greeted my parents very warmly, asked me how I felt, and before they left one of them told Dad to let him know if he needed anything. "You know the rules at the Red Cross are very strict, but there are no rules for you, okay? Whatever you need, do not hesitate to call us."

Mom and Dad thanked them, said goodbye, and stayed a little longer with me.

They left at almost 10 p.m. that night. "We're coming early tomorrow," said Mom when she bent down to kiss me.

"I hope to see you at home because I have to go to college," Tavo said, "but I'll let Frank know; don't worry." Dad also kissed me on the forehead and then they left.

I had a horrible night. During the early part of the morning, I was woken up about three times to take my vital signs, and on two of those occasions, I was given some pills. Then the pain woke me up and they gave me an injection. The next morning, I was more tired than if I had been out partying all night. Mom and Dad arrived early, but Dad left after the Jell-o they gave me for breakfast, and I stayed with Mom. "They will let you go around noon," my mother said when a familiar voice made my heart race.

"Good morning," Mrs. Margarita said from the door. Mom turned her head and for a moment she froze. I think she meant to say so many things but didn't say a word. She stood quietly watching the beautiful woman in a T-shirt and jeans, both of which fit her perfect body.

"He's the patient, right?" said the overeager doctor who was accompanying her, bursting with kindness because of the beautiful woman he was escorting. "Not too many visitors to visit at once, but we are making an exception for you." *Not too many visitors to visit?* The doctor seemed as nervous and clumsy as Jerry Lewis in his movies. But I understood that. Although it was obvious that Mrs. Margarita had put on the first thing she found, but those clothes so form-fitting to her curves it seemed as if Michelangelo himself had chiseled her. Even Mom could not help but admire her from top to bottom, and before she could say anything two more doctors came in to check the empty bed next to me, putting their hands over the sheet as if they wanted to iron it.

Then they asked the patient in the other bed if he was all right, even though they were only looking at Mrs. Margarita. One of them asked three times, "How are you?" with a foolish face that would have made anyone laugh.

Mom breathed a long sigh, caressed my face, and kissed me on the forehead. "I'm going out to get some breakfast. I'll be right back." She went to the door and when she passed Mrs. Margarita, she stopped for a moment and looked her in the eyes.

Mrs. Margarita looked up and said, "I know I should not be here, but I needed to know he's okay." Mom did not say anything, but in her eyes, there was some understanding and gratitude. She left and the three doctors did the same thing. Mrs. Margarita walked toward me and tears streamed down her face every step of the way. She took my hand and smiled at me. "How are you feeling, babe?"

"Better, but I think another part of my body is swelling up," I told her with what I was trying to be a mischievous smile, but I immediately felt the stabbing pain in my lip and the smile turned into a grimace.

She smiled as my hand rose to her lips, and after a delicate kiss, she placed her cheek on the back of it, which made me feel the wetness of her tears. "What happened?" she asked worriedly.

"I think I was mugged."

"Do you think?" she was in deep thought for a moment and then she bit her lower lip before continuing, "Do you think…Samuel did it?"

"I do not know. They were cops, but there was something they said that left me confused."

"What?"

"*So, you think you're a badass.* One of them told me."

She pondered the meaning for a few seconds. "I don't think he sent them. He does have friends at the police department. In fact, the runover toad face is a big deal there, but last night when Frank called me to tell me, I asked Samuel and he didn't know anything. And I do believe him because I know him, and he's bad at lying. I always know. That's why I always found out about his infidelity." She paused a little as if thinking about something else. "I cannot be sure anyway. It's all been so weird, and the best thing is for us not to see each other anymore, babe. For your own good."

"That has nothing to do with it," I told her, though I was not very convinced.

"Well, we'll talk about it later. How are you feeling?" We talked until Mom came back a few minutes later.

Mrs. Margarita said goodbye and Mom stopped her. "I want to talk to you."

"Of course," she replied, and they both looked each other in the eyes without challenging each other. Just woman to woman.

"Out there," Mom said and they left, leaving me with a heart about to burst.

Chapter 21

I had gotten my job back at the Camino Real where I worked from 3 p.m. to 12 p.m. so I could continue studying during the day. I left work and walked to the Lynis restaurant to wait for Mrs. Margarita, who worked as a waitress. She got off at 1 a.m. I always did my usual walk with enough caution, since there were many robberies around there, and after the beating I had received in September, I thought everyone seemed suspicious if they got too close to me on the street.

I took Mariano Escobedo Avenue and then Presidente Masaryk, which were very busy, and slightly safer avenues. I liked to see the colorful lights that decorated the streets indicating it was Christmas and a new decade would be arriving soon; 1980 was practically around the corner. Like every day when I arrived at the restaurant, I sat in the waiting area because if I sat at a table I had to eat, and my budget was quite meager. Now we had to pay rent, electricity, gas, fare, and food. "Why did they give you the 4 p.m. to 1 a.m. shift?" I asked her somewhat annoyed the day she told me she had already found a job.

"Because Annie knows the manager."

I looked at her without understanding. "Then why didn't they put you on in the morning?"

"Actually, I was supposed to get the one at night because I'm new. You'd rather I get that one?"

"Fuck! No, no. This one's fine." It was still about half an hour before she could leave so I sat as upright as I could so I would not fall asleep.

One of the young waitresses, whose name I don't even remember, came to greet me. "Hello."

"Hi, how are you doing?"

She sat down next to me and all the fatigue and any chance of me falling asleep went away because I already knew it would cause a huge jealous scene in about 30 minutes. We did not say more than five words, but the storm was certain. When we went out to take the bus that left us at the corner of the apartment we were renting in the Cuauhtémoc neighborhood, I wanted to greet her with a kiss, but she dodged me.

"You should give it to that waitress you like so much. After all, she's your age and not as old as I am."

I rolled my eyes. I was too tired to argue or to do anything else. Almost every day we would go to sleep at about 3 a.m. and I would have to get up at 5 a.m. to go to class. Sometimes we made love and sometimes we fell asleep as soon as our heads hit the pillow, but our jealousy was becoming frequent. "Why did you smile at that guy!" I asked.

"Because it's my job," she said to me in anger.

"Your job is to bring him food, not to smile at him flirtatiously."

"I did not smile at him flirtatiously."

"No? He even gave you his phone number!"

"His phone number?!"

"I saw him give you a piece of paper."

"He paid the bill; that's all!"

We walked quietly to the corner where we were taking the bus. We were silent all the way back to the apartment. On the way, I asked myself a question that had been bouncing around in my head for several days. *How did it come to this?*

***

Mr. Samuel had assigned a private detective to his wife, and he gave him a sign of where, when, and at what time we met. At the end of October, he found us at the Insurgents' roundabout. I was about to get in the blue Caprice when he came out of god knows where, grabbed me by my collar, and pushed me back, "I warned you, you bastard! I warned you!

Much faster than Wonder Woman, Mrs. Margarita got out of the car and stood in front of him as he was coming after me. Everything happened fast. Too fast. He pulled out a gun, she opened her arms in front of me, trying to cover me. I was trying to get her off.

"Get out of the way!" he shouted at her.

"Get out of the way!" I shouted at her.

"Calm down!" shouted a traffic policeman who was in the middle of the street, paler than me, and running toward us.

Margarita fought with her husband trying to disarm him. They struggled. He lifted the gun and fired a shot into the sky which indicated to me that it was loaded and that the possibility of him killing me existed. Then the brave traffic policeman came and lunged at Samuel, taking his gun away from him. Samuel pushed him aside and ran toward me. Margarita got in the way, but he pushed her too easily. I felt a hard blow to my face. I went backward trying to keep my balance and my legs were bent, but I managed to put one hand on the ground to stay on my feet as boxer Carlos Palomino had done last June against *Mano de Piedra* Durán.

At the end of the day, a brawl broke out which caused five police patrols to arrive. The three of us were the center of attention and of a lot of gossip. They took us to the police station, but I did not want to talk to my parents until I was sure what was going to happen. After about two hours at the police station and a good amount of money paid by Mr. Samuel, plus some calls to the right friends, they let us all go. There were no charges against me, since I had been the one assaulted, and there was no way to prove adultery. As I left, I felt a morbid look coming from a familiar face that smiled vulgarly at me and joined Mr. Samuel and Mrs. Margarita in greeting them. After a second look, I recognized him completely; his face looked like a run over toad.

***

A few hours after the altercation, Margarita called me, "I need to talk to you," she said to me in a firm and determined voice. When I got to the corner of Montevideo and Insurgentes, the sun was beginning to set and the sky was turning orange and red, like fire. I was surprised she wasn't in her car but more surprised not to see the car anywhere.

"Samuel threw me out of the house, took my car, and my credit cards," she said, sitting at a table at the VIPS. "My daughters are angry, and they stayed with him. I have nowhere to take them anyway. I'll talk to them later, but the problem right now is that I do not know what I'm going to do. I only have two options: either I go ahead and see where I'm going, or I go back and work things out with him. But I'm not going to leave alone."

"No," I interrupted her. "Let's leave together."

She just stared at me for a moment as if examining me. Then she sighed. "But you must understand, going to a hotel to sleep together is not the same as living together. We must work to be able to pay for housing while we find an apartment. Then we must work to pay for the apartment. And the electricity. And the gas."

"I'm going to work. I'm leaving school."

"You are not leaving school at all. I'd rather go back before you stop studying. If you're going to follow me you'll do it by working and studying or I'll go back right now."

"Okay. I'm going to work in the afternoon. I'm sure I'll get my job back at the hotel."

"I've got some money saved up from the Las Hadas thing, but it's only going to last us a week or two at most to pay for a hotel and food. We need to find a job right now!"

We had made plans that at the end of November, we were going to celebrate our first-year anniversary at Las Hadas, in Manzanillo. But that plan, like so many other things, fell apart. My parents were shocked by the news that I was going to live with Margarita.

"And her daughters?" Mom asked, outraged.

"They stayed at home."

Mom opened her eyes so wide, I thought they were going to come out of her face.

"What you're doing is stupid," Dad said.

"You're not leaving here!" Mom said.

"I'm of legal age and I'm going to do whatever I want. Nobody's going to stop me."

"Are you out of your mind?" Dad yelled at me, more worried than angry.

"Won't you just let me live in peace! Stay out of my life!" I left my parents' house proudly, breaking Mom's heart and worrying them both about my future. The shy, studious, and kind son had become an immature, obsessive man, and a perfect imbecile incapable of reasoning.

***

The first night we spent together was difficult. When we arrived at the hotel room, she went to bed like a zombie and sat down, in deep thought, worried. There were times when she was filled with tears, and times when she was absorbed in her own thoughts, without speaking, lost. Her face, still fresh and lush the previous day, looked emaciated and sad. "I never thought I'd do something like this in my life," she told me through a sea of tears. "Leaving my daughters. Do you realize what I'm doing?"

"But he kicked you out."

"I could have fixed it and I did not. He kicked me out because I chose you," she looked me in the eyes, hers still soaked in tears. "I'm not trying to make you feel bad, babe, but I hope you realize what I'm doing because of the love I have for you." She collapsed on the bed and her body was convulsing because she was crying so heavily. "I'm insane! How could I leave my daughters!" I hugged her trying to comfort her and we laid on one side on the bed for a long time, facing each other. Once she had calmed down I began to kiss her slowly, drinking the tears that covered much of her face, as if I could take in the pain that was torturing her as well. I wished I could do something to ease her torment, but I could not think of anything. "I love you," she said, taking my face in her hands.

"I love you too," I said excitedly.

"Are you going to leave me?" she asked with a certain amount of despair.

"Never!" I said, kissing her on the lips. "Never! I want to be with you always."

"Always?" Her pupils were dilated as her kisses became more passionate.

"Always!" I repeated, still excited.

"Do you swear?"

"I swear! I love you! I love you!" I was yelling at her while we were stripping off our clothes without taking our lips off each other. It was as if by doing so we were reinforcing the promised "always" love to one another. We stayed in that long and passionate kiss, so that, once naked, we would begin to make love as if it were the last time we could do so. It was slow, soft, strong, sweet, and impetuous. Wild and tender.

Because of how emotionally sensitive the moment was, the pleasure we experienced was intense. Every orgasm was quick and instead of joy, we cried as if we were living in the most tragic way. We had taken a room in a hotel on San Cosme Avenue called Geneve, which was recommended by her friend Annie. The rooms were comfortable and did not cost much. The radio was managed by the front desk and we only had three options to choose from. At that moment it was on Radio Joya, a romantic station that played mostly hits from the past. Julio Jaramillo, who had died the previous year, sang "Nuestro Juramento," a song that had become his biggest hit.

"Have we sworn to love one another until death?" she asked me laying on my chest while alluding to the song's lyrics.

"Yes," I replied, smiling and stroking her dark hair.

"And if I die first?" she added. "Will you write the story of our love?"

"Yes," I said with a slight laugh and continued with her game of referring to Jaramillo's song. "I'll write it in blood, with ink from the heart."

She looked up and fixed her dark eyes on mine. "I'm serious. Will you love me till death?"

"Yes. Of course!"

"And you'll write our story? Are not you going to feel embarrassed by it?

"Embarrassed?" I asked surprised.

"Yes. To have fallen in love with an old woman like me." I looked at her in awe. I could not believe she was saying that. I realized that something was happening, that something in her past affected her and made her feel old. In August she had turned 37 and for the first time she did not have a big party like she used to. "I do not want to celebrate my old age anymore," she said.

"What old age? You've always had a party on your birthday."

"But not anymore." She only wanted us to celebrate it. We went out to eat and then back to the hotel as if it were just any other day. Nothing special. Her many friends had grown tired of looking for her, and the famous parties she always held for every reason under the sun were a thing of the past. "All I care about is being with you," she said. "I'm not interested in parties or anything. You and my daughters are all I want in this world."

***

November 4th was the first Sunday we had spent together since she had left home. She went to see her daughters and I went to see Frank to hear about my parents. After he told me they were fine, but extremely worried, he gave me a message from Sonya,. "Sonya says she's not having a party to celebrate her birthday, but she wants to go celebrate it with you. That you should call her. She's going to be waiting for your call."

"Oh yeah. She's 18 today, isn't she?"

"Yes, do not be a fool. Go. You're not working at the hotel today and you're free." For a moment I hesitated, but in the end I decided not to call her. I was starting a new life. Margarita was doing for me what neither of us ever imagined she would do. Even if it wasn't wrong to go with Sonya, it wasn't fair for me to leave to celebrate her birthday while Margarita went to see her daughters, to try to fix things with them; a scenario that had taken place because of me.

"No, I cannot," I told Frank decisively.

"You are such an idiot, dude!"

I went to the Geneve Hotel to wait for Margarita to return from seeing her daughters and to tell me how it went. Fortunately, she arrived very happy. She wore jeans and a blue T-shirt, and her hair was tied up in a ponytail that made her perfect face shine brighter and her thick, sensual lips stand out. "I talked to my daughters." I had not seen that smile on her face in several days.

"What did they tell you?"

"They understand that I have fallen in love and that I have the right to live my life. That they understand that their dad and I are not good for each other anymore and," she suddenly got quieter.

"And?" I asked with an inquisitive look.

She lowered her eyes for a moment to look at her fingers, which were fidgeting nervously, "They do not want anything to do with you now. But someday they're going to have to understand!" she added quickly.

I kissed her on the lips with tenderness. "Do not worry. I know one day they'll understand how much I love you."

"We love each other," she corrected me and kissed me back. She took my face in her hands and the glow in her eyes reinforced her words. "I love you." She kissed me again and began to glide the tip of her tongue around my lips in a very erotic way. Then she slipped her tongue inside my mouth. Her teeth gently bit into my lower lip, and when I began to do the same, she smiled mischievously.

She laid me down on the bed and started to undress me. She loosened her dark hair, and with the ribbon she was wearing she tied my hands together by the wrists. Her gaze was dark and sensual. "Put your hands behind your head," she ordered me. "You cannot touch me, understand?" I nodded, very excited. She grabbed my penis with her hands. "Just look at you already!" She started to stroke it and looked at me again. "Close your eyes. And do not open them until I tell you to."

I obeyed. The little game was becoming stimulating and I felt like I was about to explode. Her hands began to caress my chest and my abdomen, her tongue on my skin exploring my navel and tickling me. She took my member and stroked it again, going up and down. Slowly, smoothly. I felt her tongue go all the way from the base to the tip, and then her warm, moist mouth wrapped around the top until I felt it rubbing against the back of her throat. She kissed it, sucked it, and devoured it like she had never done before causing me to nearly climax.

"Enough!" I shouted, trying to get her to stop what was about to become inevitable. "Stop it!" But she continued to suck even harder. She pushed everything she could down her throat, and with her tongue she started stroking my testicles, all at the same time! "I'm going to cum!" I shouted in despair.

She just uttered an affirmative sound with her throat, while continuing. And I exploded! All my muscles tightened, and the tip of my penis became extremely tender, which prolonged my orgasm longer while she continued to suck and lick. My hip was spasming hard and my entire body was convulsing as she continued to stimulate me with her tongue, lips, and teeth. When she sat upright, I opened my eyes as I tried to normalize my breathing. Her smile was a mixture of pride and mischief. "This," she said, "I'd never done before. I did not even think I would ever do it." She came up to kiss me on the lips, "and it was delicious."

I was still trying to recover. I wanted to touch her, but my hands were tied. Once she released me, I laid her down on the bed and stripped her of her clothes. I took the ribbon and tied her hands, but from behind her back, putting her face down on the bed. She smiled.

"Now I," I told her, "am going to rape you."

Her smile faded instantly. Her eyes widened as if they were about to fall out of her head. Her skin turned pale and she screamed, "No! No!"

I panicked. "But I did not mean it like that. It' s just a game." She stirred in fear, trying to untie herself. "Get this off me!" she began yelling at me, terrified. I untied her immediately and hugged her. "It was just a game, my love. A game."

"I do not want you to play like that," she said. "I do not like it!"

"All right, all right."

***

The day after that Sunday, I showed up for work, and the minute I got there, Elena took me to her office.

"Sit down," she asked me, settling into her chair on the other side of the desk.

"Is something wrong?" I said worriedly as I took a seat.

She smiled at me with what I thought was a strange smile, a mixture of worry and playfulness. "I wanted to get you out of the lobby because it won't be long now until she comes, and I do not know what kind of a mess she's going to make."

"Who?"

At that moment, the door to the office opened and Elena rose like a spring, running toward her. "Calm down, Sonya."

"I'm calm," she said, closing the door calmly. "I just came to tell this asshole what he needs to hear." Elena went back to her seat and I stood still in mine. Sonya was wearing tight jeans and a tight red T-shirt that, ironically, had a sign on the front that said in bold white letters: Trouble.

"You want me to leave you two alone?" Elena seemed worried. "Do not make a fuss in here because they'll fire me," she almost begged.

Sonya gave her a snarky look. "Are you fucking kidding me?! My aunt is going to fire you? Anyway, don't worry, I'm not going to make a fuss. I'm not a stupid kid anymore." She sat on Elena's desk and stared at me with her piercing green eyes. "Look Edgar, yesterday I wanted to celebrate my birthday with you, and I gave Frank a message for you. He says he gave it to you, but it was useless. All right, no problem. If you're all head over heels for Margarita it's your problem, but I'm not going to wait for you all my life until you're done getting it out of your system. So, get your shit together already. Yes, it's true that I want to go out with you. I do not mind saying it because it's the truth. The difference between you and me is that I know exactly what I want, and you're acting like a dumbass for a lady who gave you her ass, and you're not thinking about how you two don't have a future together and that you're screwing up a lot of people's lives. So, you're both just as stupid. Why do I want to go out with you? Because I like you, but I like you for the way you are. Not for your looks because you're not handsome. Even Frank is better looking than you." I could tell how Elena, sitting on her couch behind Sonya, was tilting her head trying to hide a smile. "But when the gossip spread that you were sleeping with that lady, I was curious to know what was so special about you. And yes, you're special, but you're still too stupid. She is a beautiful lady, no one can deny it, but think of one thing too. I am a virgin and she is already very raggedy." Again, Elena had to make a great effort not to laugh, and I had to make a superhuman effort as well. "So, get your shit together because you cannot have it all or you'll end up with nothing." She got up and left without saying anything else.

Elena and I were looking at each other for a moment, then she smiled at me and with some admiration said, "That's my cousin!"

***

Being lovers was actually very simple. We were only seeing each other for pleasure. Our meetings were to enjoy life; to go to the movies, to eat, and above all to surrender to passion and to our adored god Eros. But living together was something completely different. Certain duties came into play, and passion and pleasure ceased to be the priority. They were replaced with obligations. As our responsibilities increased, so did our problems and our arguments.

Between school, Camino Real, and my homework, I had no time to sleep and my nerves were shattered. She worked in the evenings and fixed the apartment in the mornings. She did the laundry and all the other necessary things to have a clean and beautiful house, which most men do not see, and take for granted.

Anything would bother her, and she'd start an argument. If I left the towel on the floor. Argument. If I had not washed the dish I'd used. Argument. If I did not clean my shoes when I entered the house. Argument! Not to mention, she fell into constant depression because she missed her daughters, and Maribel had started to flunk out of school, which had never happened before. "It's my fault," she said.

On November 26th we had already been living together for a month and had been renting the small apartment that her friend Annie got us. On my 19th birthday, Frank passed me a message from my parents. "They invited you to dinner and want to talk to you."

"I cannot go," I told him.

"Do not be so fucking proud. What's your fucking problem, man!"

"It's not pride," I replied." I'm going to show them that I was right and that I can make it without anyone's help."

"Yes, yes, I can tell," he said sarcastically. "I see how good you're doing, you fool. You look like a damn skeleton from how skinny you got."

"Well, it's only been a month. Starting out is always difficult."

"Stop fucking around! Both of you. Her daughters need her. Cut the crap! Let her go back to her place and you go back to yours and quit the bull-shit." Maybe I should have listened to my friend, but at the time, I was not listening to anyone. There was no way to talk sense into me.

***

The next day was our first anniversary. I had barely slept an hour but woke up a little earlier than usual to give her the card I had bought for her. I began to tenderly kiss her face to wake her up and she turned to me with a great big smile on her face, though still sleepy. I hugged her, feeling the softness of her bare skin, and immediately my hormones began to react, even before I was fully awake. She felt my erection against her body. "Oh, is that my present?"

"Besides this card," I showed her the envelope.

"Which one do you want first?" She smiled and we made love. Then I gave her the card that had fallen to the ground and she pulled out a package from under the bed with a thick scarf inside, which she had weaved while I'd been at school in the mornings. That thoughtful gift meant a lot to me. We had been looking forward to that date so much, but all we could do in the evening was buy a bottle of Châteauneuf-du-Pape '74 red wine and drink it in the apartment to celebrate both my birthday and our anniversary.

"I would have wanted us to celebrate in Las Hadas as we had planned, babe, but we only have money for this bottle of wine."

"Having you with me is the best celebration I can have."

"Do not you care that I can't keep that promise?" I held her against my body and kissed her.

"Of course not! If I can wake up beside you every morning, I don't care about anything else." She smiled at me and raised her cup (we did not have any glasses). "Cheers, babe!

"Cheers!" I replied by lifting and clinking my cup against hers. After we made love again, we fell asleep. And that was the end of the celebration.

***

In December, as Christmas approached, the tension grew. "My daughters want me to spend Christmas with them at home."

I was lying in bed but stood up to concentrate on what was coming. "What about their dad?"

"Their dad, too. They are sad because they say it is going to be the first Christmas we are not spending as a family."

I was surprised that instead of sitting next to me to continue the conversation, she stood there with her arms folded, in a defensive stance. "And what are you going to do?"

"I don't know yet". Suddenly she thought she'd straighten the sheets on the bed. "I told them to ask their dad if it was okay."

I stood still for a moment as she kept staring at the sheets and passing her hand over them again and again. Finally, I was able to activate my mouth to talk again. "Are you thinking of going to spend Christmas with them?"

"With my daughters." She straightened up and now stared at me. "They are not to blame for the… things their mother does," she said with a seemingly regrettable tone.

"Of what?" I asked her angrily. "What were you going to say?"

"Of the nonsense their mother does!"

"Do you think it's silly that we're together?"

She stared at me with those dark eyes that instantly took on an icy gaze. "No, I do not think it's silly. I think it's madness. Real madness!" She turned around and left me sitting there on the bed having a nice plate of emotional bile for breakfast.

***

I was nodding off on the bus trying to stay awake unable to answer the question I had asked myself on my way up. *How did it come to this?*

"We're here," she said, jolting me from my thoughts. We got out of the vehicle and walked to the apartment.

"My college vacation's starting. I'm not going next week."

"I know," she said, still very cold.

We got to the house and I opened the door. "Are you still angry?"

She did not answer me. She went into the apartment, left her purse on the table, and went into the bathroom. I sat on the bed waiting for her to come out to talk, but when she came out she took off her clothes and went to bed without saying a word. *God, how beautiful she is!* I thought, as I watched her slide into the sheets with nothing but her soft, silky skin. Even though we were already in cold weather, we used to sleep naked and while cuddling one another to warm ourselves with each other's bodies. However, a few seconds after going to bed, she got up, opened a dresser drawer, and pulled out thick flannel pajamas. That gesture hurt me more than if she had put on a chastity belt. After tucking herself in, she went back to bed in absolute silence. I still attempted to cuddle with her. "I'm very tired! Let me sleep," she said.

I stopped immediately, straightened up, and sat on the bed. *What's happening to us?* I said to myself in silence. I turned my head to look at her and her face still looked like the most beautiful thing I had ever seen. Her silhouette under the sheets was still the most beautiful in all creation, but something was not right between us. *Now that you're the closest you've ever been to me it feels like you are the farthest away,* I thought. I went to the living room because even though I was tired, I could not sleep, and I did not want to bother her with my tossing and turning on the old mattress that Annie had given us, squeaking with every move. I sat down in the old armchair in the living room, which Annie also gave us, and I drank the last of the wine that we had opened for our anniversary. Our relationship was falling apart. The tension, the lack of money, the unjustified jealousy, and the constant fights was infecting our love. It was not a mild illness but as if a cancer was consuming it at the speed of light. We were now plunging into absolute darkness.

***

During my vacation we spent more time together and as always, we tried to solve our disagreements in bed, which worked perfectly for us, but only for a while because we did not really solve anything. We just glossed over the problem with passion and desire. However, even the passion and desire were getting stale. "When hunger comes through the door, love goes out the window," she once told me when I asked her why she was so serious and cold with me. And her words hurt me as if she put salt on a wound that was already bleeding. However, that pain was nothing compared to what was coming. The closer Christmas approached, the more irritable she became.

On December 23rd, she went to her former home to settle some things regarding her daughters with Mr. Samuel and finalize the details of the divorce. And then I got tripped up by my first setback. Now I was the husband, not the lover, and the time they had been together, the years of struggle, the separation, and so much frustration with the economic situation tipped the balance in his direction.

"I've realized that I miss my home," she said to me in the afternoon on her way back. I did not answer. I did not want to go into the subject because I had a feeling I knew what was coming. That night I noticed she was tossing and turning in bed without being able to sleep. She was nervous. Something was bothering her.

At dawn on December 24th, she went out to make a phone call and did not want me to accompany her. Upon returning, she gave me my *Christmas present*. "I'm going back to my house, where I belong. For the sake of my daughters and everyone else."

"What?!" I yelled at her, losing control.

"I'm a grown woman and it's time for me to behave like one. I love you and I'm always going to love you, but I need to get back to reality."

"You're going back to him because he has money and I do not?"

"Be careful what you say. I'm not a whore."

"Well, you're selling out, aren't you?"

The well-deserved slap hit my cheek hard and I regretted what I said, but it was too late. I wanted to hug her, but she rejected me. We talked, we argued, we cried, and even made love. But there was nothing that would change her mind. When it was time for her to leave, I went crazy and would not let her leave the apartment. I created a tragic, dramatic scene that Shakespeare himself would have never thought of. She packed her suitcase and I'd take her clothes off. She would put them back on and I'd take them off again. I behaved like what I truly was: an immature and rather stupid child.

Later, Frank came to help her get her things out and take her home, but I had stood up and did not understand why. I did not want to lose her, but I knew it was all falling apart. "Fucking traitor!" I yelled at him.

"Enough, man," he said trying to be as calm as possible. "It's going to be all right. It's the best thing for both of you."

I insulted him. he was trying to calm me down. I hit him. He kept trying to calm me down. In the end she left anyway, and I was left alone and devastated. I sat on the bed for a long time, without moving or thinking, corroborating that it was not a dream and that reality hit me in the face and in my soul shouting, *it's over!*

Later I went to my parents' house, and when they saw me I could see the joy on their faces. They did not hold the slightest grudge against me. They still loved me as much as ever. "Can I come back?" I said with my tail between my legs.

"Of course!" My dad replied instantly.

"This will always be your home," my mom said. "And you'll always be my son." They both hugged me, and I cried like a child. And then I realized that I still had a long way to go; a long way to becoming a man.

***

Cousins, uncles, and other family members arrived for Christmas Eve dinner, but I tried to stay as far away as possible. I did not feel like talking to anyone, let alone answering their questions. "How have you been in your new life?" "Do you still live with your girlfriend?" "What's your girlfriend's name?" For dinner, we had a baked turkey cooked by Mom and cod made by my aunt Josefina. We also had Aunt Edelmira's rosemary and apple salad which Aunt Miriam brought. We toasted, we opened presents, and I shamefully thanked them for the ones I received because I did not have any presents for anyone.

It was still early when I left to go to bed. My mom said goodnight to me very happily. My dad kissed me on the forehead and my brother hugged me and whispered in my ear, "Welcome back, dumbass."

The next day I woke up in my old bed and realized the reality: it was all over. Our "love nest" was no more. I got dressed and left the house. I knew exactly what I had to do: I would go look for Frank.

"Good morning," I said to his surprised, half-asleep mother. "I need to talk to Frank."

"Come on in, son." She stepped aside to let me into her house, looking at me curiously, as if trying to find out if I was drunk or something. "He's asleep but let me go wake him up."

When I finally saw him, I apologized and hugged him while feeling a lump in my throat. "First of all," he said quietly, letting me go, his face sleepy and hair standing up all over the place, "no problem. I did not take it the wrong way. Don't worry. Second, you hit like a little girl, you fucking twat, and third, don't you realize that everybody fell asleep late yesterday? It's 9 a.m. in the fucking morning, dumbass." Everything was fine with my friend. I'd taken a load off my mind. But Margarita's situation was still hurting me. How could I live without her?

CHAPTER 22

The days were eternal. Sometimes I could not sleep through the night and sometimes I slept 12 or 13 hours straight, only to wake up and not want to get out of bed. I ate a whole box of Ritz crackers, several Marinela Gansitos, some Pinguinos cupcakes, and a few of the big Toblerone chocolates before I went to work at the hotel in the evenings.

As I was on vacation from college, the minutes were hours and the hours were centuries. Frank did everything he could to get me out of the state I was in, but I always had an excuse for not going anywhere; or I would leave the house and go to the park to lie down on the grass and suffer my defeat so no one would know where I was. I did not want to go out with Sonya either.

Everyone was very excited about the beginning of the new decade, the 80s, except me. Margarita and I had made plans, months ago, that we would celebrate the new year while making love.

"At 12 o'clock I want you to be inside me making love to me. We're going to welcome 1980 by loving each other like degenerate madmen," she told me shortly before we were discovered in the Insurgentes' roundabout.

"And how are you going to get out of your house that day?" I asked excitedly, but also intrigued.

"We shall see," she replied. "There is still a long way to go."

Now there were only a few days left and life had turned our relationship upside down so much that I no longer knew where I stood. Mom and Dad were also trying to cheer me up, but I was still holding onto my depression.

Finally, the long-awaited end of the year arrived with champagne, grapes, and family. "10, 9, 8, 7," they all counted in the house while I continued with my bitter face. "6, 5, 4, 3, 2, 1. Happy New Year!" My brother almost choked on the grapes because he was in a hurry to eat them all before 12 o'clock, but I had barely eaten three when everyone had already started hugging. And while I was hugging everyone, I would mindlessly repeat as if I were a tape recorder saying, "Happy New Year, Happy New Year."

It tormented me to think that at that very moment, Margarita would be hugging and wishing her husband the best for the decade, or worse, making love to him, as she had longed to do with me.

***

Ten minutes after midnight, the doorbell rang, and I went to open the door.

It was Sonya. She wore a beautiful black dress, heels, and a thick coat that made her look like a sophisticated Hollywood star. "Hello. Happy New Year," she said to me, opening her arms.

I hugged her, feeling her warmth, and her enormous sensuality all over my body, like an electric shock. We held each other for a moment and then separated just a little bit. Our faces were facing each other; we looked into each other's eyes and then we both looked down at each other's lips…with desire. I waited for her to come to me and touch her lips to mine, as she had in the past.

"Do not even think that I'm going to kiss you," she said to me as if she could guess my thoughts. "The next time we kiss will be when you are free in body and soul of anyone else, and you are not yet." She pulled from my embrace, leaving me speechless as usual. "Shall we get in my car or do you want us to stay here?"

"Let's get in your car. It's cold here."

"How are you feeling?" She asked me once we settled into the interior of the orange Caribbean, her in the driver's side and me in the passenger seat.

"Good," I did not want to answer truthfully.

"Why are you lying, Edgar?" I looked at her as if I did not understand her question. "You're not well and you know it. You said we were friends, but you're not sincere." I shrugged. "I do not wear a mask for a living, so you don't have to wear your mask with me. When are you going to be yourself?" From all the self-help books I had read, I hadn't learned what I was learning from that 18-year-old girl who seemed to be more transparent than glass.

"You've changed a lot since we first went out," I said.

"One has to change. You cannot stay stuck on the same thing your whole life. You must move forward, grow, evolve." She paused briefly and looked me in the eye. "If you see that something is no longer helping you grow, then let it go. Do not get stuck."

"You mean Margarita?"

"Yes," she said, staring at me. "Don't you think you've learned what you had to learn and that it's time to move on?"

"That's all over now," I replied, looking down at the palms of my hands.

"That's not true."

"Why do you say it's not?"

"Because you looked down when you said it."

"Are you sure you want to study architecture?" I asked with a slight smile.

"Yeah, why?"

"You'd make a great psychologist."

"I'm not interested in psychology. And do not change the subject."

I laughed quietly. "Can I ask you a question?" I said to her.

"Yeah, but if you're going to ask me a question, just ask it. Do not ask my permission."

I laughed again while admiring her beauty and above all, her way of being. Sonya was very different from all the people I had met. "Why don't you have a boyfriend?"

"You of all people are asking me that? Because the one I want is blinded by a lady who gave him her ass and is clinging to a relationship that has no future."

"But," I began to say a bit sheepishly. "You have many suitors."

"So what?" she interrupted. "They're all the same. They try to impress me by pretending to be something they are not. You're different. At least you don't try to be something you're not. Your problem is that you don't dare to be who you are, but there is a solution for that."

I talked to Sonya until my mom came out to tell us that they had called from her house to see if she was still with us. It was already 3 a.m.! Time had flown by. We said goodbye with a kiss on the cheek, which was a cultural custom.

"Think things over, Edgar," she said before she started the car. "Finish what you must finish but finish it well. Do not stop halfway." I watched her drive away and I went into the house. At least I felt better after talking to Sonya.

***

I sat in front of Elena at the reception office at Camino Real Hotel the second week of January, apologetically rubbing my sweaty hands for resigning again after just over two months of getting my job back. "Don't worry," she said sympathetically. "In fact, I was going to propose it to you because you looked so tired of working and studying at the same time." She gave me a cheeky look and I smiled blushing, which made her laugh out loud. "I love it when you blush."

The next day Frank picked me up from university in the Volkswagen that his parents had given him on his 18th birthday in October. We went to the cinema to see *Rocky II*, which had been playing since December. It had been a long time since we had gone out and it helped my psyche. For a moment I forgot about Margarita and all my problems. After the movie, we went to Susy's on Fortuna Street to have some tacos for dinner, and he kept hitting me like Rocky did against Apollo in the movie.

"And how are you doing with Maribel?" I wanted to know while we were waiting for our barbecue pork tacos, dodging his left jab.

"Good. And how are you doing with Margarita?" If I didn't know him, I'd think he was mistaken but I knew what was coming. "Oh, she already told you to fuck off, didn't she?" That was Frank. He had very dark humor, but he was a great friend.

"And has Maribel told you something about me?"

They brought us the tacos and we started eating. "No, she doesn't want to talk about you. The other day I was telling her something, I don't remember what, but when I mentioned your name, she said, 'I'd rather you not tell me anything about him,' and I haven't mentioned you since."

"And do you know why she doesn't want to hear about me?" I asked him, getting serious while holding the taco up to my mouth, my eyes locking with his.

"Why?" he asked with his mouth full, but still very much interested.

"Because she's in love with me, but we didn't want to tell you," I replied, trying to get back to some dark humor. But he just shook his head sideways and swallowed his food.

"No," he finally said. "She doesn't like fags."

"If she didn't like fags, she wouldn't hang out with you."

"She doesn't know we're fags yet."

"We are? *You* are!"

We kept having fun with silly conversation like we did in the past until I asked him the question I wanted him to answer truthfully. "And how is she?"

"Mrs. Margarita? Good. They're going to go to Las Hadas, I think."

I was paralyzed. "All of them?"

"She and her husband, dumbass. Marisol and Maribel are staying with their aunt. Or I think the aunt's going to stay at their place. I don't know, I'm not sure." I felt my blood freeze while fire from the volcano inside me began to rise to my head, erupting and causing me to lose all sense of reason.

CHAPTER 23

I hid in a corner outside of Mrs. Margarita's house early in the morning. I managed to see Marisol and Maribel go to school. Later, I saw Mr. Samuel leaving for work and a few minutes later the two housekeepers went out to the market to buy food as they did every day. I waited a few minutes after they left and went to ring the bell. A moment later I heard a few steps inside. "Who is it?" shouted that voice I missed so much. I was silent for a moment trying to decide whether to answer. "Who is it?" she asked again.

"Me," I finally answered.

"Who is it?!" she said again, incredulous.

"Me."

She quickly opened the door and looked at me with wide eyes.

"What are you doing here?!" She poked her head out into the street and turned sideways to see if anyone was watching. "Come in," she added, grabbing my arm and walking into the house. "What are you doing here?!" she shouted angrily at me. "You're going to get me in trouble!"

Despite the cold, she wore a long silk robe down to her calves that opened up at the legs, revealing the silky skin of her thighs, which provoked my desire, while at the same time provoked my rage at the thought that perhaps a few moments before those thighs were being caressed by other hands. "Is it true you're going to Las Hadas with that bastard?" I asked out of nowhere.

She was paralyzed as if I had emptied a bucket of ice water on her. "Who told you th…?" I interrupted her by taking her by the arms and shaking her.

"Is it true?!"

"You're hurting me," she said, turning pale. "Let go of me!"

I let her go, but the rage was blinding me. "To Las Hadas! Where we were going to celebrate our anniversary! You have no shame!"

"Do not shout, please," she asked softly as if indicating the appropriate volume to speak. "Keep your voice down."

"Answer me! Is it true?"

"Yes!" she said in an empty scream. And tears streamed down her face. I could not bear to see her cry, so without thinking I wrapped my arms around her. It was as if I had released a detonator because when I embraced her, she began to wail. I could feel the tears wetting my neck, her arms pressed against each other between my chest, and her shoulders shaking in violent convulsions. I hugged her harder, trying to calm her down, worried that I had been overly angry with her.

"Forgive me!" I begged. "Forgive me!"

She was sobbing harder and I was squeezing her against my body, wishing I could fuse hers with mine so that no one could ever separate us again. Little by little, her tears subsided. She separated a few inches from me, looking at me with her black eyes and her impetuous gaze. "Why did you come here? Why?!" She paused and stared at me. "I've already accepted being without you." I could see how her gaze was growing primitive. Wild. I knew that glow because I'd seen it before. Her face changed as if she were possessed and her hands took my face. "Why did you come here? Why? Why?"

Her lips threw themselves wildly at mine, devouring and biting them hard, so much so that I felt a sting of pain and noticed a drop of my blood on her lower lip when she separated her face from mine. She licked away the drop of blood and while looking me in the eyes with that fierce look, she pushed me backward until I was leaning against the front door. "You're a fool!" She kissed me again and bit my lip hard, pulling it with her teeth as she stepped back to fix her violent gaze on mine again. It was incredible, but the savagery was coming from her was turning me on.

In an instant, I grabbed her face and kissed her; biting her lip hard enough to cause her pain. We kissed fiercely, licking each other's blood, engaging one other in a rough battle. My hands seemed to have wings and flew toward her legs, her butt, her breasts, squeezing, stroking, holding. Suddenly, as if she were coming back to her senses, she separated from me. "Not here!" she said, breathing hard. She ran into the garage and threw the keys to the Caprice at me. "You drive!" I caught the keys, but I was still leaning on the door unable to react. "Get the car out!" she yelled at me.

I headed for the car in a hurry, feeling the adrenaline running through my body as if I were living a scene out of *Maximum Danger*. Once in the driveway, she closed the garage door, still in her silk robe, almost naked. She then got into the car on the passenger's side.

"Take me to a hotel or something," she said with desperation. Immediately after, she unzipped my pants, took out my penis, which looked like it was about to explode, and leaned over to suck violently and viciously. We did not even get to the bed in the hotel room. We were so excited and lost in passion that as we closed the door of the hotel room, we hugged each other, devouring each other like wild beasts, sliding toward the carpet.

I lowered her panties and caressed her labia with the palm of my hand and fingers, which poured out its essence like a torrent. I easily inserted my index and middle fingers to stimulate a spot on the front wall of her vagina which I realized was giving her great pleasure. Almost immediately, she began to move her pelvis up and down ferociously, screaming at the same time and moving her head violently to the side. I then felt strong contractions that were squeezing my fingers inside her. A beastly scream erupted from her throat. Her whole body became tense. Her back arched and a clear liquid came out of her vagina as if a water balloon had burst in there, soaking my hand and through the carpet. Her pelvis began to convulse and as if it were a wave effect, the spasms were going up all over her body until it reached her head, which kept moving wildly from side to side; her screaming continued as if it could not be stopped.

I stripped off my clothes in a few seconds and placed myself on top of her, getting between her legs pushing myself all the way in. She lifted her hip and with her hands on my buttocks, she pulled me toward her. We moved with force, gyrating around instead of an inward and outward movement. We breathed hard as our movements accelerated, making them faster and more vigorous. We seemed to be possessed by forces beyond our control and indeed we were possessed by passion, by obsession, by love.

"Why did you come looking for me?!" she shouted at me, taking my face with her hands and staring at mine, as she rushed to another strong orgasm.

"Because I love you," I responded increasing the movement of my hips.

"That's not true!" she shouted. And the orgasm began, rising like a giant wave. "Hit me!" She managed to say before forcefully clenching her teeth and eyes. I hit her gently on the buttocks with my open hand. "Harder!" she repeated as the orgasm continued to grow. "Punish me! Slap me!" I slapped her butt again and then her face while our hips continued to move in an almost savage way. Her orgasm reached its peak, causing her whole body to become tense again.

I, too, was approaching orgasm. I took her face in my hands and shouted at her, "You are mine! Did you hear me?! You're mine! Mine!"

"Yes!" She replied continuing to orgasm, her eyes filled with tears. "I'm yours. Only yours!"

My whole being completely unloaded into her with an explosive, almost infinite orgasm. Our bodies, drenched in sweat, remained next to each other in a total state of bliss. As if we had crossed into another dimension in which physical pleasure merged with spiritual pleasure. Where Yin and Yang found perfect harmony, where Shiva and Shakti merged into one being, in a universe where there is no pain or guilt, only pleasure. An eternal and pleasant state of ecstasy in its purest expression.

***

"Now we've complicated everything," she said with a tone of voice that indicated concern.

She was sitting in front of me on the bed with her legs crossed and I was still lying down with both hands behind my neck, looking at her sensual face and her shiny skin; just like she usually was after making love.

"I think there is no doubt that we love each other," I said.

"But I did not doubt that," she said in a firm voice. "And what's more, no one doubted it. And that is precisely the problem." Her tone softened and she stroked my chest with her hand. "We're not alone, babe."

I was aware that we were wiping out everything in our path, however, I couldn't imagine life without her. And apparently, neither could she. We had already entered a vicious cycle of breaking up and getting back together again, which we could not break. "Were you going to go to Las Hadas?" I asked.

"Yes," she replied confidently. "I was willing to forget you and the only way to do that was to face the problem directly, by grabbing the bull by the horns."

"But that's where we were going to go," I protested

"That's exactly why. I wanted to break away from this whole thing, but now I'm never going to be able to do so. You should not have come looking for me, babe." She laid down next to me and kissed me on the lips.

"Do you regret it?" I pondered.

"No, but I was not bad before you."

"Bad? You're not bad," I said, surprised.

"Yes, I am," she added, kissing me again but with passion this time. "And I need you to give me my punishment right now," she said with a naughty smile. We made love again without thinking about anything but the present.

"I have to go. I'll see you tomorrow so we can talk about how we are going to see each other," she said as she put on her silk robe again. *How* are *we going to see each other? What does she mean by that?* I looked at her hesitantly. "We have to come to an agreement, and this time we must keep it."

"To an agreement?"

"Yes, but we'll talk tomorrow. I must go now. I left the house nearly naked. Let's hope no one saw me."

When I finished getting dressed and began to tie my shoelaces, I decided to ask, "Why are you wearing such sexy underwear and a silk robe?"

She looked at her clothes and smiled at me. "Are we about to start again?" I straightened up and held her gaze waiting for an answer. "First of all, you of all people, know that all my underwear is like this." She opened her robe to let me see her set of Victoria's Secret beige lace lingerie. "Except for the strawberries and cherries one," she added with a mischievous, sweet smile. "Which I found in a shop in Europe, I think in France or Italy. And secondly, the cotton robe I've been wearing these cold days is in the laundry basket to be washed. I was going to take a bath when the bell rang, so I grabbed the first thing I found in the drawer to see who was interrupting me." She kissed me on the lips, squeezing my lower lip between her teeth and pulling it out very amusingly. "And it turned out to be a stubborn, obsessive young man who is driving me crazy, and with whom I don't know what I'm going to do."

I lured her to me, grabbing her by the waist, and lowered my hands down to her butt as I squeezed her toward my hips and kissed her. "Well, I can tell you what you could do with that scoundrel."

She kissed me back with desire and then stopped me. "We're completely insane. Do you know that? Insane! Lost!" And we got lost again in passion, in obsession. In love. In everything!

Chapter 24

In the mornings, I went to university, and in the afternoons, when Mrs. Margarita could go out, we would see each other.

"I'll call you when we can see each other. I'm not taking any chances again," she said before leaving the hotel that day after I'd gone to pick her up at her house.

"Are you going to go to Las Hadas?"

"No, I'm not sure what I'll tell Samuel, but I'm not going to go," she kissed me tenderly on the lips. "I promise you that." I never knew what she ended up making up as an excuse, but it's true that she didn't go. However, my torment and obsession with the phone got worse. When I got home from school, I did my homework by the phone in case she called me because if I didn't answer, she would hang up and she might not call again until the next day or two. I ate near the phone, and when I went to the bathroom I did it as quickly as possible so that I could keep an eye on the device.

There were evenings when she called me just to say hello, but we did not see each other, and there were others when she did not call at all. Having to study and do homework distracted me a little and relieved my anguish of always being by the phone. I also continued with the construction of my 19-story Lego building, which was already well underway.

"We're going to breakfast," Mom said to me on a Sunday morning. Are you coming with us?" Unconsciously I turned to look at the phone.

"No, I have to study because I have final exams."

Mom approached me, "It's Sunday. Why don't you take a break?" I was going to say something, but she would not let me. "I know why you do not want to leave, and you spend your time shut away, but did you notice that she never calls you on Sundays?" I wanted to say something again, but she raised her hand and told me she had not finished speaking. "You live glued to the phone and you only get out when she decides you can get out. You are 19-years-old and you are giving your youth to a woman who depends on another man to know if she can come out and see you or not." She paused to let me take in her words. "Go out, son. Have fun. Enjoy your life before it's gone forever." I kept my head down and listened to her without daring to look up because I knew she was right. Mrs. Margarita did not call me on Sundays because it was a day when she and her husband went out somewhere as a family. I'd spent six months like this, waiting by the phone and for her to come out so we could see each other. "Think about it, Eddy. Think about it," Mom continued. "We'd like to have you back in the family, not just in the house." She turned around and walked out of my room without saying anything more.

***

"Another round!" Frank shouted to the waiter who was waiting for us, as he waved his hand and gestured with a circular motion and pointed at the four of us at the table. He had been wanting us to go out for a long time, but I refused because I did not want to go out anywhere unless it was with Mrs. Margarita. But that night was something special, so I could not object.

We had a friend named Aldo, who also grew up with us in the neighborhood. His father owned some of the most important fabric stores in the northern part of the city. The funny thing is that his father's name was Alfonso. Because Poncho is a nickname for Alfonso, Aldo had been teased all his life about how his father's shops should have been called Fa-bri-Poncho *Te-las-Poncho.*[2]

A few weeks earlier, Aldo had invited us to dinner at a street quesadilla stand on a corner near where we lived. One of those places where a humble lady has a stove, butter, dough and everything necessary to make delicious quesadillas, sopes and tostadas. After having stuffed his face with almost a dozen quesadillas and told us to get whatever we wanted, Aldo addressed the modest lady, "How much do I owe you?"

She brought the check and he pulled out his credit card to the woman's surprise. Frank and I thought he was joking, but we soon realized he was serious. "Don't you accept credit cards?" Aldo asked the bewildered lady.

---

2 Slang that could be translated to English like "I fuck you"

"No, young man," she said, very innocently and embarrassed.

"C'mon!" said Frank. "Pay up, dude."

"I don't have any cash," said Aldo, playing dumb.

"Did you really think they would accept credit cards at a quesadilla stand? Don't be stupid!"

"Seriously, I do not have any cash. Don't you have any? I just have the card." Frank took out his wallet and paid the lady. I took out mine and gave Frank half of the bill. Aldo played dumb, "I'll pay you later." Since then, Frank said he was going to throw one back at Aldo someday. That day had come.

We were at the bar at the Camino Real Hotel. *Couldn't they have picked a better place?!* Gathered at a little round table was Aldo, Frank, my brother Tavo, whom Frank had convinced to go after explaining what the move against Aldo would be, and me. I do not know how many rounds Frank had already ordered, but we all slurred our words and everything was blurry and double. Plus, I kept remembering my visit to that hotel with Mrs. Margarita.

The waiter came in with the next round and the singer at the piano put the cherry on top: he began to sing, "You Arrived Late," (*Llegaste tarde*), by the composer Wello Rivas, and when I heard the first sentences of the song —"You arrived late, in the twilight of my sad life, and my tender words confused you, and for the first time, you wanted to love"— I started to cry.

"I was late," I said, trying to steady my tongue, which at the time was completely subdued by the alcohol I consumed. I turned to Aldo putting my face a few inches from his. I placed my arm around his shoulders. "I was late, you bastard. I was late!"

"No dude!" He also put his arm over my shoulder. "You're just in time, motherfucker. Just in time!"

"No way! No-way-y! I was late. I was late. I finally found a woman and who is she? Who is she?!" I raised my voice so he could hear me, though my face was still a couple of inches from his. Apparently the whole bar heard because every head turned to look at me.

"Shut up, you fucking drunk!" Frank said to me, slapping on the head.

"Who is she?" I said again not paying any attention to being slapped and bringing my face so close to Aldo's that it looked like I was going to kiss him. "She's the most beautiful woman in the fucking world. But married! Married, you prick!" I cried even harder and hid my head on my arm leaning against the table, but only for a couple of seconds because I got up again to say, "What a shame!" and again I collapsed on the table to cry.

I felt a hand give me a loving tap on the head. I stood up to see who it was. My brother looked at me with a smile on his face that seemed sympathetic, and now he was lovingly tapping me on the cheek. "Calm down, brother." Frank looked at me too, but his smile was not as understanding as Tavo's. It was more entertained. "Calm down, dude. Calm down."

"I was late!" I said trying to pronounce the letter T, which was the hardest letter for me to pronounce at the time.

"Be cool, motherfucker. Because if not, they're going to kick us out of here early," he smiled ironically. Aldo and Tavo joined him in laughter. I remained silent for a moment and then approached Aldo again; the only one who seemed interested in my tragedy.

"And then Sonya! Sonya!" I told him as if I had suddenly remembered her.

"Fucking Sonya is hot," Aldo said, sipping his drink.

"Isn't that right, my friend?"

"Really hot!" A lascivious smile appeared on his face and I think I may have felt a slight sting of jealousy.

"So?! Then what?!" I hid my face back into my arm on the table and listened to my brother's and my friends' laughter due to how ridiculous I was being. We continued drinking, listening to the piano singer, and talking, although I tried at every opportunity to divert the conversation to Mrs. Margarita and Sonya. But Frank would shut me up by slapping me. The next day I did not know if my headache was from a hangover or being slapped so many times.

After midnight, Frank asked for the bill which amounted to more than a thousand pesos. He examined it and pretended to take out his wallet.

"Do you have your credit card with you?" he asked Aldo, who then took out his wallet and looked for a credit card.

"Yes. How do we divide it up?"

"Have you got any money, you fucking drunk?" Frank asked me.

"No," I replied a little surprised because he told me not to bring any.

Now he turned to Tavo. "You don't either, do you?" My brother shook his head, pretending to be worried.

"Pay with your card and we'll pay you back because no one has cash. Fortunately, here they accept your card; not like the old lady from the quesadilla stand."

Aldo sobered up at that point. "No way!" he practically shouted.

"Seriously, dude," Frank said, taking his card and putting it in the check presenter. "We'll pay you back."

"But pay me back! Don't fuck around!"

"Sure, man. Don't make a big deal about it."

Frank lifted the bill with the card inside for the waiter to see. The waiter came by, took the bill and left, leaving Aldo almost completely sober and with a skin color somewhere between white and transparent. I felt like everything was spinning around and I wished I could sober up as fast as he did, but the worst was yet to come. The hangover!

The next day I could not stand the slightest movement of my head, and when the phone rang it was as if someone had blown up a grenade in my ears. "Hello?" I said, my throat frogged and swollen. There was silence on the other end. After clearing my throat I repeated myself. "Hello."

"I did not recognize your voice," Mrs. Margarita said at last. "Are you ill?"

"No," I straightened up in bed feeling as if my brain was spinning inside my head. "I'm fine. "

"See you this afternoon at 3 p.m.? I only have half an hour, but I want to see you and tell you something."

"Yes, of course." She hung up and I looked at the clock. I still had time.

I was dying of thirst, so I got up to get a drink of water. When I arrived at the kitchen, my mother was leaning over the sink with her arms crossed, watching me. "Good morning," I said to her, expecting a well-deserved scolding, but to my surprise, she smiled at me.

"That was not exactly the way I wanted you to get out of your seclusion, but it's okay. At least you went out." She prepared a pitcher full of water with ice and slices of lemon. I crave every drop as if it were the most delicious thing I had ever seen. She poured me a glass and I drank it with absolute desperation. It tasted like glory.

"Sit down and have some breakfast." She put the pitcher of water on the table while I sat down and served myself again. "Your brother already drank two of those pitchers and ate two plates of chilaquiles before he left."

I kept drinking and she put me a big plate of chilaquiles with chicken, cream, cheese, and chopped onion. Suddenly I was very hungry and devoured the tasty delicacy before me. "Thank you, Mom," I said after I finished with two pitchers of water and three plates of chilaquiles.

She nodded her head and tossed my hair around lovingly. "Get in the bath. You smell like a drunk." I kissed her on the cheek, and she smiled warmly at me. I went to the bathroom but stopped.

It'd been a while since I wanted to ask her something, but I didn't dare. Either I ask her now or never. "Mom." She stared at me waiting for me to continue. "The day I was at the Red Cross, when you went outside to talk." She kept her gaze on me as I was having a hard time speaking. "Uh...what did you tell her?"

She paused briefly as if pondering the question. "She didn't tell you?"

"No. Every time I ask her, she tells me 'mom stuff' and that I'll never know."

She smiled and walked a few steps toward me. "Well, it's true. That's what we talked about; 'mom stuff.'"

I resigned myself knowing that they'd never tell me. When I was leaving again, her voice stopped me. "I asked her not to tell you anything, but not because it was something bad, but because I wanted to see how deep her love for you was." I frowned without understanding. "I asked her that, if she loved you so much, she'd never tell you what we talked about." All the discomfort I had from the hangover disappeared as if by magic. "And I'm not going to tell you either. I just want you to know that I told her how much I love you. And I asked her not to hurt you ever." A lump formed in my throat. "That's all you can know."

I stood there for a few seconds not knowing what to do. I then walked up to her, hugged her, and kissed her again. "Thank you, Mom." That was all I could say.

Chapter 25

Our relationship after the reunion had become even more carnal than ever. Since we didn't know when we would see each other again, we'd rather go worship Eros between the four walls than go to the movies or dinner. But as much as I loved making love to her, I was getting tired of the fact that we did not see each other very much, and when we did it was in a hurry. And the jealousy was torturing me. I think there is nothing worse and stupid, in terms of jealousy, than imagining the woman you love, cheating on you with her own husband.

"We do not see each other like we used to," I complained on a hot April afternoon. She had picked me up from college and we were now lying naked and sweaty in a hotel on the Tlalpan driveway.

"Because I cannot anymore. If Samuel pays another detective to follow me and finds out about us, he'll kill us both. I cannot even let him get suspicious anymore."

I couldn't say anything in my defense. The simple fact of remembering the tremendous failure of moving in together left me speechless. "And how come he doesn't suspect anything anymore?" I asked fearing the answer. She raised her head to look me in the eye. "He used to be suspicious because you rejected him when he wanted to make love to you. How come he's quiet and unsuspecting now?"

Her gaze grew cold and her thick lips became a thin line.

"Look, babe. First, I'm not going to answer that question. Secondly, you knew I was married, and thirdly, I never said he did not suspect anything anymore."

"But…" I tried to protest, but she interrupted me.

"I'm not going to talk about it with you."

That was enough to drive me crazy. "Then with whom? Aren't you and I supposed to be a couple?" She rolled her eyes, growing angry. "And he's just the father of your daughters? That's what you told me."

"What do you know about what I have to do to get out of trouble for seeing you?!" She got out of bed to face me standing up. "I'm doing my best to get out to see you. I've become a liar, and not only with him. I lie to my daughters too so I can go out with you, and instead of valuing that, you complain to me and make me feel like a whore." I jumped up. In no way did I want to make her feel like a whore. "I told you, you're just like everyone else!" She started to cry, "Ugh! I hate myself! I hate myself for always crying!"

I hugged her. "Forgive me. You're right. Forgive me." She cried on my shoulder without turning me away. She was right. I didn't even imagine what she had to go through to be able to see me on the sly. The difficulties she had to face for loving me. I kissed her on the lips gently, but she refused to kiss me back. I smiled at her and very slowly passed my tongue between her lips to separate them. I passed it through her teeth and little by little she responded to my kiss. Suddenly she bit my lower lip hard, causing me some pain.

"I hate you," she said and then kissed me passionately, making her tongue play with mine. I drew her to me by grabbing her buttocks and she immediately felt my erection. I kissed the tears that had poured down her cheeks and neck. Our hips automatically moved rhythmically to one side and the other, rubbing against her clitoris. My kisses made their way toward her breasts. I began sucking her nipples, which caused her to groan slightly. She started getting wet right away. Very skillfully, she settled in, so my erect member slid into her. I put my weight on my heels to keep my balance and held onto her buttocks. We were moving at the same speed, increasing it gradually, but without being in a hurry.

She lifted her legs and wrapped them around my waist while I kept holding her by her buttocks. In that position, I was able to penetrate deeper. She began to move more and more aggressively, each movement roughed than the next. I tried to synch to her rhythm thrusting faster and harder each time. Her moans intensified as the orgasm grew within her, preparing to erupt in a burst of pleasure. Fluid dripped from her vagina and was running down my thighs. She moaned loudly, which was then muffled as she bit my shoulder. Her fingernails scraped my back and her body tightened.

I continued to move forcefully as she clung to me.

"Enough!" she yelled.

"No!" I shouted at the same time. "Feel it more. Feel it more!"

The contractions of her orgasm continued, and she screamed again, clinging tightly to me, throwing her head back and forth, then sideways, uncontrollably.

"I'm going to die!" she shouted at me, and tears welled up in her eyes, but this time for a different reason. This time, it was pure and true pleasure.

After our erotic meeting, we each went home; she in her car and I in the subway. The whole way home, I thought about what my future might be like with her. I loved her and was sure of it; she loved me too and I had no doubt about it. But something had happened that could threaten our relationship. Our romance was becoming endangered and the decision to save or destroy it was going to depend solely on me.

CHAPTER 26

"Let me know when you get the letter from London," said Professor Marquez, my math teacher, on the last day of school.

"Yes, professor, I'll let you know."

"It should not take long because if you get accepted, you'll start next semester."

I nodded slightly.

"In fact, they are already late. It should have reached you by now," he said.

"Maybe they did not accept me."

He looked at me, pressing his lips together and moving his head sideways, as if he were certain of something. "No, I do not think so. I think it should be here soon. You meet all the requirements to be accepted. I do not see why they would turn you down."

"There are candidates from all over the world."

"Believe me, you have everything to compete with the best, so do not be discouraged."

My letter of acceptance at the Architectural Association in London would not take long to come if I were accepted. This also meant the end of my romance with Mrs. Margarita. If I were accepted, I'd have to choose between her and my career. It was Professor Márquez who recommended me for the scholarship to the AA, one of the best architecture schools in the world. Mom and Dad were happy with the opportunity and so was I, but I had not decided yet. I was not willing to leave Mrs. Margarita for anything or anyone.

***

The summer holiday seemed to go on forever even though it had just started. Days without school were torturous. I was stuck to the phone waiting for it to ring so I could hear Mrs. Margarita's voice telling me we'd see each other that day. My Lego building was almost finished and I really liked the way it turned out. I knew that once I finished it, I was going to be upset because it meant something very important to me: it was the first building I designed by myself. We, humans, are so strange. When we like something and are satisfied with it, we don't want it to end, even if it means that we have completed a process of growth and learning.

On one of the first few days of vacation, Sonya came to pick me up at my house. "Come on, I'll buy you a cup of coffee."

Her tone suggested she wasn't going to take "no" for an answer. So, I got into her wine-colored Le Baron. "Your dad finally lent you the Le Baron?"

"No." She headed for Insurgentes Avenue. "My mom's out in her Caribbean and my dad's asleep. I took the keys so I wouldn't wake him up."

We went to a coffee shop I wasn't familiar with. We sat at a table and she asked for a soda and I asked for coffee. When the waitress left, Sonya opened her purse, reached in, and stopped for a moment to ask me:

"Can you read in English?"

I had studied English since kindergarten at Tepeyac College. "Yes, of course."

Then she pulled out a book that looked like the Bible at first because it was so thick. "This book is called *Atlas Shrugged*. It's by Ayn Rand and it's very good. You can borrow it. I read it last year and it changed the way I view things. I think it'll be good for you too."

It was hardcover and had a drawing of a train headlight and tracks. It also had the title of the book and the author's name. I went to the last page, curious to see how many pages it had. "1,168!" I exclaimed alarmed. "What's it about?"

"Read it so you can find out for yourself, but one of the things I liked the most is what it says about integrity."

"Integrity?" I put the heavy book on the table and leaned backward, interested in whatever she was about to say.

The waitress came over and left us the soda and coffee. "Are you going to want anything else?"

"Not at the moment," Sonya answered without taking her eyes off me. Once the waitress left, she went on, "Integrity. For you to be whole, for your mind and body to aim toward the same goal. For example, if you're doing something you have to hide for," she laid her green eyes on me and inched forward, leaning on the table, "then don't do it. That is a lack of integrity. Your mind is saying, 'This is not right' and your body is doing it anyway because even though the mind is telling you it's not right, it prefers the momentary pleasure it causes, betraying its integrity. That's why feelings of guilt come up. A man of integrity has no feelings of guilt. He always does what is right for him. He always seeks the truth and does not deceive himself."

"Oh," I exclaimed, realizing that described me to a tee. I looked at the book still on the table and touched it as if I could absorb the message. I looked up and she was still staring at me.

"Are you going to read it?"

"Yes, of course."

"How's it going with the scholarship in London?" She leaned back on the chair and changed the conversation like she used to.

"They have not answered me yet."

"I hope they'll accept you. That's one of the best universities in the world for architecture."

"Yes, it would be a good opportunity if they would accept me," I said thinking that it meant my relationship with Mrs. Margarita would end.

"Oh, Edgar! Really?"

I looked at her in surprise. "Really what?"

"You don't want to get accepted because you don't want to leave her?" *Does this girl have special powers?! How does she know what I'm thinking?!* I didn't know what to say. I was stunned.

"I could tell by the look on your face. Anyone else would be excited to have the chance to be accepted, and you made a face as if you didn't want to leave. And the only thing that could be stopping you from leaving is her." I looked at her like a scolded child. It was worse than talking to my mom. "Would you really be willing to bet your entire future on a piece of ass? In 20 years, you could be at the top of your career as an architect, and by that time that ass that drives you so crazy is going to be as saggy as yours. You'll have missed the chance of a lifetime for something so stupid." *I have a saggy ass?* Well, it was true. But did she have to say it like that?

"If I have so many flaws, why do you want to hang out with me?" I asked fearful of her reaction.

"We all have defects, but what do you mean?"

"The other day you told me I'm not handsome and now I have a saggy butt."

She stared at me as I went over what she had said in my mind to see if I had gone too far and she was going to throw hot coffee or her soda with all the ice.

"Do you think I want to be with you because of your body? That's the last thing I care about!" She softened her tone a little and nodded her head to one side. She continued, "Apparently you're good at making love, otherwise, the Mrs. would not be so crazy for you. And that's important to me. Why do I want someone next to me who won't even give me an orgasm? But that's not everything and physical beauty has nothing to do with those skills." I began to blush and looked down at my pants, searching for lint or anything else to distract me. "Of course, a good body can be exciting, but I never said you were ugly. Just because you're not as handsome as most people I know does not mean I don't like you." She paused and I kept examining my pants. "Look at me," she added in a slightly harsher tone of voice. "Your pants are clean, there's nothing on them. Do not be afraid of me." Now her voice became sensual and exciting. "I'm not going to eat you…yet." I swallowed saliva and knew I was redder than an Irapuato strawberry. "I told you," she steadied her tone of voice, "I'm not going to do anything until you're completely free of that madness you have in your head." She settled into the chair. "I never have, but I'm sure I could make love pretty well. What do you think?" *Why is she asking me that question?!* She laughed cheerfully. "I love turning you red."

I smiled at her and took a sip of coffee, but I wasn't thirsty. I had to do something, anything. Then she got very serious. "I've waited Edgar, but I'm not waiting any longer. I know you like me."

And who doesn't!?

"And I'm sure we could make a good couple because I know that once you get over that nonsense you're going to focus on what you should and you'll be a great architect, and above all, you can be a happy man, which is any human being's goal." *How old does this girl say she is?!* In one year, she had matured to a level that many people fail to do so in a lifetime, including me. "But I'm getting desperate and disappointed. I thought you'd get over this much sooner, but I realize it's even interfering with your career, your dreams, and your entire future. Opportunities come only once and we either seize them or waste them. If you're going to choose that lady who gives you her ass, instead of one of the best architecture schools in the world, then that means I've been wrong and you're not as smart as I thought you were." She put her arms on the table again to get closer to me. "I told you once, Edgar. You want it all and you are going to end up with nothing. Mrs. Margarita will end up staying with her husband and daughters. She is not stupid and knows perfectly well that sooner or later this will end and that's why she won't let go of the sure thing. She prefers to hold on. Obviously, of the two of you, you are the most likely to be able to rebuild your life, but if you miss the opportunity to study in London, you will be missing an opportunity that you may never get again, and that will change the course of your life forever. She will continue to live the life she has been living and her husband will forgive her. In fact, he already did because he really loves her. You opened his eyes and thanks to you, he realized what he had and was losing, but neither you nor she can open your eyes. She's about 40 and you're almost 20 and you're both worse off than a couple of hot teenagers."

I kept listening to her without saying a word. Sonya had this strange ability to put my feet on the ground and think about what I was trying to avoid because I knew she was right.

Mrs. Margarita was my first and only love. She taught me what it was like to love, she took me out of the bubble I lived in, she gave me self-confidence. Even though no one understood it, I loved her, and she loved me. I knew that and it was something that only she and I could understand. We loved each other above all. And if Sonya had taken an interest in me, it was precisely because Mrs. Margarita had already done so. Maybe Sonya didn't even know I existed before.

But she was also right that, in time, age would become an impediment. Even if the woman lived her fullness to the age of 30 or 40 or more, in the end, the balance would tip the other way. An 18-year age gap is a lot of years. Another thing that affected me was the experience of moving in together. Everything changed between us since then. What we thought would be a dream turned into a terrible nightmare. It was true that I did not want to go to London and leave her, but it was also true that I wanted to study architecture at that university with all my heart.

"Shall we go?" Sonya's voice jolted me from my thoughts.

"Already?" I reacted in surprise.

"Well, you are silent and lost in your thoughts, and I'm just staring at you like an idiot."

"No. Sorry. I was just… I was thinking that you're partly right."

"Partly, Edgar?" She tilted her head to the side again and her blonde hair fell over her shoulder, giving her a very sexy touch. "Which part?"

"Eh, with the age thing. It's true but…" I kept quiet again, not knowing what to say. *Goddamn it! Why do I always keep quiet?*

"You do not need to explain anything to me, Edgar. I do not believe in words; I believe in actions. I believe in what I see, not what I am told, so save your breath. We'll still be friends and see what happens. What do you think?"

I nodded silently, shrugging my shoulders.

CHAPTER 27

"It's a done deal. He told me he'd already reviewed the business plan and he'll lend us the money." Annie was sitting across from us at the Vips of Tonala.

"Oh, that's great!" Mrs. Margarita hugged me very excitedly.

"Now we're talking," Annie said. "You're going to be a real businesswoman." She laughed out loud, and we seconded her. "We'll see!" she said.

The sparkle in her eyes was back to its usual shine. "So tomorrow we're going to see Mrs. Tere, right?"

"Tomorrow, my friend," replied Annie. I could only stare at them both, unable to avoid smiling widely because their joy was contagious.

"And how do you know the man who's going to lend you the money?" I asked Annie.

She smiled mischievously at me and Mrs. Margarita laughed again. I returned Annie's mischievous smile, understanding. "How we met is that… we've been…very good." She was having fun making the answer suspenseful, "let's say, friends."

Mrs. Margarita laughed again. "But the best of friends!" She laughed out loud at her friend.

Once the laughter subsided a bit, Annie explained to me, "I know this man very well. He's got a lot of money. A lot! He owns a few fabric stores."

I did not let her finish. "Mr. Alfonso?" Both remained silent for a moment, very serious, and they suddenly laughed out loud at the same time.

Laughing, Mrs. Margarita asked me, "Do you know him?"

"That's Aldo's dad, isn't it?"

Another booming laugh from both. People were starting to turn around and stare at us from the fuss we were making. "Yes, his son's name is Aldo," said Annie almost drowning with tears rolling down her cheeks.

"That's right, my friend," Mrs. Margarita was also crying with laughter and could barely speak. "Everybody here knows each other." And then they burst out laughing again while I was turning completely red from the disapproving glances of others. They had finally found someone to lend them the money to start their beauty products business. It turned out, they knew a lady, Mrs. Tere, who was a cosmetologist and married to a chemical engineer; both had created beauty treatments that seemed to be a very good and promising business.

"I want to start my own business. I do not want to be dependent on Samuel anymore," Mrs. Margarita told me the afternoon I saw her after I had eaten three plates of chilaquiles. "If we were to get rediscovered and have to move in together," and that was like music to my ears. "I do not want the same thing that happened to us last time; the economic situation really fucked us."

"So, you are going to leave him?"

She rolled her eyes. "Babe, we're doing great, do not mess it up, please. We've talked about this many times and I told you that I'm not going to leave him, but if he finds out about us again, he'll either kill us or he'll kick me out of the house."

"Okay," I said disappointed. "Keep telling me about the business."

"The point is that I do not want to start my business with Samuel's money. That's why Annie is networking to get the capital we need, and if she does we'll each take 50% ownership." Apparently, Annie networked very well. The curious thing was with whom.

***

"I would have liked to have had your child," Mrs. Margarita said.

Sitting in the living room of Mrs. Tere's house while to pick up the first big order of cosmetics from her, we were watching her children, two children, about six and seven years old, each of them playing with a Rubik's cube, trying to put the colors in order, without paying the slightest attention to us.

"And we can't?" I stroked her cheek with my hand.

"No." She took my hand before I removed it and put it to her lips. "And the reason is that I've already had surgery. If I had not, I'd already be pregnant. And I would not mind if Samuel kicked me out of the house or if you left one day because I would have some of you around for the rest of my life."

"You're not getting rid of me for the rest of your life anyway."

She smiled sadly.

"You're going to be leaving real soon babe." Suddenly the subject changed, "And what happened to the scholarship in London?"

"That's what I wanted to talk to you about."

Then Mrs. Tere came in. "Good morning," she said with a lovely smile. She was a very beautiful woman, well-taken care of with a nice complexion and a slim and aesthetic body.

Mrs. Margarita introduced me as Edgar and did not say anything else. Mrs. Tere shook my hand and I wondered why they called her Mrs. *She must not be more than 30 years old.* "Sit down," she said. We did and they started talking about business. From what I heard, the business had started off very well and looked to have a promising future with enough profit to realize her desire to be financially independent in a very short time. They were still talking when the doorbell rang, and she apologized to go and open the door.

When she came back, she introduced us to a young man who was a little older than me. "My son."

I thought she was joking around. "Your son?" I asked with a smile and shook the boy's hand.

"Yes, from my first marriage." I realized it was not a joke.

"Is it true that he doesn't look like her son?" Mrs. Margarita intervened excitedly. Addressing Mrs. Tere, she added, "Tell him how old you are."

"Forty-five," she replied with a sweet smile.

I stared at her, looking over her skin, her complexion, her eyes, and everything my eyes could detect in her without looking like a stalker.

"The cosmetics really do work then!" Was the first thing I thought of saying, which made everyone laugh. And time proved me right. Her business was a success and in a few years, she was not only an economically independent woman but had enormous profits which included lots of zeroes to the right.

***

When we left, I was very impressed with how effective the products she was going to sell were, and with how happy she was. She had that special glow in her eyes again that made me dream of a future full of light for us. "I'm so excited, babe," she said after we put the products in the trunk of the car. She stood in front of me and held me by the waist. "Thank you," she added by kissing me on the lips.

I was confused because I had done nothing at all to help make her business happen. I did not give any money or anything. "I've wanted to do this for a long time, but I did not have the courage to do it. And on the day that Mrs. Tere proposed it to us, I said to myself if I've had the guts to get where I am with my babe, I can get anywhere I want to go. You gave me that strength and courage. I love you." We kissed with tenderness and passion. Then she stepped away as if she remembered something. "What happened to London?"

"Oh, that's right."

"Did you get it yet?" Her eyes glowed with excitement.

I smiled at her and took out the envelope I was carrying folded up in the inside pocket of my leather jacket. "It came to me this morning, but I have not said anything to anyone." I gave it to her, and she took it while still smiling.

"Did you get accepted?" She opened it and after reading, she gave a muffled cry of excitement. "Congratulations, babe!" She hugged me again very tightly. "And why have you not told anyone?" She looked me in the eyes which were teary and sparkling. "You wanted me to know first?"

"Partly, yes."

"Partly?" She said to me confused.

"If I leave we won't see each other anymore."

She wiped the smile off her face and got very serious. "Look, babe." She let me go and leaned on the car without taking her gaze off me. "If you miss this opportunity for us, you're going to hate me for the rest of your life, and I'm going to hate myself too. As time goes by, you will regret it and I will feel guilty for having been the cause of your frustration."

"What frustration? One must make decisions in life. Either take one path or another. I'm choosing the path I want to take."

"I love you very much too, babe, but I cannot let you do that."

"No one knows I've already been accepted."

"I do," she said flatly.

"I want you. If I have to change my whole life for you, I'd do it in a heart-beat." She interrupted me, putting her fingers on my lips to shut me up. "Do not say anything." Her black eyes glowed that special way they did only when she was excited. She kissed me softly, devouring my lips while I delighted in their fruity taste. Then she pulled back a few inches and looked at me with wondering eyes. "Do you really love me that much?"

"Much more than you can imagine." I held her tight and kissed her.

***

After delivering the products we went to the El Dorado Hotel where we had gone the first time we got together. On the way, we bought a bottle of wine to celebrate her first big delivery and the start of great success on her new path as an entrepreneur.

We took a room with a Jacuzzi. I had never been in one, and neither had she, so we had to figure out how to operate it. It wasn't too complicated. We slid into the water and I sat inside the tub. She sat facing me with her knees on either side of my hips. She then wrapped her arms around my neck and kissed me. My growing erection immediately contacted her vaginal lips, causing a slight groan of excitement.

"I love you," she told me while she was adjusting herself to put me inside her body. "I'm never..." I totally penetrated her and we both took a deep breath, "going to leave you." The movement of our bodies made the water splash and the banging against her clitoris and against my testicles was very exciting.

"I'm not going to stop loving you," I told her on pauses because, although we had just started, we were already moving quickly and she was getting closer to orgasm. As I was about to feel it, I stopped and squeezed her hips tightly to stop her from moving. She opened her eyes in surprise.

"Do not stop!" She was trying to move, and I squeezed her even harder. "What's going on?!"

"I do not want you to cum yet."

"Why?!"

She stopped and looked at me in surprise. Then I continued moving, but very slowly.

"Like that," she said beginning to orgasm, but when she was about to I stopped again. "What are you doing?!" she yelled at me again.

"Making your orgasm grow."

"No!"

I went back to moving slowly again and began flicking my tongue on her nipples. She squeezed my head tightly against her chest and started to move harder, trying to keep me from stopping her again, but I did it anyway.

"Please, please," she begged me. Suddenly, I pushed my hip up to get it out of the water and started moving as fast as I could in and out, in and out, in and out. Hard. She started screaming, dug her fingernails to my back and bit my shoulder as the orgasm spread all over her body. Although the position was quite uncomfortable for me, I didn't want to stop until she was satisfied.

Once her orgasm was over, she kissed me while we both tried to steady our breathing. I put my hip back into the tub and while still penetrating her, I turned her around, leaving her on her back to me and facing the water jet that rushed powerfully from the Jacuzzi. She leaned on me, guessing what I was about to do. With my fingers I began to caress her outer lips and separated them, getting closer to the water jet, wanting it to hit the clitoris directly.

When she felt the pressure on her clitoris, more sensitive after having just orgasmed, she began to moan. I kept her vaginal lips apart so that the water would be constantly flowing over her, and I started to move in and out again, but this time very slowly because the water would not let me move quickly. The pressure of the liquid also stimulated my testicles, so I was having trouble holding on and not finishing before her. This time she did not move. She left her hip fixed on the water jet and had a strong orgasm…and another, and another. It seemed like it would never end. The orgasmic sensation also spread throughout my body and I climaxed with the strength of a waterfall.

The movement of the water was still very exciting, and when it was over, she was still receiving the pressure from the water jet, so she tightened her vaginal muscles and began to move slowly, not letting me lose my erection. We continue to enjoy the aquatic orgasms for a few more minutes until we felt depleted and exhausted. We stayed in the tub and cuddled side by side, relaxing. "I do not want this to ever end," she said.

"It does not have to end."

She looked me in the eyes. "You're really not going to London?"

"If you go with me, I will."

"I cannot, babe. It would mean giving up my daughters and that's something I'm never going to do. It would be one thing to live together, you and me, but financially sound while keeping an eye on my daughters. It's another thing to go and leave them here." She put her head on my chest and started stroking my penis as if it was no big deal. "I know that one day they are going to go away and have their own lives, and then, I will go with you wherever you want, but not now."

"Then, I'll stay, and we can wait together for them to have their own lives."

She looked at me in an inquisitive way, as if trying to search the depths of my soul. "Why do you want me so much?"

"I do not want you. I love you, and I will always love you." She kissed me tenderly on the lips. "And stop moving it around, you've got me all turned on again."

She smiled at me. "I noticed that."

We went to the big bed and we did it until it was time to go pick up her daughters. Before we left the room, she hugged me very tightly. "I love you. Very, very much!"

"Me too."

She smiled enthusiastically at me. "I have a lot of faith in the business. I know we're going to do very well."

"I'm sure of it, too. It's going to be a success, you'll see."

"We're going to be able to be together without worrying about money, but will you wait for me until my daughters are independent?"

"I'll wait for you always." She kissed me. "You still taste like fruit to me," I said. She laughed.

"You're crazy!" And we kissed again with tenderness, with passion, as if it were the last kiss we'd ever have. And it was.

CHAPTER 28

Two days after I got the letter from London, I went to college to talk to my math teacher. I made up a thousand excuses as to why I could not accept the scholarship, and he got upset. I knew he did, even though he tried to hide it without much success. "Hundreds of people would give their lives for this opportunity. You should think about it some more." I promised him I would and went home convinced that my relationship with Mrs. Margarita was going well. She would be a great businesswoman, and I could start working in an architectural firm and finish my degree at UNAM. There was nothing wrong with that. After all, UNAM was also one of the best universities in the world.

I got off at the Indios Verdes subway station and decided to walk home, which was almost 5 kilometers away. When I got to Insurgentes Avenue and felt the heat, I regretted it. Then a curious thing happened. A big black car approached the sidewalk where I was walking, and when I looked out to see who it was, I was surprised. "Are you going home?" His little cold eyes were watching me behind his ridiculous Coke-bottle glasses; his drooling smile twisted to one side in that filthy toad face.

"Yes."

"Get in. I'm heading there." I did not feel like getting in the toad's car. I didn't want to put up with his lustful nonsense all the way there. But I thought about how far away I was and how hot it was, so I opened the door and climbed in.

"Where are you coming from?"

His nearsighted eyes examined me from head to toe. "From the university," I answered, looking away and staring straight ahead.

"Aren't you on vacation? You've started up again?"

"We start in August next semester, but I had to go talk to a teacher."

"Because of your scholarship to London?" His smile was quite disgusting, but I stared at him with my eyes and mouth wide open. *How does this bastard know about my scholarship?!*

"How did you…?" I began to say.

"How do I know about your scholarship?" He chuckled and the spittle danced between his prominent lower lip and crooked teeth. I looked away disgusted, but very interested in his response. "There are many things about me you do not know." A thousand thoughts began to invade my mind. *Who is this bastard? Is he spying on me?*

"Call Me," by Blondie had just started playing on the radio and during the chorus, the toad began to croak, "Call me, my love. na na, call me any way or time. Call me." He sang terribly out of tune.

"Call me. my love. You can call me any day or night. Call me," sang Blondie.

Any way or time?! Where did this bastard learn English? I made a great effort not to laugh, but fortunately, he stopped singing, or croaking, rather. "I must pick up some things at a house I'm using as a warehouse on Miraflores street, but it won't take long. Is that all right? *Cover me with kisses baby,*" he kept butchering Blondie's song.

In fact, my house was coming up before that but since we were on Insurgentes Avenue, he would have to take an early exit to drop me off and then get onto Miraflores, so I agreed to accompany him. That way he could continue to Robles Domínguez Avenue and go straight to where he wanted to go. "Yes, no problem."

"Llámame" He said in an oddly sexy manner at the same time as Blondie, only she said it in Italian and he in Spanish, and then in French. "A pel muá"! *Come on, he speaks French too!* While he followed the rhythm of the song with his fingers on the steering wheel, he said, "You know, I also keep things for your partner in that house."

My partner? I turned to look at him, confused, and his face contorted into a weird and disgusting smile. "Samuel, your partner." I looked forward again without answering but feeling the rage boiling in my blood, invading every cell. "What do you give women, huh? You make them all crazy. What, do you have a big one or what?" I fixed my stare on his Coke-bottle glasses, but I couldn't say a word. He laughed and tapped me on the leg with his hand which I removed immediately. "Do not be angry. I'm kidding, but you must have something." We arrived at Miraflores Street and parked in front of a house with a large window and a black metal door. He turned off the engine and I stayed in the seat, with no intention of getting out. "Get out," he said, "I'm going to need you to help me move some boxes. We won't be long." Even though something inside me told me not to do it, I did not have the courage to refuse.

Apart from two chairs and a small table with a telephone, there was no other furniture in the room, which was crammed with boxes piled up and scattered everywhere. He headed for one of the rooms. "Here!" he shouted at me. I found him standing next to the one chair in the center of the room. I tried to guess why he wanted me there since besides the chair there was only an old wooden table with a bottle of Tehuacán sparkling soda on it as well as a stereo and a thick rope. I looked around the place, but I only saw a closed door that I assumed was for a closet. "Sit down," he said with his idiotic smile.

I tried to make sure I had heard him correctly.

"What do you mean?"

"Sit here," he said waving his hand slightly while pointing to the chair. My legs went numb and they would not respond when I told them to get the hell out of there.

"What for?"

He put his hand inside his jacket and when my legs finally felt they could run, it was too late. I saw the barrel of the gun pointing in my direction and him walking toward me with the other hand outstretched to grab my hair. He put the tip of the gun to my forehead and pulled me toward the chair to sit down.

"Sit down, I said!" Blood was pumping through my veins and his disgusting, repugnant, runover toad face was starting to make me nauseous. When

I sat down, he still had a hold of my hair with the gun in my face. *Why?* I thought. *What did I do?*

Still pointing the gun at me, he walked over to the little table and grabbed the rope, threw it at me, and said, "Tie yourself up with this." The rope hit me in the face and fell on my legs, then slid down to the ground. I turned to him as if to ask for permission to move. I guess he realized how scared I was because he was smiling the entire time with a disgusting grin. "Pick it up," he said, waving his gun at the rope that was still at my feet.

I bent down slowly, so he wouldn't think I wanted to run away, which I was sure would end up getting me shot. But my slow movement apparently made him angry, and bang, I felt a punch in the face that knocked me out of the chair when one of his Ringo boots from the Canada shoe store hit me right in the face. I immediately felt my lips swell and had the taste of blood in my mouth. I instinctively began to pass my tongue through my teeth to make sure none of them had been knocked out. I had them all, but my lips were getting numb. I grabbed the rope, got up, and sat down very nervous, not knowing what to do with it. "Tie yourself up!"

And how the hell do I tie myself up, asshole?!

I looked at him, scared, and trying to tie myself up like he asked but without success.

"Pass it back," he said standing behind me. "Now, put your arms at your sides. Slowly. Don't try to be clever."

Do you really think I'd try to be clever?

He put the gun back in his coat because when he walked past me and turned around with the rope, his hands were busy holding me so tight that I could hardly breathe. I was so scared that I suddenly felt an uncontrollable urge to pee and cry. I held the pee a bit longer, but not the tears.

As he tied me up with the thick rope, I thought Mr. Samuel probably hired the bastard, and they were going to kill me. I was a goner. I had no way of even asking for help. Unless I could get to the phone in the other room and if the phone worked.

***

When he had me tied up, he took out a cigarette and lit it, then went to the other room to get another chair. When he returned he put it in front of me with his backrest pointing in my direction. He sat down with his legs open placing his arms on the edge of the backrest and put his hands on his chin. Even in that position, he wasn't able make his enormous lower lip and upper lip touch so he could shut his big snout.

He gave his cigarette a big inhale, while still looking at me with his bulging eyes through those thick glasses. He blew the smoke on my face. "So, you think you're a badass?, huh?" *Where had I heard that?* "So, the beating I had arranged for you did not change anything." He took another puff of his cigarette and blew the smoke on the face. "You're stubborn, you bastard!" He reached out his hand with his cigarette and put it out on my jeans, burning them and burning me too.

I cried out in pain as I felt my thigh skin scorching, and he got up from the chair with his stupid smile. The cigarette fell to the floor, but my leg was still burning, tears were still pouring, and I could not hold my pee anymore. I urinated. A mixture of impotence, rage, and shame interweaved within me and turned to hatred in its purest expression. Hatred of myself and of the freak that was currently mocking my misfortune.

"You are such a fag!" He laughed out loud again. "And we were just getting started." He approached me, his ugly face now a few inches from mine. "I hope you're not going to shit yourself." Then he took my face with his fat hand, placing his thumb on one cheek and his fingers on my other, pressing my lips forward. Then one of the most disgusting and repugnant things I have ever experienced happened. He put his lips on mine and put his tongue in my mouth, in what was the most horrible kiss I ever had.

My stomach turned and I almost threw up. Nausea started to take effect and my belly started to convulse, but all I could do was spit with disgust. "Are you disgusted, asshole?" His chubby hand crashed hard against my cheek, leaving me with a burning sensation that was still preferable to having to put up with his hideous snout on any part of my body. "Now you'll know what's good," he said, clutching his genitals grotesquely over his pants.

Oh, no! This son of a bitch is going to rape me.

He went to the table and turned on the stereo, pressed a button, and the cassette compartment suddenly opened. He pulled out the tape, checked it, and put it back in. He closed the little door and pressed the switch. I listened to the tape running at high speed until it stopped on its own. Then he pressed another button and after a few seconds, it began to fill the room with beautiful music that was not at all in the same mood as what was happening at that moment. I could recognize the first soft and slow notes of Ravel's famous "Boléro."

"Have you made love to Ravel's 'Boléro'?" This motherfucker thinks he is Bo Derek! I looked up at him, frightened and surprised. I saw him take the bottle of Tehuacán and uncap it with his teeth. Then he approached me again. I tried to move and untie myself. I was ready to fight this madman, but he had tied me up so tightly that I could not even loosen the rope a little.

When he stood in front of me he covered the hole with his thumb and shook it vigorously. With the other hand, he grabbed my hair to prevent my head from moving. He placed the bottle of Tehuacán closer to my face and opened the hole to let all the liquid explode into my nose. I have always thought that drowning must be one of the most terrible deaths anyone can suffer, and I think that moment was one of the closest I have ever had to that experience. I felt the gaseous liquid suddenly entering my brain, causing me to feel an unbearable and desperate feeling of suffocation. As soon as I could, I screamed. "No! Please!" I pleaded in tears.

He looked at me with a funny smile, as if he were enjoying an innocent hobby. Ravel's music increased in intensity, as did my panic. He again shook the bottle of Tehuacán and emptied it into my nose, which brought back the feeling of suffocation and despair. Then he took off his coat and put it on the table. The gun was tucked between his pants and his big belly. He pulled it out and put it next to the stereo. Ravel's music continued in crescendo as he walked toward me very slowly, rubbing his genitals vulgarly over his pants. "Are you going to give me a blowjob?"

What?! God, please, let me wake up from this nightmare! He brought his disgusting face back to mine and I thought he was going to kiss me again.

"I've always hated guys like you," he said to me, "they think they are all that and they're nothing more than fags." He started to unbuckle his belt and my nausea started to return. He took it off and folded it in half, as Dad had done the only time he had punished me with a couple of slaps with the belt. I had tried to cure our sick dog giving it almost all the medicine in the medicine cabinet. Of course, I killed him, but I didn't mean to. I was only seven years old.

I felt the thud of the thin leather on my leg and I shouted, but after the Tehuacán, my body was lethargic and could not take the pain very well. I felt one more blow and heard his nasty laugh. "I'd always wanted to fuck that old woman, but I never could."

So you're not a faggot, man? Who can understand you?

He kept stimulating his disgusting genitals and said. "Tell me how you fuck her before you blow me. What does she like? Tell me." I felt another blow, but this time to the face. "I said tell me, motherfucker!" I had the feeling that I was going to faint. My head was hanging forward. It felt so heavy that I was unable to hold it upright. His voice now sounded distant and echoed a bit. "Now faint, dumbass." I thought he'd given me a few light slaps on the cheek as if trying to wake me up. "It does not matter, we have time," I heard him say. Suddenly I felt water on my face, and I reacted right away.

He was in front of me with the bottle of Tehuacán in his hand. He sat in front of me again with his arms on the back of his chair. "You know, I don't know what I'm going to do with you. After I fuck you, of course. Because you will know everything that old bitch missed because she never listened to me. But I mean, what am I going to do after I make you happy with the amazing fuck I'm going to give you?" He laughed out loud with a thunderous, morbid laugh. "Of course, you'll never see sunshine, nor will you see another sunrise."

What a poet you turned out to be, you fucking toad.

"But the point is, should I ask your parents for some money to take advantage of the situation? You know what I mean? That certainly was not my purpose. I'm no ordinary kidnapper, but that would not be a bad idea" He reached out his hand and stroked my hair as he smiled at me with what he tried to be a sweet smile. "What do you think, Daddy?" I did not say anything. I only felt more disgusted. "Maybe I could even fuck your mom. "

I looked on with as much repugnance as I could. "Your mom is not bad looking. She's got great tits." I didn't think I'd ever felt like killing anyone until then. "What a fine feast you must've had when you were drinking her milk, huh?" I wanted to kill him. I really wanted to kill him! "Anyway, back to the subject. How is it possible that Margarita has chosen you, a fucking brat, a faggot, and an asshole, and yet despised me!" He rose from his chair and placed his hands on his large, flabby waist, taking a foolishly proud pose. "You know I played with the Miami Dolphins?"

What? How is it possible that this madman has been set loose?

"I made the Dolphins win the Super Bowl, scoring a touchdown at the last minute." I could not help but smile in disbelief as my mind thought of how disturbed this disgusting toad was. "You don't believe me, asshole?" *Shit!* I felt a blow in my stomach and was struggling for air when, suddenly, another voice was heard in the room over the most intense part of Ravel's Bolero. We both jumped.

"Did you get him? Perfect! Why didn't you let me know?" Mr. Samuel was standing in the doorway dressed in a suit as usual and watching me with a satisfied smile. The toad face ran to the table and picked up the gun. I kept trying to gasp for air. "Take it easy," said Mr. Samuel. "We don't have to kill him yet. I want the son of a bitch to suffer."

The run over toad's face was colored in surprise and mine in total and absolute panic. Mr. Samuel approached me walking slowly. Ravel's music could no longer be heard. I didn't notice whether it was over or if someone had turned it off. He bent down to put his face in front of mine. *This motherfucker's gonna kiss me, too.* "Did you pee, faggot?" he asked with a smile. He looked at my swollen lip and dried blood and turned to look at the fucking motherfucker toad. "Did you beat him?"

"I gave him a few blows," said the putrid amphibian. "I was about to call you to let you know that I had him here," the son of a bitch lied.

"Thank you." He straightened up and reached out to shake his hand. "You know I'm going to pay you back for this favor." The toad face's satisfied smile filled me with rage. "I have a little surprise for you," said Mr. Samuel, smiling sarcastically and then paused briefly as if waiting to see how I would react. Then he turned to the door and said, "Come on in."

I heard a few steps and suddenly I saw him come in. The whole world fell on me! All the emotions I was able to feel, positive and negative, exploded inside me the moment I saw him with his ironic smile. The toad pointed the gun at him. "No," said Mr. Samuel calmly, "he comes with me. It's not a problem." He did not put the gun down, though. But he kept walking toward me without flinching. He stood in front of me and I looked at him with my mouth open, feeling that my heart would stop even though it was beating very fast. He crouched down, drawing his face closer to mine in the same way Mr. Samuel had just done. He told me scathingly, "Remember the hit you gave me, dumbass? Did you think it was going to stay at that?"

I saw his hand approaching my face and I felt the blow. It hurt, but the physical pain was nothing compared to what I felt in my soul. I could not believe that Frank, my lifelong friend, had betrayed me.

CHAPTER 29

The toad stuck his gun under his belt and began to laugh at the blow Frank had given me, though he still looked on with suspicion.

"This dude is the one who went to help my wife bring her things when she came back to my house," Mr. Samuel explained the toad.

"Yes, I know."

"But this asshole beat him up," continued Mr. Samuel while nodding his head. "Besides, I offered him half a million pesos if he helped get rid of this useless guy. It looks like you've earned them."

The frog's face swelled like a peacock and Frank turned to see Mr. Samuel, bewildered. "Do not worry," he said, "you're going to get a big cut anyway."

Frank smiled, though not very convincingly. *I'm dreaming. This cannot be happening.* I was in a complete state of confusion. Now I understood why he insisted so much on ending that relationship. *"Do not be stupid anymore you two!"* the hypocrite said to me. That's why he worked with Mr. Samuel. That's why he took Mrs. Margarita from the apartment. I regretted not killing him at the time. He had sold me out for a few fucking pesos. However, more than anger, what hurt me was the disappointment of having been betrayed by my only friend.

I was sure they were going to kill me. They could not let me live because they knew I could report them. I turned to look at Frank. His cold look and ironic smile made tears run down my face. "You are going to cry, you little twat?" His voice was mocking and the pain I felt turned to pure rage. I gave him a look of hatred and resentment and he did not have the balls to bear it. He turned around, trying to flee from my presence like the fucking coward he was. The crazy toad kept laughing, practically celebrating Frank's joke.

I don't know if it's the same for everyone, but when I thought I was going to die my mind went into a state of drowsiness. It was as if I was trying to stay numb to avoid the pain. The fear disappeared inexplicably and there was only anger, disappointment, and a strange feeling of helplessness because I wasn't able to do anything about it. "I want to talk to you," the cuckold said and then walked out of the room. Frank came out behind him and the run over toad was the last one, pulling the gun out of his huge waist.

From there I could hear their conversation perfectly. The first one to speak was Mr. Samuel. "We already know we cannot leave him alive. We'll have to make him disappear."

"Of course," said the toad.

"Is it necessary?" I thought there was a certain tone of sadness in Frank's voice.

You damn hypocrite! "Definitely," replied Mr. Samuel. "We cannot risk him reporting us. Or would you rather spend the rest of your life in jail?"

"No, but I'd rather not be present when you do it."

"You can't get out of here," said the toad. "At least not until we're done with everything."

"No, I mean I don't want to be in the room when it happens."

"All right don't worry," interrupted Mr. Samuel. "I want the son of a bitch to suffer first. He needs to pay for what he's done to me."

Sons of bitches, they're going to torture me! God, give me strength, please!

"I'm quite an expert at that," the toad said and laughed out loud.

"Another important thing is who is going to get rid of the body," added the cuckold.

"I can take care of that." The toad's voice sounded proud. "I know people who can do it, but it's going to cost."

"Do not worry about money."

"Okay. I'll take care of it then." All three of them came back in. "You smell like piss, you sissy," said the bovine husband with a stupid smile while the other two laughed at the joke.

"Do you have a knife?" he asked the toad.

"No, what for?"

The cuckold walked toward me very slowly, "Because we're going to do a little surgery on Don Juan's miserable little dick ." The guy looked pathetic in his fancy suit and his vulgar thug attitude. There is no doubt that you can put lipstick on a pig, but it's still a pig.

"There's probably one in the other room."

"Let's see," he said, and the three of them left the room again. First Frank, then Mr. Samuel, and again, behind them the run over toad, who continued with the gun in his hand. My whole life passed in my mind like a torrent of images: my family, mom and dad, my brother, Mrs. Margarita, and even Sonya came to my mind. Even Frank. I could not believe it. I cried again; I did not care about anything. Nothing at all.

The cuckold, the traitor, and the filthy toad returned to the room. "Look what we found," Mr. Samuel said showing me a kitchen knife and smiling from ear to ear. I wanted to die, now, in that very instant! He gave the dagger to the toad.

"Miguel, do the honors."

Miguel is the name of the nauseating toad? "Meanwhile, I'll take down his pissed-on pants." The three of them laughed. Toad Miguel put the gun on the table next to the stereo and took the knife. Frank stepped aside, leaving the cuckold in the middle and the amphibious swine stepped aside from Mr. Samuel, who began to unbuckle my belt very carefully so as not to touch the wet part.

"You stink, you faggot," he said with an unpleasant gesture.

He turned to the table and asked, "Did you strap him down for waterboarding?"

"Yes," replied the chubby toad.

"Pass me the bottle," he said, looking at me with a mocking smile. I've always wanted to do it to someone. The toad went for the bottle without letting go of the knife, came back, and gave it to him. Mr. Samuel took it and bowed to me.

"How does it feel, huh? Nice?" The run over toad laughed and stood beside him watching me. I saw the hand holding the bottle rise in the air and closed my eyes. I heard a thud, but I didn't feel anything. I then heard a thud followed by the sound of glass breaking. Steps, a groan, another thud that sounded like something had fallen to the ground. I heard words that I didn't understand. And I still did not feel anything.

I opened my eyes and I saw the toad Miguel kneeling in front of Mr. Samuel with a stream of blood pouring from his face and his Coke-bottle glasses hanging crooked, the knife still in his hand. Mr. Samuel released the broken bottle, which fell to the ground in pieces. He grabbed Miguel's head with both hands and stuck a knee in his face, causing the glasses to fly off and the knife to fall to the side. Frank was now standing at the table and came quickly with the gun as fat Miguel fell to the ground spread out just as he was, a horrid run over toad.

Frank gave the gun to Mr. Samuel, who immediately pointed it at the unconscious lump lying on the floor. "Untie him!" he yelled at Frank but he was already behind me, loosening the rope. "Are you all right?" I heard his voice behind me.

"Are you all right?" I heard Mr. Samuel in front of me. I didn't know if I could answer them or not, but it seemed to me that the whole room was starting to turn, and the floor was rushing toward my face.

CHAPTER 30

"Edgar, Edgar," I heard Frank say as I felt him tapping me on the cheek. I opened my eyes and saw him. He smiled at me, except now his smile was not sardonic but friendly. In fact, I could say it was even sweet, which was rare for him. "Are you all right, dude?" I tried to get up and he helped me to sit up. "Easy, brother, easy. How are you feeling?" I heard Mr. Samuel's voice somewhere in the house outside the room. Frank was squatting next to me. Behind him, the run over toad was tied up with the same rope he had tied me with and he was lying on the floor.

He stared at me, his eyes bulging but dull as if they were two faded, blown out headlights. He did not say anything. He just looked at me. "How are you feeling?" Mr. Samuel asked. I turned to see Mr. Samuel as he walked into the room with the gun in his hand. He was both serious and calm.

"Good, thank you." He and Frank helped me up and then sit in the chair where I had been just minutes ago, only now free of restraints.

"It should not take long for the police to come looking for this bastard," said Mr. Samuel, nodding his head at the lump of toad meat and fat lying on the floor.

"What if his friends come?" Frank's voice was uneasy.

"Don't worry, I spoke to people I trusted who are not friends with him. I also asked Chucho to come and bring some clean pants for Edgar. I warned him not to say anything to anyone. It's better if all this stays here. It's not a good idea for everyone to know."

Frank and I nodded. Chucho was Mr. Samuel's assistant. He was about 25-years-old and a bodybuilder whose physique was to be admired. I felt ashamed and my brain was still unable to process what had happened. "It would be good if he could take a bath before they bring the clothes," he said to Frank. "There's a bathroom here. There's no hot water, but cold water will be good for him."

"Are you all right, buddy?" Frank said to me. "Can you walk?" I nodded my head and got up. I felt his arms holding me up and I smiled gratefully at him. Mr. Samuel stood beside me and took me by the other arm. "Are you all right? Lean on us; don't fall." Before leaving I turned to see the toad, who was still lying on the ground with a pool of blood next to his head. He looked helpless from how quiet and frightened he looked. I felt anger take hold of me.

"That guy's crazy," Mr. Samuel said as they took me to the bathroom. "For years I've been aware of it, but I'd rather have him as a friend," he said the last word he added air quotes with his free hand. "I didn't want him as an enemy because, as you may have noticed, he's quite dangerous. He's a conman. Since he is also a lawyer, he swindles and tricks people, but he has many contacts, so I preferred to have him on my side. He has an original gold medal from the 1968 Olympics and says it's from Tibio Muñoz, the Mexican swimmer. I believe him," he paused shortly and continued. "But don't worry, I talked to people more important than him and they're going to take care of it."

We got to the bathroom. "Get in the bath. Frank will let you know when the clean pants and the police arrive."

"How did you know I was here?" I asked Frank once Mr. Samuel was gone.

"We didn't. We came here out of pure fucking luck to pick up some stuff he keeps here, and we heard all the fuss. We hid and put together a plan out of nowhere." He smiled at me with a funny grin. "Did you see what a fucking actor I am, dude? I'm going to audition at the Televisa Training Center. Maybe I'll even fuck Lucía Mendez or Veronica Castro or both at the same time. What do you think?" For the first time all day, I laughed.

"Shit!" he said to me. "I should have taken a fucking picture of you so you could see the look on your face when I came in." He laughed again. "You looked terrified!"

I was starting to feel better as I got undressed to take a bath and listened to my old friend, "Did the beating I give you hurt?"

"Yes, motherfucker. Do you think I'm made of stone or what? Fucking asshole."

"And I was going to give you some fucking kicks too, but I didn't because I didn't want to seem too involved." I looked at him and I wanted to tell him many things, but I've always been a man of few words, so I remained silent. However, as if he had guessed my thoughts, he said to me, "Me too, brother." He hit me gently on the cheek with the palm of his hand and smiled at me. "Get in the bath because you stink of piss, you fucking twat." He turned around and walked out.

Even though the water was cold, it was very comforting. My lips, my face, and my head hurt. I think my whole body hurt, but I felt much better. I can't deny that I was also terribly embarrassed. There was no doubt that destiny was having fun with me; now I owed my life to none other than Mr. Samuel. I was so embarrassed. I didn't even want to look at him.

When I came out of the bath, I saw my clothes on the toilet and a pair of denim pants, which I was sure were Chucho's because they were too big for me. But I'd rather wear a pair that was too big for me than the ones soaked in urine. While I was getting dressed I could hear voices in the room, so many that I imagined a whole crowd was in there. Finally, I left the bathroom and saw several policemen coming and going. Mr. Samuel was talking to a guy who seemed familiar. After a closer look, I realized I had seen him many times on television. He was a renowned politician and a very powerful businessman, and from the way they talked, it seemed they were also friends. Mr. Powerful gave me a cold look after Mr. Samuel said something to him and nodded his head at me.

Frank came up to me and very quietly said, "Did you see who that is?"

"Yes. Shit! Are they friends?"

"Yes, dude. When he arrived, he said, 'What's up, Samuelito?' You're done, motherfucker. This dude will have you killed and you'll never be seen again."

"Asshole! I think if he wanted to kill me, he would have done it already."

"No, dude, maybe he's waiting," he said with his classic dark humor. "Well, you're fucking his old lady, brother. Shit, I would definitely give you a few beatings and send you to hell, asshole." He paused and his eyes gleamed with malice. "You were going to suck that fat bastard really good." He laughed. "Shit, if we would've gotten here a second later, he would've already fucked you!" He laughed again. It was amazing how he could keep his humor after all that fuss.

A woman who told me she was from the prosecutor's office approached me. "I need to ask you a few questions. Come here, please." She went into the room where the nightmare had occurred and invited me to sit in one of the chairs while she sat in the other. The run over toad was gone, but the pool of his blood was still there indicating that it had not been a dream.

It was all real, it happened. and if it had not been for Frank and Mr. Samuel, that purple stain would be my own blood, I thought, still unable to believe it. I owed them both my life. When the woman finished talking to me, it was the police officer's turn to ask me the same questions, and finally two more people repeated them to me. Fortunately, not a single reporter was in the house.

I felt terribly tired when everyone left. Frank had gone into the bathroom and I had not even seen Chucho. Mr. Samuel and I were left alone. For a moment there was an awkward silence and I felt very uncomfortable. I was his wife's lover, and now I was in his debt.

When Frank came out of the toilet, Mr. Samuel sighed a long sigh and gave me a cold look, in which I could detect a slight touch of bitterness. I looked down because I did not have the courage to hold his gaze. "Frank, Chucho's out there waiting for you, he's going to take you home. I'm going to talk to Edgar." I think my legs started shaking.

"All right," said Frank.

Mr. Samuel walked toward the door. "Let's go."

My friend and I followed him. Before I left, he told me in silence, with only his lips moving, "You are screwed."

CHAPTER 31

When we arrived at the Vips of Montevideo and Insurgentes I felt my soul leaving my body. *Why here?! Doesn't anyone know of any other damn place to talk?* During the ten to fifteen-minute journey, neither of us said a single word. The silence that reigned was so awkward, the minutes felt like hours.

They gave us a table and he asked for coffee. Then he addressed me, "Do you want something to eat?"

"No, thank you very much, I'm not hungry. Just a Coke, please." While he ordered, I observed him: confident with his well-tailored suit and vest with fine fabric along with an impeccable white shirt. And despite everything we went through, he was still wearing his tie with a perfect knot; he looked like Michael Corleone.

I, on the other hand, had on pants so big they made me look like an upside-down mushroom. My shirt still reeked of sweat even though I had already bathed and I was sure I still looked scared, like a calf on my way to the slaughterhouse.

When the waitress left, he stared at me and I looked down at my hands, trying to clear my head and take in what was happening. I never imagined I'd be in a café with him.

"I'm going to tell you something," he began. "But I need you to promise me that you'll never, listen to me, *never* tell anyone. You and I are not friends and can never be friends. So, let's talk man to man, and I want you to give me your word that you can keep it a secret."

I nodded in silence. The waitress came and served us our drinks. Once she left, Mr. Samuel leaned over the table and began to speak. "I'm going to tell you a story." He continued, "When Margarita was 19, she was the most beautiful woman you'd ever seen, and she decided to enter the contest to be Miss Mexico

City to win the title of Miss Mexico 1959 and go on to Miss Universe as Ana Bertha Lepe had done in '53. I was in love with her, but we were just friends. I was very shy and saw her as far out of my reach. All of us who knew her were sure she would win, and Margarita was happy that she would realize her dream of representing Mexico in a beauty contest." He was silent for a moment as if remembering. Then he put some cream and sugar in his coffee. "While preparing for the contest she met one of the organizers, who tried to sleep with her and took her home with the pretext of arranging some of the details of the contest. He had different expectations. When she refused to sleep with him…" A gleam of sadness and anger flashed in his eyes. "He raped her."

What?! She was raped? I was stunned and wide-eyed. Then I understood why she had been frightened by the "rape game." *How stupid could I be!*

"The next day she was notified that she had been left out of the contest for sexual harassment. She was devastated." He gave his coffee a sip and I was dying to know more. I was not looking at my hands or my pants or anything anymore. I was staring at him.

"And it was worse when she realized she was pregnant," he added.

What?!

"By then, I had already opened my first store and was doing well, so Margarita came to me for help in getting an abortion. Neither of us had any experience in these matters, so it took us a while to find a doctor to do the deed. Before she had it done, the doctor talked to her and told her the baby's heart was already beating. Then she took it back. 'I am not going to kill my child,' she said to me. 'Even if it is the result of rape, it's my child and it's already alive.'" I kept listening to him attentively and imagining a young girl my age, beautiful and with many dreams torn apart by a rapist. I felt so much anger.

"She did not want anyone to know what happened because she was afraid of the scandal and had the hope that once her baby was born," he smiled sadly, "she would become an actress or a model. She still had her dreams. So, I proposed that she marry me and that we say the baby was mine." He paused as if waiting to see my reaction, but I was still in the chair with my eyes fixed on him. "Yes, that's how much I loved her. We got married, but our marriage was not consummated until shortly after Marisol was born because she could not bear me touching her. I loved her more than my life and I was patient. I took her to therapy for a while until she got over it. Nobody knows that Marisol is not my daughter because ever since she was born, I have treated her as if she were my own and I love her just as much as if she were my own flesh and blood. It was I who decided that no one should ever know. And I hope that, at least in this case, you'll be man enough to keep it a secret." I felt like my heart was about to break out of my chest. A few words came to my mind without being able to help it: *"Samuel is not a bad person, believe me".*

"Then Maribel was born," he continued. "Who carries my blood, but I have not made any distinction between my daughters. I love them both the same. I was very young then and very stupid. In fact, I was very shy, too shy, but to have married such a beautiful woman aroused the curiosity of other beautiful women and I was unable to resist myself. So, I started cheating on her. And that was my biggest mistake. I had the best one by my side, but I did not realize I was in danger of losing her. I also tried to cling to my youth through a little girl, but when I realized that not only did my youth inevitably leave me, but because of my stupidity the woman I really loved also left. My desire to stay young became the most terrible nightmare, thanks to you."

I looked down at my pants, well, at Chucho's, and I started looking for lint. Seeing that I didn't say or do anything, he went on, "Little by little her dreams of becoming an actress or model faded away because she turned out to be a woman completely devoted to her daughters. Then she began to feel old and at twenty-eight she was terrified of reaching thirty. When she reached thirty, she felt forty. Her massive parties and boundless energy were a way of clinging to the youth that hopelessly left her, taking with it her hopes and dreams. Then you came along, at the age of eighteen." He stopped for a moment and I realized that it was hard for him to say the following, "She fell in love with you like she had never fallen in love with me or anyone else." For a moment he looked down and I noticed a slight hint of defeat, but it was only for a moment. "I've realized my mistake and I think I've paid for it. But I have a proposition for you, Edgar." He leaned back in his chair and looked me straight in the eyes as if he were challenging me. "And I'm going to be totally honest. With you in the way, I can't win her back because somehow she's attracted to your youth and does not listen to reason. So, if you love her as much as I do and you think you can make her happy, I'll leave the race and

I won't bother you again." He paused again as if waiting for me to say something. But I could not say a word. Then he leaned forward again, putting his arms on the table while looking at me again. "But if not, allow me to regain the woman I love, a woman who has been my partner for almost 20 years and with whom I want to grow old with and die by her side."

I could not cease my amazement. It had finally occurred to me to ask a question that maybe wasn't the right one to ask at the time. However, my curiosity was torturing me. "And what happened to the guy who raped her? Who was it?"

From the way he looked at me, I realized that's not what he expected me to say.

"Don't worry about him," he said with serious tone. "Soon after he had an accident and did not survive." I felt cold air running all over my body.

"Think about it, Edgar. I may have been condescending. I was young too, and a real asshole like you. That's the only reason I have let you go this far. I've wished many times to kill you, but I've tried to be understanding despite everything because somehow I was just like you. The day I waited for you at the Insurgentes roundabout, I put bullets in the gun just to scare you. But I'm not going to let you keep thinking I'm stupid. I am willing to fight for my wife to the end, but I am a man of my word, and if you think you can love her as much as I love her, to accept and love her daughters as if they were your own, I'll step aside." He looked me straight in the eye and I thought I saw a glint of a smile. "But I doubt you can do it, so you better get out of the way… or I'll take you out."

The smile in his eyes suddenly became a warning sign of danger.

He was silent for a moment as if waiting for me to say something, but I couldn't find the capacity to allow my tongue and jaw to move. So, I remained speechless, with a torrent of thoughts and emotions within me. Then he got up, took the check the waitress had left with the drinks, and turned to leave. Suddenly, he turned back toward me. "Sometimes life gives us more opportunities than we deserve. And with you it has been very generous. But believe me, Edgar, this is your last chance to make the right decision." He left and I just sat there without moving. I could not. I was almost nailed to the chair. I was trying to process everything he told me. I didn't know what I was going to do. I was only sure of one thing. Never in my entire life had I felt so shitty as I did then.

Chapter 32

I walked home and stopped in a small garden on the avenue to sit on the grass. I was so tired but I didn't want to go to bed because I was sure I would fall asleep if I did. I had a lot to think about. *Samuel is not a bad person. Believe me, he's not bad.* Mrs. Margarita's words echoed in my head.

It had to decide now. I could not keep causing so much harm to people who didn't deserve it. But I couldn't live without her either; I knew that. Especially now that we had agreed that I would wait for her until her daughters were independent. We had realized that we could not live without each other, that we loved each other. We needed each other. She was willing to leave her husband as soon as her daughters were able to support themselves. And if that happened, I had no doubt that for the rest of my life I would feel even shittier than I already did. *What a mess! What do I do God? What do I do?!*

I got up and went looking for Frank. He should be home by now. His mother opened the door for me, and from the look on her face when she saw me I could tell that I was probably in a terrible state.

"What happened to you, son?" Her gaze was one of absolute amazement and her hand went straight to my lips to touch the wound. "Did they beat you?" Her eyes became inquisitive. "It was because of that lady, wasn't it?"

"No, no, no," I said, worried and trying to think of something quickly. "I had a problem in the subway and a guy hit me. Can you believe it? Just because I accidentally pushed him."

"Look at you! Come on in. I'll fix you up."

"No, do not worry, ma'am. I'll take care of myself as soon as I get home. Plus, it's nothing, I'm fine. I just wanted to talk to Frank."

"He's not here. He's not back from work. He called me earlier and told me he was going to go get something to eat with Chucho, the one who works with…" She stopped at once as if she could not say that name in my presence.

"Mr. Samuel?" I said completing her sentence and letting her know that it was all right.

"Yes son, with him."

I said goodbye and then I thought about Sonya. She would be a good choice to help me decide, although I already knew exactly which way the scale would tip. And not because it would be convenient for her, but because of her way of thinking and the influence of the philosopher Ayn Rand, the author of the book she had lent me who was also now influencing me in some way. But it was so hard for me to maintain my integrity! Even a few moments ago I lied to Frank's mom, but I could not tell her the truth either. We had agreed that no one would know.

Anyway, Sonya would be an excellent option to talk to and calm down the hurricane of thoughts taking place in my head.

"Good afternoon, sir," I greeted Sonya's tall, blond father when he opened the door. He, like Frank's mom, stared at me as if I were an alien.

"Hello," he said with his characteristic German accent, which he had not lost, despite living in Mexico for many years.

"Is Sonya here?"

"No, she went out with her mom." End of conversation. I thanked him and walked to my house, disappointed while in deep thought. *There is no doubt,* I told myself, *the decision is mine alone. No one else's.*

***

When I got home, Mom was also surprised by the blow to my mouth. I told her the same story about the guy from the subway.

"You had a fight?" She stared at me in amazement and then looked at my pants. "What's with the pants?

"I'll explain later, Mom. I want to take a bath."

I tried to go to the bathroom even though I had already taken a shower but lying to my mother was not that easy. "Come here." Her voice was authoritative.

I stopped and she looked at me with eyes that clearly said, "None of that 'I'll explain to you later.' Explain it to me right now!"

For me, lying had started to become a habit and was prompting me to continue. However, my desire to change was beginning to grow and I had to water the seed to keep myself whole. I had to try. I knew I could not tell Mom what had happened, although I had the option of retaining my right to remain silent. That was not lying. I had to start changing, and if I didn't do it now, I never would.

"Mom," I started, looking into her eyes, forcing myself not to look away, "I can't tell you what happened, but I want you to know that I'm okay." She was going to speak, but I wouldn't let her. "I know you're thinking Mr. Samuel hit me, but he didn't. Please, let me keep this to myself because I don't want to lie to you, but I don't want to say what happened either. Please, Mom, a lot has happened, and I think I've learned a lot. Today I have received so many lessons that I'm not able to process just yet. What I am sure of is that I love you very much and that I don't want to lie. Not anymore."

She looked at me without blinking and her eyes welled up. She smiled at me and I hugged her. "I love you very much." She let out a sob and I felt her tears on my neck. It felt good. I didn't lie, but I didn't break my promise to not say what happened.

I parted from her and turned to leave, but stopped again. "By the way," it was time. The decision was made and there was no turning back, for my sake and everyone else's. "I got the letter from London. They accepted me."

I've never forgotten the way her face lit up at the time. It was wonderful, her eyes shone, and her smile was one of total and complete happiness. She could not say anything from the excitement, but she hugged me again and filled my face with kisses. "That's great, son! Congratulations!" she said at last.

Dad was very happy, and as soon as my brother returned from seeing his girlfriend we went to dinner to celebrate. "Where do you want to go for dinner?" Mom asked. "You're the one being honored."

"Wherever you want," I said. "except Vips."

The next day I woke up with the slightest sense that everything had been a dream, but I knew, without a doubt, that it had been real and that it was not possible to escape from reality.

I got up and to distract myself a bit I started to finish my 19 story Lego building. I never imagine that the first building I had designed myself, the one I had begun to build with toy pieces when I began my relationship with Mrs. Margarita, would be finished precisely on the day our affair ended. And the ironic thing is that I decided to build it for real, in the city of Los Angeles, more than 30 years later as an office building that would bear Margarita's name, in tribute to her. It was there on the 19th floor of that building that I received the text message from my friend Frank.

Life has never ceased to amaze me, its irony tends to be amusing... sometimes.

After placing the last piece of Lego and with all the pain in my heart, I reaffirmed my decision: I would not continue to harm so many people. If we could not love each other in the sunlight, we could not love each other at all. If we had to do it in the dark, I'd rather go on with my life without her. It was the best thing for both of us, for everyone.

Later that day, Frank arrived. We had already talked the night before and I let him know my decision to go to London. "Do you regret it, dude?" He said as he entered my room.

"No, it's already decided."

"Well done. At least the beating I gave you yesterday was of some use. It finally brought you into contact with the two remaining fucking neurons in your brain."

I laughed and then walked to my dresser.

"Shut up! You finished it already?" He said to me, referring to the nineteen-story building I had made with my Legos. "It turned out awesome!"

"Thank you," I replied as I took an envelope from the drawer and gave it to him. He looked at it without understanding.

"Can you give it to her?" I asked him. "But not until I leave for London."

He took it and looked at me with a serious face that, despite it being so unusual for him, gave me the confidence and assurance that he would do exactly as I asked. "Sure. Don't worry about it. I'll give it to her," he said.

I had written the letter during the night. It was goodbye; the final goodbye. I did not want to see her because I knew it would be difficult for both of us, and even though my decision was firm, there was a risk that when we saw each other, we would fall back into the same vicious cycle of breaking up and getting back together that we'd fallen into before.

In the letter, I didn't tell her that I had spoken to her husband or what I had found out. However, I did tell her how much I loved her and that it was because of the great love I had for her that I was going away; so she could live in peace.

"Ever since I came into your life," I told her, "I've only hurt you. Our love became a sword, whose only mission seemed to kill just to live, to destroy. We're hurting the people who are most important to you: your family. I cannot stop loving you, but I can go away so we can avoid all this destruction. You taught me to love and to live. You awakened the fire that lay dormant within me and you etched your essence on my being in an indelible way. I carry with me your aroma, your taste."

I have never been very eloquent, so my letter was not a romantic masterpiece like Cyrano de Bergerac's, but I said what I felt, ending it with these words: *"I love you and I will never, ever forget you."*

I knew she'd be fine. She had someone by her side who loved her and would do everything possible to make her happy; she had her daughters. She had a family who loved her, and I would eventually be like one of those natural catastrophes that, despite the damage, are eventually forgotten.

At some point, we had thought that we had met in life at the wrong time, but now I realize everything happens at the right time; on time.

She came into my life when I needed her the most and I came into hers the very moment I should have. I was a parenthesis in her journey, a pause in her marriage, the necessary cause for her husband to open his eyes and notice the journey that needed to be traversed together.

As far as I heard, he was by her side until the end. He closed her eyes after her last breath. It was his right; he had earned it.

I kept her memory in the depths of my being and let her live her life without me, next to the man who truly deserved her.

I went on with my life and in time, the wound healed, but her memory stayed with me forever. I always kept a very special place in my heart for Mrs. Margarita. Always.

Epilogue

That morning I felt strange, even though I had been waking up for many years without thinking about Mrs. Margarita, except on some occasions, like when you remember part of your past as if it were exactly that, the past. It is a distant past, but it is there and you know it.

I don't know how old she was when she died. Of course, it would be easy for me to find out but I'm not interested. I want to remember her as she was: beautiful, sensual, with a unique eroticism, smiling, and full of life.

One day she said to me, "I'm going to remember you until the last minute of my life," and she did. I promised her I'd write our story and this is it.

Looking at things from a different perspective now, I realize that we made many mistakes, but if we had not made them we would not have been able to live as intensely as we did. At the end of the day, the "could've been" does not exist, and no one can take away from us what we lived through.

After all, that's what life is for, isn't it? To live and live intensely with passion and dedication.

I've been married 27 years now and I'm very happy. I've always been faithful to my wife. Partly because I've never been interested in anyone else and, partly for my own good.

Sitting at the breakfast table I see my wife, beautiful as always, even though she is over 50. I think of our two daughters, who are already living their own lives. In fact, the oldest will make us grandparents very soon.

I feel like a very lucky man for all I've been through. I have been very successful in my profession, and before moving permanently to Los Angeles, we had the opportunity to live in London, Italy, Germany, and France. I have enjoyed my life to the fullest and have the great joy of having chosen a wonderful woman as my wife, or rather, she chose me.

I remember perfectly well when we got together back in London. I was in my university room with my roommate, a German guy, who was also on a scholarship. Suddenly, the door slammed open and we both jumped out of our wits. The German was left speechless, partially in fear but also by the beauty of the woman who had so impetuously opened the door.

"You," she said to my roommate, pointing her index finger at him. "Get out of here! Now!" The German turned to look at me and immediately left the room. She closed the door and looked at me with her big, beautiful, green eyes. "You and I have something unsettled, and now nobody is going to stop me." She walked toward me with that sensuality so characteristic of her. I was unable to hold back my astonishment. With my heart beating a hundred miles an hour, I could only whisper her name, "Sonya!"

Acknowledgements

I want to thank my cousin Diana Patricia again, for sharing her extraordinary talent with me for over 10 years, since the days of Xpresándote.

To my children Alek, Rodrigo, Aleisha, Zyanya and Oliver, for being the main reason that makes me be in this world. To my grandson Damian, for living in my heart and keeping it beating.

Again to my son Alek for all the effort he put into revising and correcting the translation of this novel so that it does not lose the sense of the original.

To Aleisha and Charlie, who rechecked the entire manuscript to confirm that everything was correct; and my sister-in-law Liz, who gave the last revision to everything.

And of course to my wife, Blanche, for always being here with me.